# DARK HEART

*Recent Titles in the Mariners Series from Peter Tonkin*

THE FIRE SHIP
THE COFFIN SHIP
POWERDOWN
THUNDER BAY *
TITAN 10 *
WOLF ROCK *
RESOLUTION BURNING *
CAPE FAREWELL *
THE SHIP BREAKERS *
HIGH WIND IN JAVA *
BENIN LIGHT *
RIVER OF GHOSTS *
VOLCANO ROADS *
THE PRISON SHIP *
RED RIVER *
ICE STATION *
DARK  HEART *

*\* available from Severn House*

# DARK HEART

## A Mariner Novel

## Peter Tonkin

This first world edition published 2012
in Great Britain and in the USA by
SEVERN HOUSE PUBLISHERS LTD of
9–15 High Street, Sutton, Surrey, England, SM1 1DF.

British Library Cataloguing in Publication Data

Tonkin, Peter.
  Dark heart.
  1. Mariner, Richard (Fictitious character) – Fiction.
  2. Mariner, Robin (Fictitious character) – Fiction.
  3. Terrorism – Fiction. 4. Africa, West – Fiction.
  5. Suspense fiction.
  I. Title
  823.9'2-dc23

ISBN-13: 978-0-7278-8165-6 (cased)

*All Severn House titles are printed on acid-free paper.*

Severn House Publishers support The Forest Stewardship Council [FSC],
the leading international forest certification organisation. All our titles that
are printed on Greenpeace-approved FSC-certified paper carry the FSC logo.

MIX
Paper from
responsible sources
FSC
www.fsc.org    FSC® C018575

Typeset by Palimpsest Book Production Ltd.,
Falkirk, Stirlingshire, Scotland.
Printed and bound in Great Britain by
MPG Books Ltd., Bodmin, Cornwall.

*For*
*Cham, Guy and Mark,*
*as always.*
*And for the staff and students of Combe Bank,*
*where I was working while I completed this story.*

# ONE

## Ghost

The orchid was a Ghost: the rarest in the world. Perhaps even among the most priceless. It should have been nest-ling high in the Florida Everglades, not resting trapped in the fork of an anonymous African freshwater mangrove over-looking the sullen heave of the Great River on the lower edge of the inner delta in the newly recognized West African state of Benin la Bas.

Like thirty generations of its ancestors, the orchid had been seeded in the distant, derelict wreck of a greenhouse away in the montane high forest of the impenetrable jungle that clothed the slopes of a ridge of volcanoes a thousand miles inland. What little was left of the greenhouse stood beside the mouldering, overgrown framework of a long-abandoned facility on the shores of a lake that occupied one of the smaller bowl-shaped calderas on the side of Mount Karisoke, greatest of the volcanoes.

In the long-ago boom years of the seventies, when there had been high hopes that the heart of Africa would make much of the continent and more of the world rich, a Japanese company created the facility. They built dams and sluices to control the flow of the young river running through the lake, seeded the warm, shallow, volcanic waters with oysters and drew up plans to harvest freshwater pearls. Not just any workaday Mikimoto freshwater pearls, so popular at the time. For the lake was silted with rich jet and ebony volcanic mud, and the oysters that crowded the fecund beds would in time, it was hoped, produce lustrous, price-less, pure black pearls.

The man in charge of the project, Dr Koizumi, was an avid collector of orchids. He persuaded the engineers working on the dam system and the facility to build him a greenhouse and orchi-darium where he could propagate his priceless collection of fragrant Japanese Fu Rans and Indonesian *Dendrobium thyrsi-florums* as well as his other, rarer specimens like the Ghost.

But before the first pearl could even be harvested, the facility fell victim to the first of the civil wars that raged through central Africa in the eighties and nineties. Dr Koizumi's skeleton now lay scattered somewhere beneath the ruins of the greenhouse as those of his colleagues were buried under the mouldering facility, or strewn down the slopes towards the black lake shore. The company cut its losses as swiftly as the rebel soldiers cut their throats.

The local villages also vanished during the succeeding decades, their inhabitants scattered, slaughtered or kidnapped by restlessly marauding armies, carried away to become soldiers, sex-slaves or sacrifices. The jungle returned, empty of all but animal life – and that, too, began to die away as the rapacious, well-armed legions turned to bush meat, and then to cannibalism. The black lake passed back into half-forgotten legend and so did the black pearls it was supposed to have contained.

By the turn of the millennium, there seemed to be nothing in the whole area except the tall trees, the ruined habitations and the timeless forest spirits which had been worshipped here between the mountains and the distant coast for most of the two millennia preceding 1999. The spirits of Obi, led by the snake god Obi himself, which governed the tribes while they still lived here – and also went west with the slave ships as Obeah: voodoo. Went west, but remained here also, as is the nature of gods and spirits, alone and unworshipped. Growing hungry, perhaps, like the swarming armies that came and went through the ruined countries, looking for human sacrifice.

And Dr Koizumi's body, facility and orchidarium remained here also, undisturbed and apparently forgotten, for more than thirty years in the lost heart of that vast, vacant darkness. And, even without the tender care that the good doctor had hoped to lavish upon them, the orchids flourished through generation after generation.

Until the rains came.

That year, in a vicious meteorological irony, all the areas of the East, from Somalia to Uganda, Tanzania and Sudan, where huge populations tried to scratch a living, were all but destroyed by drought. But on the empty and forsaken forests of the interior, five years' rainfall tore down in less than a month. The upper slopes of the dormant volcano became deadly mudslides as even the tallest jungle trees began to lose their grip. The young river grew to a raging torrent almost overnight. The carefully constructed lake burst through the ancient, unmaintained dam system and added to the burgeoning river-spate. A wall of black water carried with it boulders of shattered cement, gallons of black slime, much of Dr Koizumi's greenhouse and a range of his orchids which rode the strange grey crest. Topmost amongst them, the Ghost.

Further downstream, where the river at last left Karisoke's mountain slopes, it plunged over a low, wide waterfall. At the foot of the fall there was a massive, almost circular lake, its surface a solid mat of water hyacinth, sufficiently abundant to have leeched almost all the oxygen from the water beneath it and to have killed off those few marine life forms that hadn't been caught and eaten by the passing armies.

The debris from the lake shore smashed the lethal mat of plants apart and the power of the raging torrent sent the whole lot spinning out of the lake, on downstream. The river, which carried half as much water as the Nile, had simply been called the Great River by the long-vanished villagers who had once peopled its shores. And then the River Gir by variously coloured explorers, taking the name from records made by the earliest Roman mapmakers. Here, in strange matted islands, the water hyacinth was swept on downstream towards the distant coast, the better part of seven hundred miles away. A shore which lay beyond an outer and an inner delta which had been the death of almost every explorer seeking to come east and north upstream; from the earliest Arabic and Portuguese traders to the Elizabethan slave-traders and hardy Scottish and American missionaries. The Romans, the Bedou and the wise Mandingo traders came south and west through the Sahara – and most of them survived to tell the tale.

The Ghost, also coming south and west, survived like the itinerant Mandingo traders – for the moment at least. Caught in the thickly tangled structure, the battered orchid sat high on the greenery, surrounded by other, less fortunate blooms, which were drooping, torn and broken. Most of the concrete boulders had sunk on to the lake bed at the floor of the waterfall, tearing the mat of hyacinth loose as they did so. But the hyacinth was robust enough to be buoyant still, even in smaller clumps; sufficiently strong to be carrying odds and ends from the increasingly distant facility. Wooden planks and metal struts from the greenhouse. Bunches of black vegetation from the bed of the ruptured lake. Bizarrely, Dr Koizumi's skull, apparently keeping close watch on his beloved orchids with the wide-gaping sockets of its eyes, grinning eerily at the sight of their survival.

The normally stately flow of the Great River Gir was enhanced not only by the flood from the slopes of the great volcano, but by the fact that the rains continued to pour on to the empty forests through which it was now flowing. The river spread itself into a series of meanders and lakes big enough to pass for inland seas, but still its flow remained fearsome under the unrelenting deluge that thundered down, day after day after day.

The Ghost, with its watchful keeper, swept swiftly onwards, therefore, through what had once been prosperous farms and plantations. Past the ruins of fishing villages and mining towns, which, like Dr Koizumi's facility, had flourished in the seventies only to die during the relentless onslaughts of the eighties and nineties. Every now and then there would be something newer – projects that had died at birth under the dead hand of the bribe-crippled kleptocracies that had run the place through into the noughties and early twenty-tens, before the IMF, World Bank, and interested economies from Chile to China, discovered the hard way that money invested in Central Africa was even more at risk than money invested in Iceland, Ireland, Greece and Portugal.

Until, at last, the Great River entered the inner delta. A stream that had been as broad as the Amazon at Manaos, wide enough to make a fisherman suddenly believe he was lost at sea with the two banks fallen far below his horizon, suddenly fractured, shattered, ran away into the swampy jungle in a maze of lesser streams. From outer space, on Google Earth, the River Gir seemed to be constructed like one of the great trees that stood along its lost and silent upper reaches. Twigs of streams ran down from mountainsides and in from the edges of deserts, gathering into branches that flowed inevitably into one huge trunk – a trunk more than five hundred miles long; a trunk that became twisted, wandering, widespread, but coherent. Until it met the green wall of the delta. And here, like the trunk of a tree entering the ground, it spread its roots as widely and wildly as it had spread its branches far inland. There remained a tap-root, true; one stream stronger than the rest, still calling itself the River. Still the Gir. But no longer the Great River. Its greatness was lost in the delta.

The Ghost, too, would have been lost, but for the force of the flood which held its floating island in midstream so that it followed that tap-root of the River Gir straight into the heart of the inner delta. Here the flood had all but swamped even the hardiest mangroves. But they still reached out, like deadly reefs and sand-bars, swaying and shifting, until one at last snagged the matted roots of water hyacinth. The mares' nest of vegetation swung inwards towards the shore and became more firmly anchored. It had reached its final resting place, seemingly almost as high as the simple wooden cross on top of the missionary church which was the first sign of current human habitation half a kilometre inland on a knoll miraculously above the floodwater.

Then the flood beneath both chapel and orchid crested and began to recede. The force of the falling water sucked at the hyacinth raft with sufficient force to start it breaking up. The mangroves tore at it as the current began to release them. Ripping at it as they sprang back like the claws of the great leopards that had once hunted here, with branches as powerful as the arms of the huge silverback gorillas that had once ruled the impenetrable jungle on far Mount Karisoke. The hyacinth raft began to come apart. Dr Koizumi's skull rolled away into the receding waters. Much of the rest of the matted vegetation fell into the mud of the river's shore. But the Ghost, sitting on a high, tough fork of mangrove branch, remained miraculously unscathed. As the rains eased during the next few days and the water continued to fall until the Gir at last resumed its accustomed river course, running gently enough to allow the first couple of orphans from the church school near the chapel to come down to the bank and begin to explore the aftermath of the flood, like creatures recently released from the Ark, unaware of the beautiful flower sitting like a white dove just above their heads.

Until the soldier crushed it out of existence by resting the barrel of his Kalashnikov on the tree-fork so that he could get a steady

platform for observation and assessment of a good field of fire
for the moment when the rest of the Army of Christ the Infant
caught up with him. The fork offered the soldier a sufficiently
steady lookout point for his purposes, for he was lying on what
remained of the bed of water hyacinths and it made a perfect
hiding place and observation platform. At this stage the soldier
only wanted to spy on the unsuspecting children still wandering
between the riverbank and the school, which was the army's next
objective because of the number of potential recruits its students
represented – and because of the two women who were in charge
of the place.

A bell in the chapel began to ring. It had struck perhaps half
a dozen times before its dominance over the breathless silence of
the jungle was overwhelmed by a distant roaring from high in
the sky. Thunder, perhaps – and the sultry air certainly threatened
it. Or an airliner's engines going into noisy reverse thrust somewhere high above the green jungle canopy as it settled towards
its landing at the distant Granville Harbour International Airport.
The soldier paid scant attention to the distant thunder – diminishing
already – as he watched the children hurrying towards the chapel,
blissfully unaware of his presence – and the impending arrival of
his comrades. They were a mixture of boys and girls. It was hard
to tell their ages, but they looked young to him. Young and soft
and tender. His stomach grumbled in an internal echo of the distant
thunder – and his mouth flooded with saliva.

The soldier's name was Esan, which meant 'Nine' in Yoruba.
The soldier had been nine when Moses Nlong had recruited him
into the Army of Christ the Infant by making him kill his cousin
with his sharp-bladed matchet and eat part of her heart. Not
General Nlong alone, of course, but the power of Obi that he
controlled through Ngoboi, his own terrifying devil, with its
magic mask and his matted raffia costume, who embodied the
most terrifying of the Obi spirits of the Great Dark Forest and
gave the general much of his power. A devil which would soon
be here, with the army and with General Nlong, hungry for
recruits in more ways than one.

In the years since he joined the Army of Christ the Infant,
Esan had risen to the rank of corporal and had been given the
trusted role of pathfinder and scout, for, unlike many of the
others, he was contained and icily quiet. He did not suffer from

nightmares and he did not need to be motivated with cocaine. He had grown tall and strong in body as well as in spirit. He believed in the power of the spirits the devil embodied but he wore only one small fetish – and did not rely on bizarre magical wigs, costumes or make-up to make him invincible; the green-brown camouflage of his corporal's uniform was what he preferred to wear. Consequently he blended into the forest and could be relied upon to give accurate reports. So the general came to know him. To trust him. And he had killed many more people and eaten many more hearts.

He was thirteen years old.

# TWO

## Turbulence

KLM Flight 1330 from Paris swung low over the delta, fighting to complete its landing at Benin la Bas's Granville Harbour International before the threatening weather closed in again. The Boeing 737's engines thundered as it settled into the lower air, rolling to the left as it swung on to a westerly heading, the better part of three hundred miles east of the runway, a little more than twenty minutes out. The captain's voice crackled through the PA system, 'Please ensure that your seat belts are tightened. We may experience a little turbulence.'

Richard Mariner sat, looking down out of the window below his left shoulder, his big fists motionless in his lap. His belt was already as tight as it could go – and would have been so even if he hadn't managed to get a seat with extra legroom. A necessity given his massive size, but nevertheless a slightly unnerving prospect whereby any kind of emergency landing would throw him bodily through the side wall of the lavatory if his belt proved less than perfect. In any case, he was expecting all kinds of turbulence in all sorts of ways. During the next few minutes, the next few hours, perhaps even during the next few days. His bright blue eyes were narrow and his throat felt dry – and almost as tight as his seat belt.

The sight of the delta always had that effect on him, he thought. The simple, bone-deep disgust he always felt when coming close to it. The way the cancerous outgrowth of dark green jungle and mangrove bellied into the bay and spread like a dark stain back far beyond the horizon inland. The bulbous, almost brain-like swelling of it reaching into an inner delta, then giving way to a riverine plain reaching deeper into the impenetrable jungle of the volcanic hinterland a thousand miles away.

Three quarters of a million square kilometres of mangrove and marsh – more than twice the area of Belgium – veined with a maze of rivulets, the wetland scrub lifting to secondary forest, where the earth rose into hills and ruined villages told of failed farming communities, and into timeless rainforest away back along the tap-root of the main stream, the River Gir. A wasteland that had once been home to millions, now deserted and destroyed – a mess of polluted swamps and abandoned towns. Ruined enterprises and broken dreams.

Full, still, of untold potential and fabulous fortunes for those with the confidence, the assurance, the simple blind courage, to go eastwards up the rivers and into the dark heart of the place, Richard admitted ruefully to himself. That was why, in the final analysis, the only living people you were likely to find in the delta were the marauding armies that had been chased out of Somalia, Uganda, Rwanda, Sierra Leone and the Congo. For there was much for them to try and get control of – if they could come up with the equipment and expertise to extract it in any meaningful quantities. And, of course, it wasn't only the Rwanda's genocidal Interahamwe or Uganda's Lord's Resistance Army, or Moses Nlong's newcomers the Army of Christ the Infant who were greedy for the potential riches. There were companies, corporations, national and international financial organizations and NGOs from Bretton Woods to Beijing who were drooling for a piece of the action too. That, after all, was why he was here himself.

There was oil along the coast and in the delta itself. Oil in such abundance it came flooding out of the ground, so that the disgruntled locals in their vast shanty towns at the southern edge of the capital city of Granville Harbour hardly needed to bother tapping the pipes for illegal fuel – or to ignite explosive protests. There were diamonds in the south, there was gold in the rivers;

tin, coal and copper in the mines. And the new precious metals too – plutonium, uranium and, of course, tantalum in the most sought-after form of all: the incredibly precious, ruthlessly harvested conflict mineral – jet-black coltan.

As Richard's narrow gaze swept over the matted wilderness, all dead darkness except for a momentary flash of gold where the setting sun caught the broader flow of a major artery, Richard's perspective was changed, and he found himself looking along the coast to the south. Down to where the delta's outer edges were fringed with an unsettling intensity of flames as the hundreds of oil wells there continued to flare off millions of cubic kilometres of gas, in spite of international attempts to stop the dangerous, environmentally damaging practice.

But it was more than the sight of the oil-dark, deadly jungle framed with the unsettlingly vivid fires that had his breath coming short and his belly feeling tense. More than his memories of the danger that he, his wife Robin and two young women in the hands of ruthless kidnappers had faced there on his last visit. More than the fact that Robin was there again already, waiting for him alone in their suite at the Granville Royal Lodge Hotel. More than the fact that the two young women they had risked so much to rescue – Celine Chaka, the president's estranged daughter, and Anastasia Asov, disowned and disinherited daughter of his Russian business associate Max Asov – were somewhere upriver running a rescue station and mission school for orphans in the heart of the delta itself. More than the patently dangerous wall of thunderheads massing in black battlements out over the Atlantic, racing eastwards in over the airport as they were racing west to slip beneath them – turbulence or no.

It was not what lay below him or behind. It was what lay ahead.

When General Dr Julius Chaka, President of Benin la Bas, had asked Richard and Robin as representatives of Heritage Mariner to attend the conference with their Africa financial team, Richard's first instinct had been to go to Jim Bourne, head of the massive shipping company's intelligence section, London Centre. It was the better part of four years since Julius Chaka had assumed control of the country – with the Mariners' almost accidental connivance. Richard tried to remain distanced from the country and his company's involvement in transporting the oil from its wells to the refineries in Europe, but like someone worrying a loose tooth or rubbing an old wound, he found himself incapable of leaving it utterly alone. He ordered London Centre to keep an eye on developments in Benin la Bas; had found his own attention drawn to news reports, political discussions and financial commentaries about the place.

Robin shared neither his unease nor his distaste – and she felt a positive friendship for Celine and Anastasia – which was only strengthened, of course, by their disinheritance. Her only hesitation about accepting Julius Chaka's invitation was that, as a friend and champion of the daughters, she might find it hard to take the required positive attitude to the fathers – even though they represented so much political and financial power. 'Max Asov will be there?' she asked in confirmation, looking down at the old-fashioned, gold-embossed invitation on the morning it first arrived at Heritage Mariner.

'Max, several other big Russian players, all the usual international teams . . .' he answered.

Robin interrupted with a cynical laugh. 'Chaka's after money. This is a loan and investment hunt.'

'Looks like it,' he admitted. 'But in the right hands it could be a sweet deal.'

'Are we interested?' she asked quizzically.

'I don't know,' he answered slowly. 'But I know who I can ask.'

'Jim,' she had said at once. 'Jim Bourne at London Centre.'


'Under the late President Liye Banda, the place was a kleptocracy,' Richard said to Jim Bourne in the main office at London Centre later that same day. 'Like the Congo under Mobutu in the nineties. Like Zimbabwe under Mugabe. The country was going down the drain in every way and nothing got done except by bribery and corruption. Everyone skimmed their cut off every deal from the president on down. It was the only way to survive for most of the country, and anyone who didn't have a position of power just went to the wall. Or rather, to the shanties and the slums where they simply starved to death.

'President Chaka's had four years since Banda died and he

assumed power, and now he's after international funding – from Heritage Mariner amongst other possible sources. From *every* possible source, as far as I can see, in fact. But has he managed to pull things round? Has all the graft and corruption stopped? Is Benin la Bas a good risk nowadays?'

Jim Bourne looked at Richard with a lopsided grin, pulling his pencil-thin Rhett Butler moustache awry. 'Best way to find that out, Boss, is to take a look-see for yourself. Let Robin take the company jet and go in first class like they expect. Let her follow the red carpet route with all the other big wheels. Keep her feet clean and her eyes blinkered by the wonderful welcome . . .'

'While I go in like a tourist. Commercial flight. Keeping out of first or business class. No fuss or fanfare. See how far I get down and dirty on the ground. Find out how much it really costs to get anywhere in Benin la Bas nowadays.'

'It'll set you back about five hundred dollars one-way for the airfare,' said Jim wryly. 'Rumour has it that's about the amount it used to take to get you safely through the airport immediately after you landed . . .'

'Do tell. I wonder if it still does? Perhaps I *had* better take a close look for myself. If I can convince Robin to go in with the team and leave me to my own devices . . .'

It had seemed like a good idea at the time.

But now, as the Boeing's wheels thumped on to the runway and the sky above was shattered with lightning and split with instant thunder, Richard found his breath short, his heart racing, his scrotum and sphincter clenched – like a scuba-diver spotting a shark.

Out over the dull green canopy, a single bird soared, its movement almost unique in that dead place, and the phrase '*Chil the Kite*' slipped unbidden into his mind. It took a moment for him to track its relevance down to his reading of Kipling's *Jungle Book* as a child.

*Ere Mor the Peacock flutters, ere the Monkey People cry,*
*Ere Chil the Kite swoops down a furlong sheer,*
*Through the Jungle very softly flits a shadow and a sigh –*
*He is Fear, O Little Hunter, he is Fear!*

And at last Richard's mouth lifted into a wry smile as he began to laugh at himself – not to mention at his childish fears. 'Get a grip, Mariner,' he growled.

During the moments of inevitable confusion following the landing, Richard checked the most vital things, like a soldier going into combat. He slipped the green cardboard security card he had filled in prior to landing into his passport at the first vacant visa page and put the passport in the breast pocket of his jacket. He checked the carefully folded US dollar bills in his left jacket pocket. His BlackBerry in his left trouser pocket with his handkerchief. The local network Benincom cellphone that Jim had given him slipped safely in his right jacket pocket, pre-programmed with a local number that would summon immediate help if the going got too tough after all . . .

He pulled his hand luggage out of the overhead cabinet and slid an Apple Mac laptop into place. A 17" MacBook Pro worth £2000 and counting when he had bought it. If that went missing, he thought with a grim chuckle, the cost of getting through the airport was likely to go on to a whole new level. But then the same would be true for either of his suitcases, though his most expensive – most vital and formal – kit had come on the company jet with Robin and the financial team Heritage Mariner habitually sent to functions such as this. He squared his shoulders, stooped a little to keep the top of his head clear of the cabin ceiling, and joined the queue of passengers shuffling towards the exit.

It was the heat that hit him first, then, on the first breath, the stench. An overpowering, humid sultriness, packed with the scents of avgas, rubber, concrete, metal, bodies and garbage all heated far too hot for comfort. Immediately aware of the perspiration prickling on every fold and wrinkle from his scalp to the soles of his feet, he stepped down the disembarkation stairs and strode across the apron to the waiting bus.

The air conditioning in the long vehicle was nullified in an instant by the number of sweating bodies close-packed all around him. The vehicle lurched into motion even as he tried to ease his laptop case out of the small of his nearest neighbour's back. An action he felt he should attempt at once as the neighbour in question was a young woman in a formal business outfit. An action also cancelled out by the lurching movement of the bus which sent everyone staggering and slammed the corner of the bag into her spine once again.

'Hey . . .' she began, trying to swing round and face her assailant. She got far enough for him to see black curls and a cinnamon-brown cheek. But she, like him, was wedged in place. Her skin was a different colour to most of the passengers – no matter what their ethnic background. But her accent, dripping over that one syllable like molasses, sounded American to him.

'Sorry,' he answered, fatuously, sounding painfully English.

The coach drew up outside the arrivals terminal and the doors hissed open. People fell out rather than stepped out. The young woman shrugged and strode off ahead of Richard, who followed, frowning. The path up to the tall glass doors was just long enough to let him check his passport, money and Benincom cellphone once again. Only as an afterthought, as the glass portals hissed wide in front of him, did he think to check his BlackBerry.

Then he was in. The girl with cinnamon skin walked immediately in front of him, directed by white-uniformed security guards to the visa section. Still behind her, he joined a short queue. Taking a moment to look around and try to orientate himself as the air conditioning began to cool things down in all sorts of ways. After the visa section there was a security portal by the looks of things, then a passport and security check. Then baggage reclaim in the distance. And what looked like another security check before the customs hall. Further inside the huge building, the white-uniformed security men were joined by others in camos and fatigues. The ubiquitous sidearms were joined by submachine guns with skeleton butts, stubby barrels and short, square magazines. Richard recognized the uniforms from the last time he had been here – and had a less than satisfactory brush with Major Laurent Kebila, the man who had apparently risen to the rank of colonel and the position of head of army security under General Chaka. Kebila had clearly taken the opportunity to rearm his men – replacing the questionably efficient British SA80s with American Ruger MP-9s by the look of things – and to spread his tentacles a little wider into the bargain. Airport security and army security. Not a nice combination. Nor, Richard suspected, a cheap one. Unconsciously he slipped his hand into his pocket and ran his thumbnail over the edges of the carefully folded dollars.

'What visa do you want?' demanded the man in the visa booth in French.

Richard looked down. The official was talking to the girl.

'I don't know . . .' she responded, also in French. 'I'm here for the finance meeting . . .'

New Orleans? wondered Richard inconsequentially. Did they let folks from Dixie into the hallowed halls of Bretton Woods, New Hampshire, where the IMF and the World Bank had their headquarters? But who else would send their employees tourist class to the conference?

'Where are you going?'

'The hotel . . . the meeting . . .' She sounded less sure of herself now, in the face of the official's abruptness.

'Show me your disembarkation form! Quick!'

'My . . .' she quavered.

'Green form! Green form you filled in on the plane. I will tell you what visa and how much!'

The young woman passed her green form through the opening in the security glass. The official glanced at it. 'Town visa,' he decided. 'Ten dollars US.'

She passed over the money. He stamped the form. As he passed it back, Richard looked at the 'EMPLOYMENT' section – 'World Bank' it said. And her name was just above it: 'Dr Bonnie Holliday'. He smiled.

Richard stepped forward, acting before the man could even speak. He passed in his green form and the ten dollar bill. Dark eyes glanced up, then down. The stamp fell like a guillotine blade.

Richard knew the security portal was going to present problems. They always did for him. Still behind the increasingly nervous-looking young woman, he put his laptop case in a plastic tray and dumped his phones, keys and steel-buckled belt on top of it. Even so, as he followed her through the gate itself, the alarm went off. She was waved to one side and subjected to a body scan. He was directed to the other side and searched. 'It's my knees,' he explained in English – and then, in the face of an uncomprehending stare, he explained again in French. 'The joints of my knees are metal. My legs were damaged in an accident . . .'

He closed his eyes for a moment, fighting his memory. Once, in the early days after the operation, he had been strip-searched at Belfast Airport before the security team there had believed him. But things were easier here. The security wand that had just passed over the woman from the World Bank passed over him as well and the man studying the screen clicked his lips in surprise as the picture indeed showed titanium knee-joints. Another twenty dollars smoothed the passage. But when he got to the tray of possessions he saw that his keys, belt and both phones seemed safe enough. So did the Apple. He re-threaded his belt and headed for passport control.

Once again he found himself behind the World Bank woman, and he began to wonder if something in his subconscious was causing him to follow her. Latent stalker or Galahad complex? Either one was possible, he thought cynically – both fitted well enough with the James Bond mode he was trying for, at any rate.

'This passport is out of date!' spat the man in passport control.

'I assure you it is not . . .' answered the woman, frowning. 'It will not expire for—'

'Five months! It must be at least six months from expiry! This is serious!'

She turned around at last, her eyes wide with shock. 'I had no idea! They called me in at the last moment! I only had twelve hours to get my stuff together and catch the flight from Boston to Paris!' She was explaining to Richard, in English.

Without a second thought he was at her side. '*How* serious?' he demanded in his brutal French. '*This* serious?' Richard produced twenty-five dollars.

The man frowned.

'*This* serious?' Richard added another twenty-five dollars. Fifty dollars now lay beside the passport.

The stamp came down. 'Remember in future,' the passport controller said. He handed up the passport. Richard took it and handed it to her. 'See you in baggage claim, Dr Holliday,' he said. She walked away hurriedly without looking back at him. He slid his own passport into the booth. There was already ten dollars in it. He was getting the hang of this, he thought.

The baggage hall was busy. There were people everywhere, many more than had just come off the KLM Boeing. A good number of them looked local. And not just the taxi-touts, the hotel drummers, or the ubiquitous men in white and camouflage with their sidearms and their submachine guns.

The cinnamon-skinned World Bank woman was nowhere to be seen, so Richard contented himself with looking for his bags. When they arrived, they were so battered that he only recognized them because he had cinched distinctive personalized straps around them. Narrow-eyed, he heaved them off the carousel and carried them through to the next security section which stood between baggage claim and customs. This time the pallets were bigger. Cases went through X-ray searches, as did his laptop, keys, belt, BlackBerry and cellphone once again. And as did his knees once more when the alarm sounded.

And he found himself another twenty dollars poorer by the time he caught up with his cases and effects.

He re-threaded his belt, slipped his BlackBerry into his breast pocket with his passport and put the Benincom cellphone in his right jacket pocket conveniently to hand. Then he put his laptop bag over his shoulder and hefted his cases into customs.

The first thing that he saw there was a selection of ladies' underwear so adventurous as to be almost shocking. It was being held up by the customs official going through a suitcase. And a second glance all too clearly revealed that the case belonged to the woman from the World Bank. Her cheeks were no longer cinnamon: they were mahogany with embarrassed blushes.

*Enough is enough*, thought Richard, and he shouldered his way through the hall and slammed his cases down beside hers. The simple noise distracted the sniggering officials. Then they registered his height and his presence. And the look on his face. The woman's underwear was roughly shoved back and her case closed then marked 'PASSED'.

'Are these bags yours?' demanded the tallest of the three in French that was almost as brutal as Richard's own.

'Yes.'

'Open them . . .'

Ten minutes later, sixty dollars poorer and lighter by most of his exclusive toiletries, Richard carried his cases out into the main arrivals hall. This was even busier than the baggage claim had been. It was as much a market as an airport. People ran here and there, jostling the new arrivals, trying to sell them knick-knacks, local fruit and produce. There were men and women, boys and girls all in a jostling crowd offering everything from help with luggage to cigarettes to local currency and promises to guide.

The woman he had been following was standing, helpless, at the heart of a crowd of feral children who were pawing at her, apparently intent on tearing the very clothing off her back. 'Hoi!' bellowed Richard without thinking, using his quarterdeck voice – the one that could carry half the length of a supertanker in the middle of a storm. Every head in the place swivelled towards him. The crowd of boys broke away from her and descended on him like piranhas. She staggered a few steps, only to find herself confronted by a soldier clutching a Ruger MP-9 submachine gun. One of Colonel Kebila's best by the look of things.

She looked over her shoulder, her eyes wide and desperate.

Richard decided that he had had enough. He dropped his cases and reached into his pocket for the Benincom cell pre-programmed with the number of someone capable of getting him out of this.

But his pocket was empty.

The phone was gone.

'Stop thief,' he yelled at once in French. 'Someone has stolen my phone!' Quick as a flash, he reached into his breast pocket and pulled out his BlackBerry. He had left it switched on and programmed with the Benincom cell's own number. He pressed speed-dial and immediately the phone began to ring. 'Help! Stop thief,' he yelled again. '*Au secours! Voleur! Arrêtez le voleur!*'

One of the urchins who had been circling the woman and Richard himself seemed to freeze, then in a flash he was gone. But the ringing carried on.

'It's here!' said the soldier with the submachine gun. And several others joined him at once. Numbly, moving like a zombie, the girl from the World Bank reached into her bag and pulled out Richard's phone. She stood there, gaping at the shrieking instrument, suddenly alone with the accusing soldiers in a widening space in the centre of a vanishing crowd. Richard strode forward, his clumsy thumb fighting to break contact with his BlackBerry.

And, as he did so, a slim wiry figure in a Colonel's uniform also stepped into the accusing vacancy. 'Ah, Captain Mariner,' purred the familiar Sandhurst-polished voice of his old adversary Laurent Kebila, Chief of State Security. 'Still having problems with the ladies, I see. Perhaps you had both better come with me.'

# THREE
## Oyster

Anastasia Asov watched Celine Chaka as she rang the chapel bell. It was six o'clock local time. Sunset would be swift and soon – especially under the gathering western storm clouds and the overspreading forest canopy. It was time for the Christians amongst their charges to hold their shortened Evensong, and for the Muslims to perform their Maghrib or sunset Salat. Then they would all have supper and start to tuck down. During the last twenty minutes or so, the two young women had rearranged the schoolroom desks and chairs into the chapel's rows of makeshift pews, and had transformed the teacher's desk on the slight platform in front of the whiteboard into a rudimentary altar. Just as the bell – a school bell in the daytime – was now transformed to a chapel bell at sunset. Now they stood, breathless and running with perspiration in the suffocating humidity of the early evening.

Above the rhythmic chime of the bell, the call of the camp's muezzin suddenly rose, the power of it still able to make the hair all over Anastasia's lean body rise in goosebumps. The two religions covered the majority of the children here – given only, Anastasia suspected darkly, that many of the older boys had already been initiated into the local forms of magic animism of the Poro secret bush societies. Certainly there was a large number of ritual scars on a good few backs and cheeks. And, she suspected, a good few of the older girls had been taken into their female equivalent – the Sande. A percentage of both genders – though blessedly few girls – had been circumcised. This in spite of the fact that most of the children here – the better part of three hundred of them at the last count – were from lost families and ruined villages. Which begged the question of who on earth was out there managing to initiate them. Obi and Ngoboi, perhaps; the great spirits of the dark places.

But the bush societies, with their emphasis on the separation of body and soul, the presence of spirits and ancestors, shared a sufficient range of ideas with the Western religions they practised here for the children to look up to the cross or bow down to Mecca with a clear conscience, thought Anastasia darkly. But she would hate to test how deep their allegiance to the foreign ideas really was.

Anastasia had no sense of being watched at all. Nor any feeling of impending danger. Instead, all she felt, as increasingly often in these long, sultry evenings, was a vague, disturbing stirring of desire for her beautiful companion. Celine was tall and slim where Anastasia was slight and wiry. Her skin was café au lait, except in those areas where she had been beaten, burned and tortured in her previous incarnation as a freedom fighter. Her body moved with something close to liquidity, as though her belly, breasts, buttocks and thighs somehow contained viscous oil – palm oil perhaps – which caused them to judder, ripple and sway when Celine moved. Every action she made was performed with an unconscious, almost balletic elegance, except that she limped occasionally, and found unexpected pains in her shoulders where she had been introduced to the strappado. But even her imperfections made her more desirable in Anastasia's eyes. The way Celine's sweat-streaked blouse clung to her now, almost transparent in places, especially as her slim arms rose and fell pulling the bell-rope above her head. Her curls glittered with water droplets as though diamonds had been scattered amid ebony shavings. What breeze there was seemed to mould her skirt to her thighs.

Anastasia sighed. Shook herself a little. Her lazy sapphic lust wasn't strong enough to get in the way of their friendship yet; for one thing, Celine gave no indication of noticing or returning it – but it was of increasing concern to the Russian woman. An itch she couldn't scratch, in the old cliché. Made all the more itchy by the fact that the two of them shared accommodation, sleeping quarters, showers, everything. On occasion even clothes and underclothes.

Anastasia and Celine were by no means the only women in the organization. But they were the only women of the same age. They shared a calling – but not the burning fervour of the others. And, even among the disparate leadership of the church school, orphanage and rescue centre, they didn't really fit in. Celine, after all, was an ex-freedom fighter, the Mother Teresa of Granville Harbour according to the media, though Anastasia thought Joan of Arc would have been more accurate. A survivor of President Banda's torture cells and daughter of the current president – for all that her father and she had managed to disown each other almost immediately after he assumed power. Largely because he had failed to hold the promised elections.

Anastasia herself, lean and boyish – scrawny, she thought herself – with her skin dimpled in all sorts of places by piercings for bars, studs and rings she no longer wore, decorated in a wide range of areas with a disturbing array of tattoos, would hardly have fitted in anywhere – other than a Goth festival or a heavy metal rock concert. A fact which underlay the separation from her own billionaire *biznizman* father and family, and she made no secret of it. For she had indeed been a groupie to a heavy metal band, a drug addict and a crack whore before she managed to pull her life back together through a combination of good luck and sheer grit. And, as with Celine and *her* survival, through the blessed intervention of Richard and Robin Mariner.

Father Antoine, who doubled as head teacher and had been camp doctor until Celine arrived, came into the chapel then, followed by Sister Faith, who doubled as deputy head and nurse, laden with service sheets. In the absence of indigenous animal life nearby – hunted to extinction by starving villagers with access to guns rather than crops – he was a giraffe and she a hippopotamus. Brother Jacob, a water buffalo, who doubled as technology teacher and camp maintenance man, was unlikely to be joining them as he had more earthly responsibilities – to wit the generator, which had not liked the wet weather at all. He and the three eldest boys, whom he was training, would be labouring to ensure that there was light to combat the gathering darkness.

Sister Hope and Sister Charity were on dinner duty tonight, hovering like superannuated vultures over their task. There were nearly three hundred to feed, after all. And they too had half a dozen helpers from amongst the older girls. Working in parallel with them, the brawny elephant Ibrahim and his boys would be preparing halal food for the elegant leonine Imam Mohammed, the songbird Muezzin Samir and their flock. Neither of these enterprises relied on Brother Jacob's power, physical or electrical – all the cooking was done over traditional fires, though what was cooked was by no means always so traditional for it depended on what the enterprise's sponsors in America, Europe and Russia could send – and what of that made it through Granville Harbour and up on *Nellie*, the bizarrely named riverboat that laboured upstream from Malebo, the nearest outpost of civilization, and kept the place supplied. Tying up at the little pier down-slope from the chapel – a rickety little construct which had only just survived the floods – or sitting out mid steam if she was too heavily laden to risk the shallows, loading goods into the little rowing boat they kept tied to the pier to act as a lighter. Celine and Anastasia taught, doctored, nursed, and provided public faces for the enterprise. They were as adept at raising cash as they were at healing and teaching the children.

Immediately after Father Antoine and Sister Faith, the first of the children arrived. There was an instant, lively bustle. These youngsters were not the desperate, downtrodden, diseased charity cases of the big charity adverts. The jungle sanctuary gave them hope, health and training. And, above all, a way out, for twice a year at least – four times in the last eighteen months. Anastasia and Celine had taken twenty or thirty of the eldest downriver with them aboard *Nellie* all the way down to Granville Harbour – a journey of three days going and four returning, never to be undertaken lightly – and passed them on to the seminaries, colleges and university there.

Those voyages haunted Anastasia, not merely because they took her away from the solitude she enjoyed and thrust her into the bustle she increasingly hated, but because of the simple depression that they brought to her spirit. For they took her through a journey into desolation as well as memory. Past roadways that had been eight- and sixteen-lane highways in the seventies but, with only the rarest exceptions, were overgrown now and impassable to everything except motorbikes. Under Captain Christophe's gentle tutelage, she learned to con *Nellie* past ruined villages and towns. Past mouldering jetties, port facilities and the rotting corpses of boats – even ships – that had once plied these waters to supply a burgeoning economy. An economy gone the way of the dinosaurs. Past the greatest folly of all: Citematadi, a piece of urban development to rival Paris, its parks and boulevards all deserted and overgrown. Its buildings vacant and rotting.

Celine and Anastasia had on more than one occasion taken

the opportunity to explore the riverbank and the strange ruins that sometimes clustered round it. Awed, saddened, spooked; like barbaric Anglo-Saxons wandering amidst the ruins of the Roman empire, wondering what terrifying giants could have created such things.

For it had been there in the city-scale ghost town – and near there, in the rebel camps upriver – that Anastasia had been held captive with Robin Mariner. Kidnapped and held to ransom by the freedom fighting army of General Dr Julius Chaka, as a gambit in the campaign that would eventually lead to the death of President Banda and Chaka's assumption of total power. It was partly a reaction to that, she supposed – to the sense of helplessness, the terror, the soul-destroying tension of knowing nothing but imagining every physical and sexual horror that might be possible – which finally knocked her off the rails. The appalling experience and the discovery that her father, deeply involved with President Banda, would have been happy to bomb the living daylights out of her kidnappers, no matter what the risk to her. In the face of the near-certainty, in fact, that if he did so, then she would die.

Almost immediately after her release, she had run off with the rock band Simian Artillery; becoming their groupie, pet and play-thing. It had all been downhill from there. Until the moment she was rescued from the addiction to crack cocaine and the lifestyle she had adopted to support her habit. Not by her outraged father but by Robin Mariner, who had shared her terrible kidnapping ordeal but had been rescued – as had Anastasia herself – by Richard. She had never asked how Robin came to find her – or why she had even bothered to look for her. But the fact that the Mariners cared so much for her had given her the strength at last to start to care for herself. And then to care for others.

As Celine stopped ringing the bell and went forward, surrounded by children, to sit at the front of the church, Anastasia felt a hand on her shoulder. She turned, to confront Ado, one of her favourites. Ado was rising fifteen – ten years Anastasia's junior – but she was wise in the ways of the forest. Wisdom garnered at the price of scars on her cheeks, back and chest – the devil's tooth marks of Sande initiation ceremonies. And Anastasia had helped Celine treat the girl for a botched circumcision. Luckily botched in Anastasia's opinion. The mutilation was minimal. Ado, in due course, would be able to take pleasure in the act of love-making where many of her tribal sisters never would. The tall, self-possessed teenage girl was silently holding out a pile of black stones towards her. It took a moment – and a whiff of fishy odour – for Anastasia to realize that Ado was holding a handful of oysters. Anastasia's black brows arched in surprise. She knew that oysters were a delicacy down in Granville Harbour but she had never seen any this far upriver. 'Where did you find these?' she asked in her rough Matadi – the local dialect.

'Down by the river,' Ado answered. 'Come and see.'

Anastasia nodded and the pair of them left together. *Anything to get out of one of Father Antoine's sermons*, thought the Russian woman cynically. It was already dark outside, and the weather seemed threatening. The compound, with its dormitory buildings, palm-thatched lean-tos that doubled as outside classrooms and refectories, was lit by a combination of flickering electric lights and candles – both now attracting the first evening moths but not – blessedly – mosquitoes. The lack of mosquitoes was the deciding factor in their choice of location. The river flowed too swiftly here for them to breed; and even after floods such as they had just experienced, the gradient of the land between the chapel and the river was too steep to allow any dangerous pools of standing water.

Beyond the illuminated area, down towards the river, there was only a deepening, velvety darkness. Anastasia and Ado crossed to Brother Jacob's generator hut, therefore, and Anastasia reached in to grab the big black steel Maglite torch that the engineer kept for emergencies. It was nearly fifty centimetres long and weighed a kilo and a half. Jacob kept the massive torch in a presentation box with an equally outsized Victorinox knife. She took that for good measure – if they found many more oysters, then she would want to start opening them. In her days as a billionaire oligarch's beloved princess, she had indulged quite a penchant for oysters, caviar and pink champagne.

Side by side, the two young women ran down the steep river-bank to the edge of the water. Anastasia did not switch on the torch at first, for she really did not want to be summoned back to the Evensong service, and her prickly conscience told her it would only take a word from Sister Charity to call her to heel. With a sense of guilty excitement, the truants ran down the bank in breathless silence until the busy chuckling slithering of the river warned them they were in danger of getting their toes wet. Then Anastasia pushed the Maglite's switch forward and shaded the eye-watering dazzle with her hand. The red mud of the river-bank slid into the darker rush of water with hardly any differen-tiation. There were no deep banks or riverine cliffs here. And yet there was flotsam piled along the smooth mud as far back as the roots of the trees above them and the roots of the mangroves that spread away downstream. Like the ubiquitous water hyacinth, the freshwater mangroves were the result of an experiment in the seventies that had got out of hand in the last forty years. The river flooded regularly enough to support them and in places the huge bushes grew to more than fifty feet in height. But there was a strange, unsettling foreignness about them.

The girls kept clear of the mangroves as they searched the bank, side by side, like children. The bright beam of the Maglite soon illuminated a big pile of ebony shells and Anastasia caught them up without a second thought. As she did so, Ado gave a startled gasp – the closest she would ever come to a scream. Anastasia looked down. There, beneath the pile of shell and weed, a skull was grinning up at them. Without a second thought, Anastasia struck out at it as though it had been a spider or a scorpion. The torch hit it like a bat striking a ball and it rolled back into the slick swirl of the river.

'Hold this,' ordered Anastasia after a moment, when her breathing returned to normal. Ado took the offered torch and Anastasia pulled the biggest blade out of the Victorinox. With an expert twist, she opened the largest oyster. She pushed the blade on to the glutinous darkness of the creature's soft body. And both girls gasped again. For the movement of the oyster's slimy flesh revealed the biggest, blackest pearl that either of them had ever seen.

They were still crouching, side by side, staring down at the jet-black wonder when the Army of Christ the Infant swept out of the jungle and into the compound behind them.

# FOUR
## Tie

'White,' said Richard incredulously. 'You did say *white*?'

'White!' confirmed Robin, calling through from her bathroom in their suite in the Granville Royal Lodge Hotel. The Nelson Mandela Suite, the best that the five star establishment had to offer. Max Asov and his latest flame were in the Presidential Suite next door. A couple from the IMF were in the Royal Suite. These three suites comprised the most exclusive in the hotel. The World Bank rep and the various government middle-rankers also in attendance were travelling without partners so no one's nose had been put too far out of joint by being offered the slightly less magnificent accommodation on the next floor down. And their teams, like Richard's Heritage Mariner associates, were scattered through the rest of the world-class hotel's lower floors.

'Not *black*?' Richard insisted, towelling his hair vigorously as he looked glumly down at the bed. Since being driven under armed escort from the airport in a police armoured car with only Dr Holliday and Colonel Kebila for company – except for the squad of soldiers with their Ruger MP-9 semi-automatics – he had checked in and showered, yelling snippets of information through to Robin in her own bathroom next door. The silence in the vehicle had been salutary. And it had frankly come as something of a relief to find that they had pulled up outside the familiar front of Granville Harbour's premier hotel instead of the equally familiar front of the city's central police station.

'*White!*' snapped Robin now. 'It's most specific! That's why I had the laundry press it, starch it and lay it out for you.'

'Bloody hell!' said Richard glumly, stepping into his underwear. 'It's just as well you brought the monkey suit with the rest of the clobber in the jet.'

'Stop complaining and get a move on,' called Robin. 'You're

already well behind schedule, what with your hare-brained airport adventure! From the sound of things it's a providence that Colonel Kebila rescued you and got you here so fast. We certainly don't want to be late, even if we do only have to take the lift down to the ballroom. And don't you dare call it a *monkey* suit outside these four walls.'

'Penguin suit then,' allowed Richard. 'Penguins shouldn't offend any sensibilities. But still and all,' he added, *sotto voce*, 'white tie!' He sighed, picking up the starched icy white cotton of his evening shirt and reaching for his white pearl studs. 'And as it turns out, the scheme at the airport was not hare-brained,' he called more loudly as he crossed to the mirror and started wrestling his wing collar into place. 'I learned a hell of a lot that will stand us in good stead when push comes to shove. And I suspect that it was by no means providential that Kebila showed up. I just can't work out what his game is, that's all. Nor what Julius Chaka's game is come to that! White tie and tails! I'll look like Fred Astaire! What is our beloved president up to?'

By the time Robin swept out in her basque and suspenders, her golden curls coiffed, her grey eyes exquisitely mascaraed, the rest of her gamin face most carefully made up, slim neck and fingers bejewelled, curvaceous body perfumed and ready to assume the exclusive creation in turquoise silk and sequins that had played Ginger Rogers to Richard's Fred Astaire outfit on the bed. He had his white braces adjusted, his turn-ups sitting squarely on his patent dancing shoes, his white tie hanging round his wing collar and his white waistcoat ready to be buttoned.

'"I just got an invitation through the mails"' he sang as he helped Robin step into the dress and then began to settle it into place. '"*Your* presence requested this evening, it's formal, a top hat, a white tie and tails."'

'Very funny,' she said as he pulled ribbons into place between her broad shoulders and her slim waist. 'I'd like to know what you're up to, sailor. I never quite trust you when you start singing apropos of nothing. No, don't tighten those too much, or I'll burst out of the top like a couple of balloons.'

'Hmm,' he answered. 'Maybe we'll try that later. You know what the sight of you in all those white frilly underthings does to me.'

'Do I ever!' she answered throatily. 'Down boy! For the moment at least. And zip me up at the side here!'

Richard obliged, then crossed to the mirror, picking up his tailcoat, and sang the next section of the song in a baritone more reminiscent of Frank Sinatra than Fred Astaire as he did what it said in the words: tying up his white tie, duding up his shirt front, putting in his shirt studs and brushing off his tails. But his eyes were narrow, and Robin, looking at his reflection, knew that the song was a cover for some very rapid thinking indeed.

Richard and Robin stepped out of the Nelson Mandela Suite at exactly the moment that Max Asov and his current partner stepped out of their suite and the couple from the IMF stepped out of theirs. 'Madame Lagrande,' said Richard, at his most suave, greeting the chic, petite economist with the suggestion of a bow – and a quick smile to her gangly, bespectacled husband. 'A pleasure to meet you again. Professor Lagrande. You remember Madame Mariner, of course. Have you met Monsieur Asov, Managing Director of Bashnev Power and the Sevmash Shipping Consortium, and his partner Mademoiselle Irina Lavrov?' Max looked very much the intellectual, with a whisper of the young Trotsky and more than a suggestion of Che Guevara. Everyone was likely to know Irina – to some extent at least. Her kick-ass blockbuster films routinely topped the box office listings if not the Oscar nominations.

Richard was relieved to see that both Max and Professor Lagrande were also in white tie. Max, surprisingly, looking urbane and at ease; almost as much the intellectual as the pair of top-flight economists beside him. Every inch the well-dressed, sophisticated man about town, he even sported a gold watch-chain; an affectation which put to shame Richard's insistence on staying with his battered but beloved steel-cased Rolex Oyster Perpetual.

'Of course, Captain Mariner,' answered Claudette Lagrande smoothly in her impeccable Oxford English. 'It is very pleasant to see you again. Shall we?' She gestured towards the lift and the doors opened as though at her command.

They made easy small-talk in the capacious elevator. Professor Lagrande was a fan of Irina's and he managed to flatter her without being overpowering. Max struck back by turning on the charm and engaging Madame Lagrande in a techno-financial conversation that made Fermat's last theorem seem positively elementary. 'So,' said Robin. 'The airport. What did you learn?'

'I don't think the president has managed to pull things round as well as he seems to think . . .' Richard began to explain.

'But Colonel Kebila pulled your chestnuts out of the fire in the end . . .' she repeated as he reached the end of his brief explanation.

'And gave us a ride to the front door,' he confirmed. 'Full military escort.'

'Hmmm. *We?*'

'Ah. Didn't I mention Dr Holliday of the World Bank?'

'I see. A doctor. An elderly masculine doctor of economics, I assume? Very much in the mould of Professor Lagrande here?'

'One out of three isn't bad . . .' he began, a little sheepishly.

The doors hissed open and the six of them stepped out into the cavernous magnificence of the Granville Royal Lodge's newly completed Gala Ballroom. The ballroom seemed to take up one entire level of the hotel. Richard gazed up genuinely impressed by the scale of the architectural vision and the simple efficiency of the civil engineering. Chandeliers hung in widening circles, the gleams from their lustres glimmering white, yellow and blue, as though they were diamonds of the first water. And the light from candle bulbs reflected equally brightly in glassware and silverware on the tables that encircled the huge, waxed, interior-sprung dance floor that matched a gargantuan porthole in the centre of the ceiling, whose massively toughened glass allowed those in the ballroom to look up into the cool blue water of the illuminated swimming pool which lay, miraculously, immediately above them.

Andre Wanago, the hotel's urbane manager, greeted the six of them as they stepped out of the lift and escorted them at once to President Chaka who was standing nearby, waiting to greet his guests, flanked by the senior members of his government. Richard scanned the faces of the exclusive group of men, recognizing all of them. The flight down here had not been wasted. The two most important, Minister of State for the Inner Delta and the Minister of State for the Outer Delta, stood at Chaka's right shoulder. And Colonel Laurent Kebila stood at his left, bringing the reception line to an unexpected end.

But then, even as the Colonel's easy presence amongst the most powerful in the land began to sink in – with the realization that Kebila was standing where Richard had expected to see the Minister of Police and Security Affairs – something else struck him. Of the whole group round Chaka, only Kebila was in anything like Western dress – the khaki army uniform with the eagle and stars on his epaulette that stated his rank. All the others were in traditional West African clothing. They were all attired in various versions of the flowing robes known locally as a grand boubou.

As Andre Wanago gracefully ushered the little group forward, Richard took the opportunity for a swift look around – aided in his endeavour by his excellent eyesight and his considerable height. Yes. There could be very little doubt. All of the locals were wearing traditional – easy, comfortable – dress. Men in the grand boubou robes; women in female equivalent, the m'boubou. All the visitors were in ball gowns or penguin suits, like Andre and his formally attired waiters. So, where the male guests were – perforce – straitjacketed in their costumes of black and white, their hosts were relaxing in a rainbow of patterned silk and cotton.

Just as the ballroom by its very existence gave a strong message, so did the difference in dress code. The ballroom said, 'Benin la Bas can do anything Western or Eastern technology can – even when it comes to cutting-edge hotel design.' And the dress code said, 'We are an African nation on the African continent. This is now our country and no longer your colony. We belong here as you men in your penguin suits do not. What we have we might share – but you will need to come to us to get any of it.'

That had been Colonel Laurent Kebila's message too, of course. He had been watching Richard from the moment he stepped off the Boeing – perhaps from the moment he had bought a ticket under his own name – all it would take was a little Trojan virus in the booking systems of the airlines connecting to Granville Harbour International. This was a twenty-first century state. Security cameras, computer databases, cellphone monitoring systems, secret security services, the lot. Everything one might expect to find in the UK, the USA, the European Union, the Russian federation; except, perhaps, democracy.

These thoughts were sufficient to take Richard along the

reception line until he found himself looking directly into the coolly intelligent eyes of his host. The handshake, too, was cool. 'Captain Mariner, welcome to Benin la Bas,' he said, his voice deep and resonant. His English every bit as fluent as his French and Russian had been. His welcome to the man who, more than any other – except for Laurent Kebila, perhaps – had helped to put him where he stood now was, to put it mildly, ambivalent.

'Thank you Mr President,' answered Richard smoothly. 'My visit has been most instructive so far.'

'Yes. Colonel Kebila was just telling me. And I'm sure you will find that it continues to be instructive.' He paused a beat. 'And profitable.' He paused another beat as he turned to Robin, his face folding into a broad and charming smile. 'And *pleasurable*, of course . . .'

As it happened, Robin found the meal instructive as much as pleasurable. The instruction started immediately she was shown to her seat. On her right sat Max, with the incandescent Irina beyond him. On her left sat Richard, and beyond him a simply breathtaking young woman with the most arresting cinnamon skin and an accent as deep and dark as molasses. As deep and dark, Robin observed wryly, as the young woman's eyes; not to mention her cleavage. All of which seemed to be aimed at Richard.

'Darling,' said her scapegrace husband at his most insouciant, 'I don't think you've met Dr Bonnie Holliday of the World Bank, have you? Dr Holliday and I met at the airport . . .'

President Chaka gave a brief speech of general welcome, forbidding all business talk on this occasion, commanding his welcome guests to get to know one another before they began to discuss in more detail why they were here. Discussion that might commence, he suggested, at a series of meetings planned for tomorrow. As Robin already knew Max Asov, and also had a good idea why he was here, and as there was no one opposite her, she focussed her attention on Richard and the dazzling girl who had shared his airport adventure.

'What is it you do at the World Bank, Doctor?' she asked.

'I am on the East Africa desk at Washington headquarters at 1818 H. The local director is stuck in Abidjan, apparently, so they scooted me out at short notice. I'm not really in finances. My doctorate is in African Studies. But I guess that's OK because

my ultimate boss may have started out at Deloitte but she came
to us via Education.'

'African Studies,' said Richard. 'What school?'

'Harvard.'

'So,' said Robin, 'at the very least you'll be able to guide us
safely through dinner. You'll need to if it's as traditional as what
our hosts are wearing.'

'As safely as your Richard guided me through the airport!'
said Dr Holliday with a dazzling smile.

*Quite*, thought Robin, smiling back. *MY Richard. And don't
you forget it. Either of you.*


But, as it happened, one section at least of Bonnie Holliday's
PhD was put to good use, for Dr Chaka was seemingly keen to
underline the point he had made by asking for his guests to wear
white tie. The first course arrived. It consisted of a small plate
of cooked rice in the middle of which was spread four lobes of
pale nut. Each plate was garnished with a bright red petal or two.
'This is the traditional West African greeting course—' said
Bonnie.

'I know,' interrupted Robin. 'Rice and kola nut. How anything
this bitter got into the recipe for Coca-Cola, heaven only knows.'
She cast a sideways glance at Dr Holliday's curves. 'Still, it kills
the appetite. A useful diet aid.'

'And it's full of caffeine,' added Dr Holliday, apparently failing
to register the implication of Robin's comment. 'And several
other stimulants. The locals use it a little like Viagra, so I believe.'

'Right,' said Richard. 'I think I'd better just try a little . . .'

A moment later, he was using sweet palm wine to try and
clear his taste buds as the kola nut was replaced by poached
oysters. 'Is it alcoholic?' he asked, sipping the milky, fragrant
liquid carefully.

'Not if it's sweet and fresh. It gets to about four percent after
a day but it starts to taste more vinegary then,' Dr Holliday
explained. 'The oysters are from the delta, I expect,' she added.
'They're famous all along the coast. There'll probably be shrimp
later too. But Benin la Bas oysters are just so famous, for their
flavour and for their . . . qualities . . .'

'More aphrodisiacs,' riposted Robin. 'It's a wonder anyone
ever got past the hors d'oeuvres!'

The doctor giggled, and her date-brown eyes flickered up to meet the cool grey glaze. There was an instant of girl bonding as they shared a knowing grin before the sweet potato and peanut soup arrived.

Blessedly, the rigour of West African food and drink eased enough to allow a South African Chenin blanc with the Scalopines of Pompano, and the sommelier was even able to find some sparkling Ashbourne Water in the cellars. As Richard sipped this, the fish was replaced by Kyinkyinga, which Bonnie explained were chicken kebabs seasoned with garlic and groundnuts. They were served on rice and Richard for one found them delicious. Fortunately, he was careful not to overindulge, for they were replaced with Egusi soup, which was more like a stew with minced lamb and shrimp on a bed of spinach seasoned with fiery chillies. That was replaced in turn by Boko-Boko – beef roasted in cumin and cinnamon, served on a bed of cracked wheat with plantains in palm oil and okra in greens. A robust Moroccan Shiraz. The Boko-Boko gave way to a light course of fresh shrimps from the outer delta – accompanied by an Algerian white Cabernet – and that in turn was replaced with Jollof rice, with chicken, rice, green beans, onions and carrots stewed together with fresh rosemary, red pepper flakes and nutmeg, partnered with another considerable North African red.

It was after this, the ninth course by Robin's reeling calcula-tion, that President Chaka stood and announced a break in the proceedings. 'Before we introduce such sweetmeats as our famous coconut Shuku-Shuku, our goat's cheese and paneer, let us pause,' he began. 'In our continuing endeavours to entertain our non-African guests . . .'

'. . . *educate*, he means . . .' whispered Robin and Bonnie gave a complicit gurgle of laughter.

'. . . we would like you to experience some of our tribal customs to go with this feast of local fare.'

As he sat down, the chandeliers dimmed. A vertical column of brightness struck straight down from the swimming pool on to the dance floor as though there were some kind of huge blue moon up there. It was shifting, shadowy, as much to do with liquid as light. No sooner had the assembled diners got used to it, and to the strange silence that followed the President's ringing announcement, than the drums started. They built to a crescendo surprisingly quickly, and were accompanied suddenly by a deafening chorus of bull-roarers that sounded as though a legion of demons was being tortured to death nearby.

Abruptly, almost magically, one of those very devils seemed to appear in the heart of the strange blue light. It was the better part of seven feet tall, a thing of mask and raffia, designed to ensure that whoever wore it was completely invisible – not unlike the Chinese demon dogs that Richard had seen dance in Hong Kong, Singapore and Shanghai. But this devil was darker, more mysterious, more disturbing. Surrounded by his lesser dancing demons, he went whirling round the dance floor in a dance more complex than anything Fred Astaire ever attempted. As though possessed by something superhuman, something timeless, something out of the depths of the delta and the heart of the jungle. His mask, a carapace of ebony brutally carved and garishly daubed, seemed to glow beneath the blue luminescence. A strange sort of frisson went round the huge room. The Western tourists were surprised, perhaps shocked. The local people reacted differently, it seemed to Richard. With something more like superstitious awe. With genuine fear, perhaps.

Richard leaned over to Bonnie Holliday who was sitting stone-still at his side. 'What is it?' he asked.

'It is Ngoboi,' she said, her voice trembling a little. 'One of the greatest, most powerful and most dangerous spirits of Obi. Ngoboi is the dancing devil that is said to control the Poro, the secret bush societies; to demand and to take their sacrifices. Hearts. Livers. Fingers. Toes. The skin from foreheads and palms and feet. Sacrifices of people, you understand. Women. Children. Warriors, even. Human. *People*.' She took a deep, shuddering breath. 'A *tourist-friendly* version of Ngoboi.' She shook herself a little, then added, 'Pray you never meet him out in the wild jungle. In the jungle where he is real. They say it is death to look on him out there.'

'Ngoboi,' said Robin, intrigued. 'Tell me about him, Bonnie. Just in case . . .'

# FIVE
## Ngoboi

The Army of Christ the Infant arrived at the chapel compound in a sudden howling rush, like a wave unexpectedly breaking into surf as it hits a reef. There was no warning rumble of engines for the roads on this side of the river were all currently impassable. The army's transport section, trucks, four-by-fours and technicals, had stopped a kilometre distant, therefore, and the troops had come through the jungle on foot. Given that most of them were aged between ten and twelve years old, they had moved surprisingly quietly. Moses Nlong thought they were attacking an easy target, and that helped – he was running low on cocaine and decided against getting the kids hopped up as he would have done had he feared any kind of resistance. On the one hand, this ensured they didn't go in screaming like ghosts and shooting. On the other hand, it meant he was going to have a problem getting them motivated when they got there. Sober soldiers were always less willing to perform the sort of acts his power relied upon. But he had a way round that particular quandary.

The first that Anastasia and Ado knew about the attack, therefore, was the sound of Evensong breaking into screaming. And then came the sound of animalistic howling and the first shots. Anastasia's first instinct was to switch the big Maglite off. Then she put her arm round Ado's shoulders and they crouched together for a moment at the bottom of the high mud slope, shaking with shock on the riverbank. The mental picture of the big black pearl seemed to fade slowly in Anastasia's memory and she blinked in the velvet darkness, forcing her eyes to clear through sheer strength of will, commanding her night vision to click in. Without thinking, she shoved the whole oyster into the left-hand pocket of her jeans, looking around, her mind racing.

Further up the bank and in the mangroves, the darkness would have been all but absolute. Out here at the river's edge there was a little leaf-shadowed starlight and the pale promise of moonrise in the east – though the black battlements of the storm front sweeping in from the west had claimed almost half of the sky above. Up at the far end of the stretch of bank, away from the mangroves and the delta downstream, their little jetty stepped hesitantly into the stream, their tiny little rowboat – hardly more than a cockleshell – tied to it, waiting for the riverboat's next visit. Without further thought, Anastasia put the rest of the oysters into the bag that Ado had brought. There was quite a weight of them now. Irrelevantly, she wondered how much of that considerable bulk was made up of big black pearls, companions to the one she had just seen. Then Father Antoine's distinctive voice rang out – only to be silenced by the flat, unceremonious *bang* of a gunshot – and the full horror of what was happening hit home.

Ado gasped in a breath but, providentially, Anastasia stopped her before she made any sound. For, just at the moment she would have screamed, a tall figure appeared from the direction of the mangroves, coalescing out of the utter darkness like one of the local forest spirits. Anastasia recognized neither him nor what he was wearing, but she knew the outline of the gun well enough. Without thinking – without even reasoning that she was probably almost invisible in her Goth-black jeans and T-shirt, she rose up in front of him, pointing the Maglite like a gun. He sensed rather than saw her movement and started to swing the Kalashnikov up. She switched on the torch and shone it full in his face. For a nanosecond she saw the features of the soldier she had blinded. Frozen, blinking, his soft brown eyes suddenly full of tears. He looked so young. Then she switched the beam off again and hit him on the left temple with the kilo and a half of black-enamelled steel that made a very effective club. He went down without a sound and she followed him on to the mud, pounding on the back of his head, to make sure.

When he was lying still as death, she set about disentangling the Kalashnikov from his lifeless arms. For a moment she cradled it to her breast, her mind racing back across five years. The rock group she had run away with were called Simian Artillery – apes with guns. It described them perfectly. They had behaved worse than apes in the end but the guns had been real. And what self-respecting extreme Russian heavy metal rock group with a name

like that would not have the odd Kalashnikov lying around? Long
before she snorted her first line of coke or experienced her first
crack party gang-bang, she had learned how to field-strip, zero
and fire an AK-47 as deftly as a Spetsnaz special forces man.

This one came apart under her fingers almost by magic. Less
than five minutes after she picked it up it was back together again
and she was deciding how best to use it. The magazine was a
standard thirty round capacity and the weight of it felt about
right for fully loaded. Short of taking the cartridges out and
wiping them all off then counting them all back in, there was
nothing more she could do other than to rely on the gun. But
that was OK because, of course, it was just about the most reliable weapon ever manufactured. It was probably an AK that cut
short the poor old priest's last sermon. Better that than one of
the local matchets – what the rest of the West called machetes.

'Hold this,' she breathed to Ado, passing the AK. Then she set
about searching the unconscious soldier. He carried no matchet,
but he did have another two curving clips. That was ninety shots
in all. She could do some serious damage with ninety shots, she
thought. As long as she stayed alive. But she sure as hell couldn't
outgun a whole fucking army. Mind racing now as the formless
howling of the attack settled into a deeply disturbing rhythmic
chanting, Anastasia took the AK back, unclipped the shoulder strap
and set about tying the soldier's wrists and ankles together with it.

'I'm going back,' she breathed, stooping to scoop a handful
of dark silt from the pile of flotsam on the river's edge. She
smeared it on her face, thinking inconsequentially of fish. It was
the black mud that came downstream with the orchid and the
oysters from the lake. 'You stay here. If it looks hopeless then
I'll come back for you and we'll try and go for help. If the soldier
stirs or makes a sound then you hit him in the head and keep
hitting him until he stops. Really. You know what they'll do to
you if they catch you.'

'I would rather fight,' said Ado. 'I would rather die.'

'Fight *him*,' said Anastasia. 'And try to stay alive. I will too.'
She clicked the safety on the AK to select single shot. And she
was gone.

The brightness of the compound's electric lighting was enough
to guide her up the bank. She slid across the mud flat on her

belly, trying to remember what little she had learned about this kind of thing from watching endless macho war films with Simian Artillery and going paintballing with her father in happier days. It seemed sensible to keep low, move slowly and use her eyes to the limit of their ability. At the back of her mind the fact that the soldier hadn't been able to distinguish her black clothing from the shadows gave her a little confidence – but not as much as the AK cradled across her forearms just under her chin. Or the spare clips she had shoved down the back of her belt to lie like sabres of ice across her buttocks. Or even the Victorinox she had in her left-hand pocket. She became distracted by the wry thought that for the first time in her life she was glad that she didn't have much of a bust – her flat chest helped her stay lower still. She didn't even register that she also had a pocket full of oysters and at least one big black pearl.

Anastasia came up behind the chapel. Like all of the compound buildings it stood on breeze blocks that raised it about three quarters of a metre off the ground. The area might have been mercifully clear of mosquitoes but the same could not be said for ants and termites. Further, it had been erected on a slight slope – the one that ran from the compound down to the river – and the breeze blocks had been used to level it so the gap on the river side was higher than the one on the camp side. A welcoming cavern, easy to enter.

Still with the AK cradled under her chin, Anastasia wriggled under this, moving slowly on elbows and knees, keeping her butt low and her chest tight to the ground, straining to see out of the shadows into the brightness of the central compound – all too well aware that she would be lucky to see much more than foot-wear, calves and knees from this angle, and trying not to think about ants, snakes, spiders, centipedes and scorpions.

But it was nothing from the insect world that came closest to making Anastasia give herself away. It was Father Antoine. She had calculated that the best place for her to place herself to start with was beneath the steps that led up from the compound to the chapel. The first step was made entirely of brick, but the next two were simple planks standing on piles of bricks, maybe forty-five centimetres high and a metre and a half apart. The lower step would form a protective wall she could hide behind. The upper steps would give her good vision and, perhaps, a secure field of fire.

But Father Antoine had been standing on the bottom step shouting at the Army of Christ the Infant when he was shot. He had fallen back on to the wooden planks and the nearest child soldiers had spent some moments ensuring his demise by chopping at him with their matchets. They had rolled him over to one side of the rudimentary stairs so that they could search the chapel itself. Anastasia was therefore confronted by the vision of his staring eyes, so wide they seemed to gleam in the shadows. His forehead had been burst by the gunshot and then chopped open in four more places by matchet blows. His crisp white hair – a blackish brown now – hung forward on his forehead and the matted strands seemed to be all that was holding his brains in place. His nose was gone and his mouth gaped unnaturally wide, tongue lolling grotesquely. Beneath the shapeless russet sack of his once snowy robe, a considerable lake of blood was slowly soaking into the red mud and dusty brickwork. His hands stuck through the planks, hanging down helplessly. All his fingers were gone.

Anastasia lay there for several minutes, considering things. She had no notion of being in rapidly deepening shock. She was wondering – albeit distantly – whether to be sick. She had been too focussed on action before to feel fear but it stabbed through her now. Not fear. Sheer stark terror. She had, perhaps, wet herself. Or it might have been Father Antoine's bodily fluids flowing downhill under her. She wondered vaguely whether there was any way she could manoeuvre the AK so that she could kill herself now and escape all this in one agonizing instant. But then she heard Celine's clear voice, and all other thoughts flew straight out of her mind.

Anastasia discovered that if she pulled herself up as close as possible to Father Antoine's corpse, she got quite a good view of the compound. The unfamiliar children – the Army of Christ the Infant – were distinguishable from her own young charges only in that they were armed, and were wearing an assortment of dirty, ragged clothing – shorts and T-shirts for the most part. And that they all needed a good bath by the look of things. The child soldiers were standing in a restless ring around the taller, fitter, better dressed and cleaner orphans, who were cowed and terrified by the guns and the matchets. Also by the death of Father Antoine and by the situation of the other adults in the camp. Imam Mohammed, the Muezzin Samir and Ibrahim were in the same state as Father Antoine, lying in the centre of the circle, hacked to death. Brother Jacob was kneeling beside them but he seemed to be alive. Just about. Celine was standing, tall and apparently fearless, in front of the three nuns. And, behind the nuns, the boys and girls they were trying so vainly to protect. There was silence and stasis after whatever she had said. So much silence, in fact, that Anastasia dared not risk pushing the selector down one more notch to automatic fire. Even though a fire-rate of 600 rounds a minute suddenly seemed worth having at her disposal – for the second or so that her clips would last for.

Anastasia wormed round until she could see whoever it was that Celine was speaking to. A group of older boys – young men – were standing round half a dozen adults whose uniforms were cleaner, pressed, more military-looking. The special guards all held AK-47s. In the centre of this group, the tallest man stood, apparently thinking. What looked like a Browning automatic hung from one listless arm. A blood-spattered matchet the better part of a metre long hung from the other, its lanyard looped up round his wrist above the huge gold watch he wore. It was hard to tell *what* he was thinking because his face was a mask of ritual scars that seemed to be set like ebony. His mouth looked like just one more scar running from side to side instead of up and down. He wore a maroon beret pulled to the line of his eyebrows. Between the beret and the scarred cheeks there was a pair of sunglasses whose silver lenses simply reflected Celine's wide-eyed stare. Anastasia had never seen any pictures of self-styled General Moses Nlong, but she reckoned that this must be him. And whatever Celine had said must have given the general pause. And the whole of his army had paused with their leader.

Then he slapped her round the face. With the flat of the matchet. It was a casual blow, with seemingly no real force behind it, but it swatted her to the ground like a left hook from a heavyweight boxer. A gasp went up right round the compound. Silence returned. He gestured, twice. Two of the tall young men stooped and pulled the reeling Celine to her feet and held her. Four others closed on Sister Faith. They dragged the struggling woman forward. As they did so, Nlong holstered the Browning. He reached out and pulled the sister's white headdress off. Then, with the matchet hanging from its lanyard, he ripped her robe wide, revealing her plump white shoulders. He pinched her upper arm and smiled. There was enough light to see a flash of his teeth. They had been filed to points. He nodded and Anastasia froze, suddenly realizing what was going to happen next. Celine yelled something, her voice slurred, but too late.

Sister Faith was on her knees and the matchet rose and fell like a guillotine. Dancing clear of the fountain of blood with practised ease, Nlong strode over to Celine, shouting wildly. But she was sagging in a dead faint between her two captors. The general took her hair and twisted her face up towards his. Then he let her drop and spat an order to the men holding her. He raised his voice and shouted to the whole of his army. Suddenly everything was in motion. The well-armed ragamuffins sprang to life. The girls and boys from the orphanage were separated. The girls were herded into one of the dormitory huts. The boys were forced back along the wall nearest to the fire and held there under guard, where they could watch. Watch and learn. While this was going on, the two men holding Celine dragged her fainting body across the compound and up the steps into the chapel. Anastasia heard the telltale thumping and scraping immediately above her which told of a body being dropped and then tied securely. By the time the two young men came out again, the rest of the army was seated at the refectory tables as Jacob the handyman, Hope and Charity served the food that would have fed their children.

Into this strange, almost domestic, scene stepped the huge, masked figure of Ngoboi, spirit of the wild jungle.

At once the atmosphere changed. Anastasia had never felt anything like it. The monstrous apparition stared around the compound, the raffia costume covering his tall frame seeming to stir as though there was a wind, the lifeless visage of his painted ebony mask catching both light and shadow. Two helpers in masks and raffia skirts over shorts and T-shirts danced forward to help him. They carried matchets that looked even longer than the one the general had used to decapitate Sister Faith.

In the sinister silence, Ngoboi started to move around the pale bulk of the nun's corpse. Shuffling at first, then beginning to twirl and leap in a complicated ritual dance, the strange forest

devil whirled around and around the fallen woman, moving to
the relentless beat of a drum he could only hear in his head. His
skirted helpers capered around him, also increasingly wildly, until
suddenly he gestured, mid-bound. And they fell upon Sister
Faith's corpse, their matchets rising and falling in practised
sequence. Every eye in the place was riveted on the horrific
performance, captivated by the terrible magic. As the matchets
rose and fell above the butchered nun, first the general and then
his army began to pound the tables with their fists, giving voice
at last to the rhythm inside Ngoboi's ebony and raffia head.

Anastasia put her AK down, its barrel resting on the first
wooden step, then she wriggled through the gap between that
and the third step, using the pale bulk of Father Antoine's
corpse and the depth of the shadow it cast. In an instant she
was inside the chapel, standing with her back to the wall, the
door-frame at her right shoulder, looking down to where Celine
lay bound and helpless on the floor. Her eyes were wide and
her lips were parted, panting with shock and horror. Three long
steps took Anastasia to her side. She went down on one knee,
pulling the Victorinox from her pocket and snapping out the
longest blade. As she sawed at Celine's bonds, the girl gasped,
almost whimpering with terror and tension as the thunderous
pounding rose and rose outside.

It took only a moment to cut Celine free, then the pair of them
were side by side pressed against the wall inside the door. There
was no other way out. No windows. No weaknesses in the sturdy
floor – raised above the depredations of the termites that might
have weakened it. Anastasia gasped and gulped an explanation
of how she had got here from the riverbank. The best way back
by the look of things. Their only chance of survival. Their only
hope of somehow getting help and coming back for the others.
'I'll go first,' she concluded. 'Then I'll signal the best moment
for you to follow . . .' Celine nodded.

Anastasia oozed out through the door on her belly like a slug,
falling into Father Antoine's shadow at once and slipping between
the planks to cradle the AK like an old, dear friend. She looked
along the barrel just in time to see Ngoboi straighten from a
crouching position over Sister Faith. An acolyte at his shoulder
straightened too. Ngoboi had no hands; the helper held Sister
Faith's heart in one fist and what looked like her liver in the

other. Held the bloody trophies high as Ngoboi took off again, twirling and dancing. The rest of his helpers fell on the corpse again and Anastasia realized they were literally butchering it – cutting it into joints like a carcass in a meat shop.

Sister Faith's organs were carried towards the general. Anastasia had very little doubt about what he was planning to do with them. Once again, every eye in the place was riveted to the gruesome spectacle. The pounding rose even higher, thundering through the jungle in a terrific tempest of sound. Anastasia thumped on the floorboards above her head, then moved the AK over out of Celine's way, for the ex-freedom fighter was much larger than her Russian would-be rescuer. And dressed in more bulky clothing of a much lighter shade.

Anastasia blinked and shook her head, trying to clear the sweat and black mud from her eyes. When she looked again, General Nlong, standing in Father Antoine's place of honour at the top table under the palm-roofed lean-to, was raising Sister Faith's heart to his lips. Everyone was watching him. The drumming was fading away as the pounding fists stilled in anticipation. Such was the horrific power of the ghastly moment that the general seemed to be illuminated by an instant of the brightest white light. It flickered as his strange sharp teeth bit down, and was gone. Anastasia realized she still had not switched the selector over to automatic. Another opportunity lost.

Celine came crawling out of the chapel door then. With some difficulty – and far too slowly for Anastasia's taste – she began to wriggle between the steps. A great sound went up. Not a cheer. Something too feral and brutal for that. The pounding started again, a hollow thundering taken up by the sky itself as the threatened storm finally arrived. But Ngoboi had stopped dancing. He was standing looking towards the chapel. Shouting. Shouting and gesturing. Fighting to make himself heard above the thunder. Fighting to make the others understand. Celine flopped in beside Anastasia.

'GO!' screamed Anastasia and pulled the AK's trigger, simply aiming towards the centre of the compound where Ngoboi was still capering. The muzzle flash exploded at the same instant as the next great blaze of lightning; its flat report lost amid the faltering beating on the tables and the instant explosion of thunder overhead. Ngoboi staggered back a step and suddenly sat down.

Anastasia rolled away from the step, and, holding the AK by its hot muzzle, she wormed her way under the chapel as quickly as she could. The thunder echoed through the jungle and began to fade away. But at once its diminishing rumble was replaced by the arrival of the rain. She rolled out on to the upper slope of the bank and saw Celine beginning to pick herself up. 'Go!' yelled Anastasia again, and side by side they pounded towards the river, slipping and sliding in the instantly disorientating deluge.

Blessedly, Ado had not been idle in their absence. She had pulled the little rowing boat down from its place beside the pier and – in a moment of bizarre inspiration – had secured it by tying it to the unconscious soldier. As the two women came sliding down the bank towards her, she flashed the Maglite once to guide them. 'Get in!' shouted Anastasia as soon as she understood what Ado had done. And Ado obeyed. Celine stepped in next and Anastasia herself brought up the rear. Kneeling in the bow of the rowing boat, she turned back to try and untie the rope. But Ado had made too good a job. The knot securing the little vessel to the unconscious soldier was far too tight and complex for her trembling fingers to loosen. And the rain only made matters worse. She felt back along the straining rope only to find a tangled mare's nest beneath her knees.

Celine's hand came down on her shoulder then and she looked up. Along the top of the ridge, silhouetted by the flickering lights of the compound, a row of figures stood looking down into the darkness. Uncertain yellow light gleamed fitfully on matchets and AKs as they were brandished above the howling soldiers' heads. 'Get him!' Anastasia shouted. 'Get him in the boat!'

Celine reached down and together they wrestled the dead weight of their living anchor in over the gunwale. And the river took them at once, sweeping the four of them down towards the mangroves. Lightning pounced down, lighting up the wild crowd of their pursuers, with the general in their midst, mouth wide, crocodile teeth gleaming, chin red with Sister Faith's heart's-blood, face slick and streaming. And, in that instant of brightness, he saw them. His eyes locked with Anastasia's, and he raised the Browning even as she fought to bring up the AK. This time she took more careful aim.

They fired at the same instant, though neither was able to see where their bullets went, for the little rowing boat was whirled round the out-thrust of the mangroves, as though propelled by the recoil of the AK itself, and was gathered into the midst of the river as it twisted round a sharp bend and plunged down into the delta proper.

# SIX

## Craft

As Ngoboi and his assistants at last whirled off the dance floor, the chandeliers brightened once again and Bonnie's whispered commentary stilled, Richard leaned over towards Robin, his eyes narrow and his face crafty. 'While we savour dessert and coffee as promised, my darling, why don't I bring you up to speed with some of the background I read up on during the flight down here?'

'OK,' said Robin, equally craftily; well aware that showing off to her would distract him from the delectable Dr Holliday. 'Do tell, my darling.'

'The minister for the outer delta is that huge, short-necked bull of a man at the table over there. His name is Dr Bala Ngama and he is every bit as powerful as he looks. His responsibilities run from the lower edge of the inner delta right out to the boundary of Benin la Bas's territorial waters. His purview is, therefore, very wide indeed, and his influence, inevitably, just as far-reaching. Only Chaka himself outguns him, so they say. There's oil in the outer delta, of course, and under the continental shelf beneath the ocean waters to the south of it.'

'Oil that Max Asov's Bashnev drills and we at Heritage Mariner ship to and from the refineries in Northern Europe. I know that, my love.'

'Quite. Oil that everyone else is trying to get hold of too. At any price. But the minister, like the rest of Chaka's government, has the reputation of being untouchably honest. But you know how dirty big oil can get. Still, that's why Minister Ngama works so closely with the minister for petroleum resources. That scrawny-looking chap with the black-rimmed spectacles. Keeping an eye on each other, perhaps. As pristine as Caesar's wife.'

'But he's just responsible for the outer delta and the oil, isn't he? I mean he's not responsible for mines and so forth as well, is he?' Robin asked, frowning.

'That's right,' answered Richard. 'It's the minister for the inner delta who's responsible for the mineral wealth of the area – and he works most closely with the Ministry of Mines and Metals, not to mention the nearly nationalized Minière Benin la Bas diamond cartel. Those gentlemen you took such a shine to as you went down the reception line.'

'Gold and diamonds,' she countered cheerfully. 'I can't *think* what the attraction was . . .'

'Well, he and Bala Ngama, fortunately, are brothers or there might have been some danger of rivalry between them. Especially as the minister for the outer delta, the elder, more powerful of the two, has yet more strings to his bow, many of them involving Colonel Kebila in his various security guises and his family in several of theirs.'

'Now that I didn't know,' she admitted, more seriously. 'Do fill me in.'

'Minister Ngama is currently responsible for the customs service, which Kebila oversees in a semi-official capacity. By extension, he is responsible for the port and docking facilities in Port Granville Harbour and, again with a little help from his friend, for the security of the port as a whole. He's equally responsible for the protection of the platforms, pipelines and facilities both ashore and in the offshore oilfields. Responsibility for Benin la Bas's navy comes under his purview, therefore – both the riverine and maritime sections of it – and the coastguard, with which there is naturally some overlap. The senior repre- sentative for naval affairs, however, is Captain Caleb Maina, who has day-to-day oversight of naval matters in the bay and up the river.'

'Which one is he?' demanded Robin. 'You know how I feel about naval men . . .'

'He's the only other one in uniform,' said Richard with some asperity. 'In dress whites, in fact. Over there beside Kebila. They're cousins, apparently.'

'So that's why they look so similar! Two Denzel Washingtons

for the price of one. One with moustache, one without. And does he have a command of his own, this Captain Caleb?'

'Two, as a matter of fact – though how he exercises both I can't imagine. When he's out with the big boys in the blue-water navy, he shares command of a neat corvette called the *Otobo*. But when he's assigned brown-water duties along the coast or sent off upriver, he has a pretty hairy Israeli-made Shaldag Mark Three fast patrol boat which is a bit like John F. Kennedy's PT109 on steroids. On steroids with guns.'

'Now he sounds like someone I'd give quite a lot to meet!' said Robin.

'*Me too*,' added Dr Holliday quite unexpectedly. 'And he's the guy in white, you say?'

'You're going to have a race on your hands, girls, judging by the way one or two of the other guests have been eyeing him up,' said Richard, more than a little amused. 'Though to be fair, Robin, you'll have your chance tomorrow. We're scheduled to meet Minister Ngama and his team – which includes your new heart-throb – tomorrow morning. Apparently Max wants to try and flog the minister one of Sevmash's updated Zubr hovercraft – which is just about designed to fill the gap between the Shaldag and the corvette, I'd say. Perhaps even cancel them both out.'

'Why is that?' asked Dr Holliday, no doubt hoping to have something to talk to Captain Caleb about if she got him on the dance floor later.

'It's the biggest hovercraft ever built,' said Richard easily. 'It's just under sixty metres long and twenty-five wide. It has a displacement of five hundred and fifty tons but when the cushion is up it has a draft of less than two metres, though it sits just over twenty metres high. It can carry more than one hundred tons – three T80 main battle tanks for instance, and it goes at nearly fifty knots – that's the better part of sixty miles per hour. It's bristling with rocket launchers, thirty millimetre cannons, air and missile defence systems. Or it would be if Max was allowed to import fully functioning armaments – which he's not. It has an armoured command post and sealed combat stations for when the going gets tough. That's almost as much firepower as his corvette on a platform that moves as fast as his Shaldag, with a draft only half a metre deeper than the patrol boat has. Max thinks he'll find it irresistible. And Sevmash have plenty more where that came from. A million US dollars apiece, apparently. A snip at twice the price.'

'That poor girl,' said Robin lazily some time later, as they were wandering back through the Nelson Mandela Suite, all footsore and danced out. 'I thought you were going to start trying to sell her a used car or some life insurance.'

'She asked,' said Richard, shrugging off his tails and pulling his bow tie apart. 'And, from what I observed on the dance floor later, she was making good use of what I told her.'

'You weren't supposed to be looking at *her* on the dance floor!' snapped Robin, outraged. 'You were supposed to be looking at *me*!'

'I was,' he answered, wounded, looking at her reflection over his shoulder as he undid the stud at the front of his collar. 'I was watching you eyeing Colonel Kebila sitting all alone and forlorn.'

'That was different,' she said, giving a little pirouette as she floated round the end of their massive bed. 'I was feeling sorry for him.'

'Perhaps you should have asked him to dance,' suggested Richard as he unscrewed the pearl studs down the front of his shirt and waistcoat.

'Wouldn't have done any good,' she announced a tad over dramatically, plumping herself down a trifle inaccurately on the edge of the bed. 'He's heartbroken. Everyone knows, apparently. That's what Bonnie Holliday reported back at any rate. What his gorgeous cousin Captain Caleb said.' She collapsed back, arms spread.

'Once you started grilling her over that South African brandy,' said Richard, dropping his waistcoat on a chair and shrugging off his braces. 'How much did you have to drink yourself?' He stepped out of his shoes and began unbuttoning his trousers.

'A perfect amount. An inelegant suff . . . sufff –' she gave up on 'sufficiency' and continued – '*suffishanchips*. And don't change the subject.' She rolled over, the movement threatening to make her burst out of her dress after all. She looked across at him, her eyes huge and fathomless.

'OK. Why is poor Colonel Kebila heartbroken?' He stepped out of his trousers and folded them neatly, placed them carefully over the back of the chair then watched them slither gracefully on to the floor.

'*Celine Chaka*,' she announced triumphantly. 'He loves her with a love that burns unrequited in his breast. Especially since his boss, her father, has publicly disowned and abandoned her.'

'Has he? Does he? Is that from a poem? *Burns unrequited*? Or a Barbara Cartland novel, perhaps?' He slipped off his shirt and threw it at the chair, turning before he saw it land. There was a quiet rattle of studs and cufflinks hitting the floor.

'No. I made it up. And now that you mention burning *unrequited* . . .'

'Yes?' he hopped from one foot to the other, pulling off his socks.

'That's exactly how *I* feel. Come here and get me out of this dress and requite me. I hope you had a lot of those koala bear nuts and oysters. Because, believe me, sailor, you are going to need them!'

By something akin to a miracle, they both woke bright-eyed, bushy-tailed, clear-headed and ravenous a little over six hours later. An hour later still, Richard and Robin were side by side in the most striking office either of them had ever visited. Richard was relieved to see that, as with the food, last night's traditional costume had been dispensed with. Minister for the Outer Delta Bala Ngama met them in a lightweight business suit made of beige merino, apparently cut and crafted for him in Paris, London or New York. It was very much a match for Richard's own tropical lightweight, from Gieves & Hawkes, his favourite London tailors. There were a couple of dozen others in the room; most of them men, most of them in business suits of some kind.

'I have several offices,' the minister explained as the Heritage Mariner team assembled together with the Sevmash Consortium people, led by Max Asov. 'But this one seemed the most apposite, given the main focus of today's first meeting.' He raised a broad hand, gesturing proudly around. Richard, Robin, Max and the others looked appreciatively – even the members of Ngama's own team – as the minister's staff passed around them offering cool drinks, coffee and biscuits.

Richard's mind raced, picking up on subliminal messages designed to underline what had been so forcefully not stated last night – the opposite of what he had experienced at the airport. That Benin la Bas had changed from a broken kleptocracy with a moribund economy and a starving population simmering on the edge of revolution to a modern, wealthy, self-sufficient state. That President Chaka and his governments – both national and local – had pulled the country round and stood on the verge of achieving the African dream, thereby becoming a place where investment might be welcomed – and for the lucky acceptable few, would be enormously profitable. The whole of their current environment said this in no uncertain terms. Especially to someone like Richard who had known the place in the bad old days.

The office was in one of the smart new low-rise government buildings that had been erected on the land that had housed the shanty towns and slums the last time Richard was here. What had been a riverside mess of shacks and tents constructed of clapboard, bamboo, timber pilfered from the wreckage of the nearest suburbs and ubiquitous plastic sheeting, was now a carefully planned complex of manicured public gardens and municipal offices. The position of this particular office could hardly have been better from the minister's point of view. The broad front of the building opened through a series of glass doors on to a convex curving veranda that seemed to command a view of everything for which he stood responsible. To the left, the mouth of the River Gir opened, as wide as the Thames at Greenwich. Where the jungle used to cluster right up to the edge of the city, now there stood river docks, bustling with river craft, some freighters, more dredgers, and a pair of the neat little Shaldag fast riverboats that Caleb Maina was supposed to captain on his brownwater days. And a neat marina, filled with pleasure craft of all sorts, from pirogues to gin palaces, that could have been transported here directly from San Francisco or St Tropez.

With a slight shrug, Richard turned back to the breathtaking view. Straight ahead, on the far bank, the forest and jungle of the delta itself swept out across the bay. But where in the old days that had been an environmental disaster of oil-polluted mangroves peopled with restlessly dissatisfied freedom fighters, now it reflected order and care. Pipework looked new. There seemed to be no leaks. Some distant figures were working there, wearing a range of coloured overalls, clearly about legitimate business.

To the right, the bay itself stretched away to southern and western horizons, ringed with rigs of various sizes at various distances – the farthest only visible as columns of smoke and flame. A range of vessels moved busily among them, and Richard found himself wishing for binoculars as he strained to see the telltale house colours of Heritage Mariner. Hard right, looking almost north-west along the city's coastline, there stood the new dock facilities. The last time Richard had seen the place it had been a blazing ruin after the late president's helicopter had caused a supertanker to explode with near nuclear force. Now it was all rebuilt – quite a feat in less than five years, he allowed. The port frontage extended right down to the office complex itself; the minister's waterside office seeming to stand as the dividing point between seagoing and river-going vessels, between commercial craft and pleasure boats. Right at the hub of Granville Harbour. At the heart of Benin la Bas.

No sooner had Richard completed these thoughts than there was a sharp rap on the door and Captain Caleb Maina entered. 'Everything is ready, Minister,' he announced.

'Good. Then we can begin. Mr Asov, you will take the lead in due course but for the moment, please allow the captain and myself to be your guides. It is only a short walk, I assure you . . .' He gestured expansively once again. And Richard realized he was pointing towards the nearest of the vessels tied up on the seaward side of the docks to their right. A neat-looking corvette. The *Otobo*. Captain Maina's blue-water command, no doubt. He looked out across the bay, suddenly, working out what was going on here.

About half a mile offshore was a freighter he had overlooked in his keenness to search out Heritage Mariner house colours. The freighter was in Sevmash colours and it had its cranes up, busily lowering something over the side. He blinked. Gasped. It was all very well to be talking about Max's plans to sell equipment to the local navy, but it looked as though they were just about to get a closer look at the deal than he had calculated.

'A little surprise,' breathed Max, as he passed close by Richard's shoulder, simply bubbling with excitement.

'You can say that again!' said Richard, straining for a closer look at what the freighter was lowering into the bay – even as the pressure of all the bodies around him forced him to move towards the door.

'What is it?' demanded Robin.

'It's Max's hovercraft,' said Richard. 'The Zubr. Look at the size of the thing. It's almost as long as Captain Caleb's corvette, twice as wide and a great deal better armed. Or, as I said, it would be—'

'Except for the fact that I was forbidden to bring her full range of weaponry with me,' Max threw back over his shoulder. Then he was gone.

'So what's the actual plan, then?' she demanded as they walked out of the building and on to the dock where the corvette's gangplank awaited them.

'I think,' he answered quietly, 'that we're just about to join in a little war-game . . .'

# SEVEN

## Shell

'Bail!' shouted Anastasia. 'Bail or we'll all drown!'

The tiny cockleshell of a rowing boat whirled out into the middle of the Great River. There was water everywhere – slopping over the sides, thundering down from the sky. The whole universe seemed to be made of liquid – and it was all swamping the boat at a terrifying rate. Another fork of lightning made everything bright for a second – just enough time for Anastasia to see how wide the river had suddenly become. How far from the shores they were already. How near their gunwales were to the heaving, boiling surface. For an instant she regretted her failure to blow her own brains out with the AK. Things seemed to be getting worse by the moment. A quick, clean quiet death might have had its attractions after all.

Her scrabbling fingers kept skinning themselves against the AK in the bottom of the boat beside her. She tore a nail loose on an oar submerged beside it, then her hand became briefly entangled in the plastic bag. There was another oar and a grappling hook down there as well, she knew. And a big can of petrol – against which she bruised her knuckles. That was for the ancient two-stroke motor she had neither the time nor the knowledge to power up. But at last she found something that felt like a cup. She started pouring water over the side with feverish haste. 'Bail!' she screamed again.

She felt Celine moving beside her, her motion jerky and spasmodic, but she assumed that this was just some part of the young woman's long-past injuries, like her limp, like her stiff and painful shoulder joints. 'Ado!' she shouted. 'Are you bailing?'

'I can't find anything to bail with!' came the distant, desperate answer.

'Shine the torch around . . .' she ordered, thinking: *We have to be well out of sight of them now*.

The Maglite's beam struck out across the vast darkness, showing only sheets of pouring rain and the wildly dimpled foaming surface their massive drops were falling on to. There was no longer any sign of the bank. Then Ado swung the beam inboard and gasped. 'The soldier. His face is under water! It is deep. He may drown.'

'See what you can do. But be quick or we're *all* going to drown! Can you see anything?'

'I have an old bait tin here. I must just turn him . . .' The light wavered wildly. The boat rocked even more unsettlingly. Then the darkness returned and the three of them continued bailing.

After half an hour – which none of them counted or calculated – the rain eased. After a further hour, which whipped by equally unnoticed, the cloud cover broke up and a low, full moon came out. Had they been in the forest, it would have made no difference to them at all, for it would have been blotted out by the canopy and they would still have been lost in shadow. But they were in the middle of a wide river – slowing now because it had grown so broad. So there were no leafy branches above them – simply the big sky, the stars and the moon.

The pace of their bailing slowed to a stop. The bottom of the boat was by no means dry, but they were too exhausted to continue. They sat, slumped, arms hanging and eyes vacant. The little boat sailed on, pulled unerringly by the current towards the heart of the delta and on towards the sea, hundreds of miles downriver. Only the whispering chuckle of the water sounded sibilantly near at hand. There was no life in the river to breach and breathe, to jump and splash. There was no life in the jungle on the far banks to hoot, howl, roar or call. There was no wind to whisper in the distant leaves. There was only the patter of the fallen raindrops dripping down from leaf to leaf, from grass to ground. And, like their mighty cousin the river, whispering and chuckling as they did so, like the thread-thin ghostly voices of the great spirits and long dead ancestors crowding the deepest shades.

The soldier groaned.

'At least he's still alive,' Anastasia voiced her thought without realizing it. And, because of this, she spoke in English. She had been thinking in English for some time now. 'But that's a fact which could cut both ways. Is he tied up tightly?'

'Yes,' answered Ado, the little school's star pupil, fluent in English and Russian as well as her native Matadi. 'But he's in pain. I think he's cramping badly. And you tied him really tightly . . .'

'Probably has a nasty headache as well,' said Anastasia wearily. 'But you're right. I'll see what I can do.' She pulled herself slowly and carefully down the boat, aching in every muscle, moving like a very old lady.

The braided nylon line came undone surprisingly easily now that no one was chasing them. Especially under the bright beam of the Maglite. And it looked as though it would make a far more efficient restraint than the AK's webbing sling. The boy was still groggy enough for Anastasia to risk loosening his wrists from his ankles and straightening him out before she re-secured him. Just to make doubly sure, however, she called over her shoulder to Celine, 'Hold the gun on him while I do this, would you?'

Ten minutes later, he was lying on his back in the bottom of the boat – a useful piece of ballast if nothing else. His shoulders were wedged between the oars and the boathook was under his spine along the keel where he couldn't get at it. His wrists were lashed together, as were his ankles. Anastasia had been generous with the rope and it looked as though they wouldn't be tying up to any jetty in the immediate future. He also had a band around his chest and another round his knees securing him to the oars and the boathook – in case he took it into his head to start rolling around or kicking out.

'All right, Celine,' said Anastasia. 'You can stop covering him now.' She turned to her friend, looking at her properly for the first time since their escape.

Celine was slumped with the AK across her knees pointing at the boy. But her finger was nowhere near the trigger. Her arms were hanging limply, her hands resting in her lap like a pair of lilies. Her head was bowed and only the curve of the boat's side was holding her erect. One side of her blouse was dark with blood. And Anastasia realized with a pang of utter horror that the woman she loved had been shot.

'Don't die!' snarled Anastasia. 'Don't you dare die on me!'

Celine was lying on her back on top of the semi-conscious soldier. She was still unconscious. Her head was held by the ill-fitting combat boots that completed the soldier boy's uniform and her own feet rested astride his battered face. Ado, at the left-hand side of the boat's prow, was trying to balance Anastasia who was sitting on the right side of the stern, her backside on the only seat aboard, her torso leaning in over her friend's right shoulder, her own shoulder hard against the outboard motor's control lever as she worked. Celine's blouse was open wide. The blood-soaked right cup of her bra gleamed under the still-bright beam of the Maglite. The strap that should have supported it was snapped right at the crest of her shoulder, above her collar bone where the bullet from Moses Nlong's automatic had gone right through her trapezius muscle, about seven centimetres out from her neck. Anastasia tore the bra off, seeking a second, fatal bullet hole before it registered that there had been just one shot fired at them. She tore her eyes away from the liquid perfection of Celine's right breast and concentrated on the damage that she could see.

Anastasia looked in horror down at the wound, her mind racing, with no idea just how lucky the wounded woman had been. As wounds went, it was about as neat as could be expected. The bullet had simply gone straight in and straight out.

Memory kicked in. The last time Anastasia had seen anything like this was when the lead singer of Simian Artillery had acci-dentally shot his lead guitarist during a variation on Russian Roulette that had formed the centrepiece of a marathon drinking session at the Ermitage Hotel after a sell-out concert in St Petersburg. Anastasia, the soberest of the group, had packed the entry and exit wounds with clean cloth, bound tight, and phoned the hotel's doctor. Who, as it turned out, had complimented her work and said she had missed her vocation as a nurse. Just before the disgruntled night manager threw them all out of his exclusive hotel – and suggested they try the Baskov Hotel instead.

She knew what to do, therefore – but she wasn't so sure she had the wherewithal to do it. The cleanest piece of cloth on board was likely to be Ado's blouse or the T-shirt she wore beneath it. They, unlike Anastasia's or Celine's own, had not been rolling around in God knew what underneath the chapel. The blouse was cotton and too flimsy. The T-shirt was more substantial however. And, although Ado was by no means fully grown, there was a good deal more of her than there was of Anastasia – and a good deal more T-shirt, therefore.

'Ado,' said the Russian after a moment, 'pass me the Victorinox and your T-shirt.'

By midnight the wound was bound. Celine was resting more comfortably and both Ado and the prisoner seemed to be sound asleep. Anastasia wearily relieved herself over the stern, trying not to take too seriously the mental picture of a crocodile rising to bite off her backside. Then she too slumped sideways on the seat, trying without much success to make herself comfortable as she leaned back on to the top of the outboard motor. But even so, she went to sleep. It was only in her dreams that she began to come to terms with what had happened – what was happening still – at the chapel and the compound. But by the time she woke, she knew with a bone-deep certainty that she was going to have to do something about it.

Anastasia sprang awake six hours later as the sun rose behind her and sent its first rays like a golden hammer to batter the back of her skull. Without thinking, she sat up, stretched, and reached down into the river to scoop a handful of blessedly cool water. She poured this over her head. It ran down her face and she licked her lips. It tasted sweet. She looked over the side. The river's surface was glassy and clear. Her gaze plunged down into the crystal depths. Only at the deepest reach did shadowy hints of river-bed come and go, like reflected clouds far, far below. She scooped more water from the upper reaches. Drank and began to look around.

She looked down at Celine first and was relieved to see her apparently sleeping peacefully. The white pads she had fashioned from Ado's T-shirt were still in place, and still white. Their pressure had stopped the bleeding at least. Anastasia reached down to pull the wounded woman's blouse together in a vain attempt to cover up her breasts. Then she looked up and out a little further. And met Ado's wise eyes. 'Thanks for the T-shirt,' she said in Matadi. 'The bandage seems to be holding well.'

Ado nodded, her face still serious and thoughtful. Her blouse was little more substantial than Celine's but at least it was decorously buttoned.

'You didn't kill me!' a wondering, masculine voice announced from the bottom of the boat. 'I thought you had killed me.' The prisoner spoke Yoruba, but Matadi was a sub-dialect of the West African *lingua franca* and they could all understand each other.

'We probably should have,' snapped Anastasia. 'Your friends have killed our friends – killed them and eaten them. And taken our students as slaves and soldiers. We need fewer like you, not more!'

'But we do not slay our enemies,' said Ado simply. 'We love them. And we do good to those that hate us. It is what Father Antoine said.'

'Father Antoine,' answered Anastasia brutally, 'was the first to die.'

'Anastasia!' Celine's gentle voice came from beside the Russian's foot. The tone of the word was that of a parent chiding a child. But instead of berating her, Celine simply said, 'I'm thirsty.'

Celine was too weak to sit on the seat beside the outboard, but some cautious wriggling soon had her resting at a slight angle with her back against the curve of the side and her wounded shoulder in the shade of the seat above her. Anastasia scooped handful after handful of sweet water from the river and fed it to her friend – and Ado did the same for the soldier at her feet. The Russian woman at last took the opportunity to look around and get a clearer measure of their wider situation.

The river had narrowed again, but it was still the better part of a kilometre wide. Because it had narrowed, it was flowing more swiftly, but still smoothly, between walls of green vegetation trailing down over banks that only revealed themselves every now and then. On their right, the occasional glimpses of red earth seemed to be smooth and slick, sloping back gently, like the bank beneath the chapel back at the compound. On their left there were steeper red mud walls that once or twice attained enough height to count as cliffs. And above increasingly lengthy sections of these, the jungle appeared to have been cut back, so that Anastasia began wracking her brains trying to remember if there was some kind of a roadway up there. And, if there was, where it might lead to.

'Citematadi,' said Celine when Anastasia broke down and finally asked her. 'The city may still be a long way off, and there isn't anything much there in any case.'

'Nothing at all,' added the young soldier. 'We were there not long ago. There's nothing in Citematadi.'

There was silence for a moment, then Ado said, 'My name's Ado. That is Celine and the woman with the gun is Anastasia. What's your name?'

'Esan.'

'Esan? That's not a name, it's a number.'

'It's the name the general and Ngoboi gave me when I became a Soldier of Christ the Infant. When I became a man.'

'Let's not ask how he became a man,' said Anastasia wearily. 'It'll have involved killing, eating and raping if last night was anything to go by . . .'

That bitter observation crushed the boy to silence, but it also had an unexpected consequence. 'Anastasia! The others!' Celine was suddenly sitting upright, her movements enough to make the boat rock dangerously, her eyes wide with shock and bright with fever. 'We have to go back! We have to help them!'

'We have to help ourselves first,' answered Anastasia sharply. 'And there's no going back. Not for the moment at least. Mind you,' she added, 'when I do go back I want to go in there, as the Americans say, like *gangbusters*!'

'We can help them,' insisted Ado. 'We can pray for them!'

That idea seemed to calm Celine a little, and she and Ado began to pray quietly together. In the meantime, the less spiritual Anastasia set about checking over the outboard, all too well aware that they were going to need more than the power of prayer. And pretty soon, too. For it seemed to her that the river was gathering pace, with a strong current running over to the left, at the foot of those red mud cliffs. And that current was sucking the rowing boat faster and faster over towards the high-walled southern bank. But the engine was no AK and she had had no experience at all in making them work. 'Look,' she said at last. 'Does either of you know anything about outboards? Or anything about motors at all?'

'I do,' answered Esan unexpectedly. 'I have worked with Captain Ojogo. He is in charge of transport for the army. He has trained me in all sorts of matters to do with engines.'

Anastasia looked at the other two. Celine frowned, hesitating, but Anastasia had no idea whether that was because she didn't trust the soldier or because her brain was slowed by shock and fever. Ado nodded decisively. And that was what made the difference.

It took longer to untie Esan from the oars, loosen his hands – though not his feet – and help him along the length of the boat – all the while keeping the AK trained on him – than it did for him to get the motor started. Then, as he sat back down in the bottom of the little craft, balancing Celine, with his shoulders at the bow, Anastasia tried to take them in a smooth arc away from the relentlessly approaching shore.

But what seemed like a big step forward proved very nearly disastrous. Anastasia had never handled an outboard before and she couldn't get used to the counter-intuitive way it seemed to work. To go right, she had to push the handle left, and vice-versa. All too swiftly she found that her attempts to break out of the current were simply pushing them more firmly into its rapidly tightening grip. The red cliffs of the shore seemed to exercise some kind of magical attraction for the little vessel. The persistent beating of the late-morning sun on her unprotected head simply added to the gathering feeling that things were slipping out of control.

She had not panicked last night because she had felt confident with the AK-47; because she was focussed on rescuing Celine. She came close to panic now because she did not understand the boat or feel that she was really in control of it. But this time she was completely responsible for Celine and her continued welfare. Not to mention Ado and this strange boy-soldier. And it occurred to her now at the worst possible moment that if the boat went over, the tied-up boy would drown at once and Celine would not even be able to swim for safety with her shoulder in the state it was.

So when a tongue of the shore suddenly appeared, stuck out

in a low, curving hook that seemed little more than a sandbar just above the racing surface immediately ahead of them, she pulled the outboard's rudder-arm firmly in to her side without a moment's hesitation and ran the boat hard up on to it.

# EIGHT
## War-game

R ichard ran up the gangplank on to Captain Caleb Maina's command with almost boyish excitement. Unable to stop himself, he trailed his fingers along the sleek vessel's side as he moved, making a deep and personal contact. The neat, spare ship reminded him vividly of Heritage Mariner's *Poseidon*, for she was also basically a corvette. The immediate difference was that, as he reached the top of the companionway and turned to step aboard, he could see that on *Otobo*'s foredeck there was a 125mm naval gun in its grey-white pillbox housing instead of the bright yellow deep-sea exploration vessel *Neptune*.

A glance upward past this showed Richard enclosed bridge wings and the blank one-step design of the bridge-house front was pretty similar to *Poseidon*'s too. He had time to look around, for as he stepped down on to the weather deck at the head of the companionway, he was met by a small armed guard led by the man who was clearly the ship's security officer – who handed him a plastic-coated ID badge complete with photo to pin on his lapel before allowing him to proceed. While he did all this, the captain waited courteously a few steps ahead. Then they were off.

Aware of Robin, almost equally excitedly striding along at his shoulder, also securing her ID, Richard followed Captain Caleb along the familiar weather deck and in through the bulkhead door into the dark coolness of the air-conditioned bridge house. The captain swung round at the foot of the companionway, his long eyes crinkling into a smile. 'I believe I may rely on you to know your way around,' he said. 'Now that you have your IDs, please feel free to proceed up to the command bridge while I return to

the companionway and see to the greeting and disposition of
the other, less shipshape, guests. This is A Deck, of course. The
command bridge is on D. My watch officer, First Lieutenant
Sanda, is waiting to show you around. Mr Asov will join you
immediately, I'm sure, and I will be up in a moment.'

Richard needed no further bidding and went leaping up the
stairway with Robin close behind. As Caleb Maina guessed, their
experiences aboard a range of vessels made the layout of this
one almost second nature to them. They pounded up three decks,
therefore, then on up the final short flight to the command bridge
itself.

The bridge was busy, if not actually crowded yet, thought
Richard. There were perhaps a dozen stations in an angular
horseshoe, most of them facing forward so that their occupants
could look over the flat computer screens and through the angled
clearview along the foredeck. A quick scan showed him all that
he had expected to see, as they grouped astride the central ship's
handling system – the one that replaced the binnacle, helm and
engine room telegraph handles on older vessels. He leaned over
and half whispered to Robin, 'Computer-enhanced navigation
systems, pilot and electronic chart systems, collision alarms,
weather monitors, ship's system monitors, engine room slave
monitors, sonar, several weapons control systems, echo sounder,
GPS . . . Most of them 3D by the looks of things, like the Doppler
radar.'

'I see it all,' she answered. 'And that must be communications
away to the port. Speed and engine monitors on the starboard.
It looks like a modern, integrated, top-of-the line system to me.'

As Richard nodded, a wiry young man with 'SANDA' embroi-
dered on a badge sewn to his white shirt pocket turned from his
position at the helmsman's shoulder and smiled welcomingly.
'She's pretty impressive, don't you think?'

'She is indeed,' boomed Max Asov, as he bounded up the
steps behind Robin. 'But she doesn't stand a chance against my
Zubr!' He held up a Benincom cellphone. 'Just tell me when to
unleash the dogs of war. Though sharks would be more appropriate, I think. You reckon Shakespeare would approve? Sharks
of war?'

'I beg to differ, sir,' riposted Sanda easily, disregarding all the
Shakespeare stuff. 'She stands a very good chance against your

hovercraft. You have not taken into account the twin caterpillar 3616 diesels or the variable pitch propellers . . .'

'Delivering, what, twenty-five knots? Thirty? My craft tops fifty. Even with a T80U main battle tank in her cargo hold. She'll run rings round you!' He nudged Richard knowingly. Richard realized right from the start that Max's war-game had started as soon as he stepped aboard. Phase one was psyching out the opponent.

'Perhaps,' allowed the Lieutenant, losing just a little of his bonhomie. 'But only because this is a game, sir. In a real encounter, I assure you our 125 millimetre gun and the RIM 116 missile system—'

'Got several of those and then some. Or would have if this was for real!' exulted the Russian, cheerfully turning this into a game of 'Mine is bigger than yours' as phase one of his war-game evolved into phase two. 'And four missile defence systems to go with them. Your 125 millimetre gun is pretty impressive, though, especially in the face of my poor little 30 millimetre Gatlings. It is the same size as the gun on my T80 Tank, in fact. But I have several Gatlings, though I see you have one of them yourself mounted at the rear beside your helipad. Very useful when you turn tail and run for cover! My Ogons are 140 millimetre, though. And I have minelayers too. Guns are just so old-fashioned, aren't they? Even guns with a twenty kilometre range. And I still say that speed and manoeuvrability will have the edge . . .'

'We'll see,' concluded Captain Caleb, as he came up on to the bridge himself. 'We'll see.'

Twenty minutes later, all necessary formalities complete and the dockside rapidly diminishing behind them, Caleb ordered, 'Full ahead both, please, Mister Sanda. You know the heading.' The lieutenant, back at the helmsman's shoulder, nodded and repeated the order, which the helmsman echoed in turn. And the corvette *Otobo* surged towards thirty knots. Richard was bouncing on the balls of his feet with excitement and Robin grudgingly felt his contagious enthusiasm beginning to infect her too.

'Just say when you want the war-games to begin,' said Max, at Richard's shoulder, his eyes fixed on the warship's battle displays – in which the Zubr featured sizeably and centrally, as it wallowed apparently powerlessly beside the Sevmash freighter which had brought it here. 'You just need to say the word,' he emphasized, pressing his cellphone to his ear. 'I can call Captain Zhukov any time you want . . .'

'Very well.' Caleb turned. 'Gentlemen,' he announced formally in English to the bridge. 'We are at war.'

What Max said to Captain Zhukov was lost in the clamour of the emergency stations alarm that Sanda set off on his captain's word, but the effect on the huge Zubr hovercraft was electrifying. It simply vanished from the displays.

Richard looked up, hardly able to believe his eyes. Away ahead, the Sevmash freighter sat solidly, as though painted against the hard blue sky. But the Zubr was no longer anywhere near her. Clearly Captain Zhukov had not merely readied his toothless weapon systems, he had inflated the hovercraft's skirt and put the massive fans on idle. And on Max's word he had gone to full astern. Without any water resistance to drag at a keel that hardly broke the surface, he had gone from dead stop to fifty knots in a heartbeat. Fifty knots in the opposite direction to the one he was expected to be heading in. It was simply astonishing.

'Incoming!' called one of the men stationed in front.

'Hard left,' ordered Caleb and *Otobo* heeled into a screaming turn towards the distant delta. Running across the incoming swell, she started to pitch and roll as the one motor pushed her hard forward while the other pulled her hard back. She had an impressively tight turning circle, but inevitably she was fighting the physics of being half submerged in a way the hovercraft would never have to do. 'Deploy countermeasures,' Captain Caleb concluded his order. 'Gun. Do you have him?'

'The tracking is too slow, Captain,' answered the gunnery officer. 'We latch on to him but he slips away before we can engage . . .'

'Press the fire mechanism as soon as you engage,' ordered the captain. 'The system will register a hit without actually firing the gun.'

'Really?' answered Asov. 'You put my mind at rest of course. But where's the fun?'

The last comment seemed to bypass Captain Caleb, who was already issuing his next command. 'The 30 millimetre Gatling may fire as it engages. Its system is nimbler than the big gun's, you see, Mr Asov. And I must observe that we are not running for cover.'

As he spoke, a lone missile exploded harmlessly in the air high above them, its powder-filled warhead sending a puff of blue smoke drifting down the wind.

'Countermeasures effective, Captain . . .'

'But it wasn't a real missile,' teased Max. 'It was just a little rocket. A toy. Like on May Day in Moscow, you know?'

'Thank you. Now, please engage the Gatling.'

'Engaged,' sang out the assistant gunnery officer. 'No . . .'

Richard crossed behind the engine monitoring station and looked out of the starboard bridge-wing window. The huge hover-craft was speeding full ahead now, skipping across the water like a skimmed stone. It was on a parallel course to the corvette, but running at least twice as fast.

'But then,' needled Max's voice from behind him, 'if you can engage your one little Gatling then I can engage all of mine! Though I observe that Captain Zhukov is keeping just out of range – just on the two point five kilometre mark, I see. And what else is he doing? Oh yes! He's running rings round you!'

*Otobo* completed her turn and ran straight ahead. As she steadied and came level, Richard stepped back to look over the top of the Doppler radar station, out over the hump of the gun, dead ahead. It was a dangerous but impressive manoeuvre because the Zubr was sitting exactly between the corvette and the grey-green hulk of the delta, its shoreline a little less than ten kilometres ahead according to the radar. Sideways on, the hovercraft presented an excellent target with a profile sixty metres long and fifteen metres high to the top of its radar mast. The three six metre fans on the stern gave out a tempting heat signal. 'Gun?' demanded Captain Caleb.

'Any minute now, Captain . . .'

'Armaments, ready the RIM missiles. They're heat-seeking . . .'

'Incoming, Captain!' warned the armaments officer again.

'Ha! You see I have missiles too, Captain!' exulted Max. 'More than simple little May Day rockets!'

'But are you supposed to have *fired* them?' asked Robin, shaken.

Even Richard was taken aback. The Zubr was in motion again,

streaking to *Otobo*'s port, running across the opening of River Gir itself. Richard glanced down at the Doppler radar and gasped. The monster was moving at sixty-five knots – more than seventy mph. He had never seen anything like it! In the air behind the quicksilver vessel, a series of black trails showed where the hovercraft had launched its missiles at them.

'Chaff!' spat Caleb. 'Hard left. Full speed. Into the red! Are you mad, Mr Asov? Those things carry one and a half kilo warheads. You were forbidden to import them. If they hit . . .'

The corvette raced forward, wrenching herself left across the river mouth, in a vain attempt to keep the speeding hovercraft under her gun. But Richard saw at once that the manoeuvre was doomed. Quite apart from anything else, the river washed out great tongues of silt which formed shallows and sandbars that shifted unpredictably across the channel they were heading for. He realized, with something of a start, that these would mean less than nothing to the Zubr. Water or mud, deep sea or sandbar, she would skim across it all. Not so the corvette. She had a solid keel that sat four metres below the surface and that was that.

And even as Richard realized the implications the sonar station began to sound its alarm. 'Sandbar,' called the operator. Shelving to two metres dead ahead! My God! He's dropped mines. Mines dead ahead!'

'Come right! Come right!' snarled Caleb.

The corvette did her level best to obey, but as she swung back, engines on full power, reversing her course in an instant, there was a BANG! like an explosion that seemed to echo throughout the ship and her wild turn slowed. 'Stop all!' ordered Caleb.

'That sounded like one of your propeller shafts going pop,' Max crowed. 'That's another thing Captain Zhukov doesn't have to worry about, incidentally.'

The corvette settled and started to roll as the way came off her. Richard looked out of the starboard bridge windows, watching the Zubr reversing at full speed into the dangerous river mouth, its blunt wedge-bow facing them, all its armaments and weapons systems zeroed.

'Game, set and match,' he breathed to Robin.

But Robin didn't answer. She was looking with nothing short of horror at the vapour trails of the three incoming missiles.

As the crippled vessel slowed, inevitably and helplessly,

Captain Zhukov's missiles arrived. They thumped relentlessly into her side. And, as Caleb had said, each of them carried a one and a half kilo warhead. But the high explosive had been replaced with paint. And as the ship shuddered three times, her port side was painted with huge humiliating blotches of red, yellow and black.

'Your country's national colours I believe,' said Max. 'Now what could be more fitting than that?' And as he spoke, the first of the apparent mines bobbed up – nothing more than half-inflated beach balls, also coloured yellow, red and black. Max positively beamed. 'And a present for your children into the bargain! It has been a pleasure playing with you, gentlemen.' He put his cellphone to his ear. 'Thank you, Captain Zhukov. A most impressive little game. But I'm afraid we're going to need a chopper to take us home while the Captain arranges a tow . . .'

# NINE
## Truck

More by luck than judgement, Anastasia had beached right at the beginning of the low spit. The boat rode up the smooth flank of the sandbar, swinging inwards under a ragged overhang of bank, into a blessed pool of shadow. Then it came to a halt, grounded securely and leaning over towards its left side, as though still attracted by the shore. The propeller caught on the bed of the shallow behind and the outboard stalled at once. '*Govno*,' she said, safe in the knowledge that of all the languages spoken in the boat only she understood Russian swear words. Then she switched to English. 'Is everyone all right?'

'Fine,' said Ado intrepidly, though she sounded shaken.

'Me too,' added Esan. 'Though I don't want to do that again, so maybe I should steer in future.'

'When we know that we can trust you,' said Anastasia. 'We'll take it one step at a time. First we'll untie you. Then we'll see. But we won't rush into that too quickly either. Celine? How are you?'

'Like the olive in James Bond's martini,' answered Celine faintly. 'Shaken.'

They all lay back, considering their new situation. At rest for the first time since their terrible ordeal began. There was a short silence. Which extended itself. Then stretched out further still . . .

Anastasia jumped awake. The sun was shining into her face, but much of the midday fierceness had gone out of it. She stared blearily ahead, looking downriver from the relative protection of her overgrown little mud cliff. Apart from the river, there was little to see. The far bank, all but lost in a low haze, was a wall of unvarying green that stretched unbroken, she knew, all the way down to the little settlement of Malebo, God knew how many miles distant still. The near bank curved to her left, vanishing along the back of a little bay whose extent was concealed by the edge of the mud cliff they were sitting under, not reappearing again until a good deal further downstream. The jungle stretched along this bank until it heaved over a low, mountainous ridge and swooped down into the broad basin that contained the ruined metropolis of Citematadi. Or that was the way she remembered things from her trips downriver and back aboard the superannuated little steamer *Nellie*.

The thought of *Nellie* turned her mind back to Malebo, where the supply boat was usually docked. Where the nearest aid of any kind might be found. The best hope of communicating with the outside world and trying to get some proper help. Maybe she should trust the boy soldier after all and pray he had enough skill – and the rowboat had enough petrol – to get that far down and across the river.

But then the needs of her body took over from the workings of her mind with a sudden vividness that was almost breathtaking. Without further thought, she scrambled out of the boat and started looking around for some kind of privacy. Half a dozen steps straight ahead took her across the bankside end of the hook and round the cliff which had been blocking her view. There was a little bay there, reaching back as she had suspected. It seemed to have been formed when an overhang of the red mud precipice had been undermined by the floods and collapsed. There was a jumbled slope, made into rough steps by the sections of vegetation that had come down with it. Anastasia was scrambling up it in an instant and a moment later she was up on top of the bank, perhaps five metres above the surface of the river itself.

The collapse had pulled down a complete wall of shrub and stubby jungle trees and their downfall revealed behind them a grassy space several hundred metres broad. And beyond that, was a road. It looked to be a wide road; a six-lane highway with a central reservation where there still, miraculously, stood a sign which announced in several local languages and English 'Citematadi 30kms', with an arrow pointing downriver. Anastasia was so surprised to see it that she overlooked the most obvious thing of all at first. The road was not overgrown and impassable. Someone was keeping it clear enough to drive along. Someone was using it.

But then her bodily needs reasserted themselves forcefully – and the answer to almost all of them appeared beyond the roadway. A banana plantation. It was wild to be sure. No doubt the trees had been decimated – all but wiped out by the starving peoples who had come through here in the last thirty years – destroying the local animal populations in their search for bush-meat, and even the creatures that had once inhabited the river itself. But the bananas had come back now that the starving hordes were a thing of the past.

Anastasia ran across the road, pulling her T-shirt out of her jeans. She contained herself for just long enough to find some privacy and tear down a handful of banana leaves before she dropped her pants and squatted. It was only when she was finished and pulling her clothes back into position that she paused to laugh at herself. Privacy from whom? The whole fucking delta was empty, apart from the army Esan belonged to and the village of Malebo – both more than a day's hard travelling distant. In opposite directions. On the far side of the river. But then her laughter stilled and she frowned as she thought again about the road. Face folded in a thoughtful scowl, she pulled the Victorinox from her pocket and cut down a hand of the ripest-looking bananas she could reach. She banged it against the ground to make sure there were no nasty surprises lurking in it, and she put it on her shoulder. As she recrossed the road, she paused, leaning against the surprisingly solid sign, looking both ways and glowering as her mind raced over a range of unknowable possibilities. Then she went on across the grass verge and scrambled back down to the river's edge.

An hour later, all but the greenest bananas were gone, their bright yellow skins floating away downriver like strange lilies – though Anastasia noticed that Celine had hardly touched anything while Esan packed away enough for a small army – and the banana plantation had been well watered and fertilized one way or another. Both Celine and Esan had been harder for Anastasia to deal with, right from the start, in fact. The wounded woman had needed a great deal of help to get up the bank – and even to meet the calls of nature, forcing Anastasia, one way or another, into much more intimacy than she had ever dreamed of enjoying. Esan presented the opposite problem – how to allow him enough rope to permit privacy without giving him an irresistible chance to escape. But a tightly knotted loop round his throat seemed to answer the conundrum. It allowed him freedom to use his hands and feet while presenting him with something he could hardly have untied even had he been able to see it. Which, of course, he could not. The only problem, as it turned out, was that Anastasia couldn't untie it either. So she ended up cutting it free with the trusty Victorinox. And, against her better judgement, she was impressed by the way the boy calmly let her saw away at the cable, the spine of her blade moving back and forward across his jugular. She might not yet trust him, but it seemed that he was ready to trust her.

As soon as Esan was free, Ado suggested that he had been tied up for long enough. It was time for less trussing and more trusting. Anastasia reluctantly acquiesced – though she kept both the knife and AK close at hand, still firmly in charge. 'As I see it, we still have very limited choices,' she said, her glance sweeping round the other three. 'We relaunch the boat and hope we can get it to Malebo. Get help, make contact with the outside world, see if we can get the authorities to help us rescue *our* people from *your* people . . .' This last to Esan. Who sat and watched her like an anthracite statue.

'The downsides, of course, are the time it will take, and the difficulty it will present,' Anastasia continued after a while. 'We can only just all fit in the boat in the first place and it's at least another day to the village. We can't rely on coming safely ashore near food and shelter like this whenever we want to. Certainly not with me at the tiller. We can't stock up the boat with two days' supply of food and water. It would simply swamp us – even if we could come up with containers for the water and be content with a diet of bananas. We can't rely on the river to run clean – particularly after we get past Citematadi. And talking of Citematadi, Celine and I at least know the big problem there. The road bridge across the river collapsed years ago. It's effectively a man-made set of rapids now. They've had trouble getting *Nellie* safely past it every time I've been downriver; it was the only bit Captain Christophe wouldn't let me steer the boat through. And this rowboat is nowhere near the vessel that *Nellie* is. I quite honestly think we'd be lucky to survive, even if the petrol lasted that far and we could rely on the motor to push us through.'

'We drift,' suggested Esan. 'Drift downstream and only use the motor to keep us safe or to bring us ashore or to try and avoid these rapids you talk of.'

'It will take too long!' countered Anastasia, her voice tense with frustration. She did not add that Esan's plan relied on them trusting him absolutely. No one else would be able to guide the boat in the way that he suggested. 'Drifting might take us four days to reach Malebo,' she said instead. 'Your army will have moved; vanished. Our people will have vanished with them – those that haven't been butchered. We would never be able to find them, let alone get them back again.' She did not add that it was also her burning ambition to see the men who ran the army brought to justice. Or simply executed at the earliest possible moment.

'There is another problem with time,' interjected Ado suddenly.

'What?' asked Anastasia.

Ado simply pointed with her chin in the Matadi fashion. Celine was slumped over and shaking. Her blouse was transparent with perspiration. 'Madame Celine may not have much of it,' she observed.

Anastasia felt Celine's forehead. She was running a very high temperature indeed, and it seemed to have sprung up since the pair of them had climbed up to the banana grove and back. Her heart sank. 'We'd better not move her too far anyway,' she decided. Then she looked around. 'But we can't stay down here either. If it rains or if the river rises at all, we'll all be washed away. We have to get her back up into that banana grove. Find some way to keep her warm. Light a fire, maybe.'

Then the afternoon turned for Anastasia into a living enactment of a puzzle she lad loved as a child. One of Kordemsky's famous Moscow Puzzles – where a farmer has to row a piglet, a goat and a wolf across the river in a boat only big enough to take two animals. The goat and the piglet are friends. The goat and the wolf fight if they are left alone. The wolf eats the piglet if they are left alone. This time the conundrum concerned a fit – if exhausted – woman with a knife and a gun, a sick woman who needed to be moved, a girl whose loyalties were beginning to shift and a boy soldier who just might be planning to slaughter the lot of them – especially if he could get his hands on the gun or the knife.

Eventually, Ado and Esan helped Celine back up the bank while Anastasia followed with the AK. Then Ado made her teacher as comfortable as possible on a bed of banana leaves while Anastasia watched Esan pull the boat further ashore and secure it to a solid-looking tree – with the AK cradled across her breast. Then, as darkness gathered, the increasingly active and decisive youngsters moved confidently through the grove and the jungle surrounding it. They made Celine's bed, though Anastasia sacrificed her T-shirt as a pillow while Esan offered his combat jacket as a rudimentary blanket. The torsos thus revealed could hardly have been more different on one level – more similar on another. His was smoothly muscled, deep-chested, marked with the scars that told of his initiation into Poro jungle society. Hers was scrawny but strong, modestly breasted – her bra verged on being an unnecessary vanity. And, like his, her skin was covered in the marks that proclaimed her member-ship of certain societies. A leopard was tattooed across her belly, seeming to leap out of her jeans, its ear-tips brushing the lower curves of the loose black bra, level with its fore-claws. Its snarl filled the hollow of her solar plexus. And, when she turned, a silverback gorilla stood guard on her back, clutching an AK-47. Each of them looked askance at the other, then came to terms with such primitive ritualism with a shrug.

Esan and Ado erected a low shelter over the sleeping woman by putting up a simple frame of branches and covering it with banana leaves. Then Esan built a fire like an accomplished member of the Russian Federation of Scouts and Navigators, and showed Anastasia how to light it – a process aided by a cupful of petrol from the fuel can in the boat and a shot from the AK, its muzzle buried in the petrol-soaked kindling. Then the children rose and began to walk towards the darkening jungle. 'Wait!' said Anastasia, raising the AK. 'Where are you going?'

Esan turned back, just at the edge of the darkness – hardly more than a series of golden planes and glitters in the reflection of the little fire's flames. 'I am Poro,' he said simply. 'I know the jungle. I will find her medicine.'

'In the dark?'

'It is only dark near the fire. I know what I'm looking for. I will be quick.'

'Ado?' called Anastasia, feeling the initiative, the power, slipping away from her. Ado turned, a ghostly figure in her pale blouse and skirt.

'I am Sande. I know as much as he does. I will go with him. We will bring medicines for Madame Celine.'

And, without a further word, or any sound at all, they were gone.

Anastasia sat cradling the AK and watching her friend as she slept her restless, feverish sleep. Long ago, in the days immediately after her adventures with Simian Artillery, there had been an Anastasia who was depressive, negative, always expecting the worst from a life she could not control, which was always headed from bad to worse and regularly kicking her in the teeth. That had been the life she had tried to hide from in numberless bottles – mostly of Stoli and Russian Standard – then cheap Polish potato vodka and worse – then, finally, behind lines of coke and crack.

But that was the old Anastasia. This one, the new Anastasia – post-Robin Mariner, post-detox, post-psychiatric help and support – knew that if life threw problems at her then she could overcome them. It was just that if the problems got bigger they required more energy, more self-reliance, more faith in herself. Certainly not more alcohol or more cocaine or more group sex or gang-bangs. Even so, when she looked down at Celine tossing from side to side in the firelight, she felt she would have given almost anything for a decent belt of original Red Label Stolichnaya.

Quite when the grumbling of the truck's engine first insinuated itself into Anastasia's reverie she didn't know. But when she

suddenly sprang alert, it was already quite loud. She jumped to
her feet and looked around. The noise could have been coming
from anywhere – like the roar of a hunting leopard. But she felt
it was coming from upriver, moving down, along the road they
had been following on the water. She looked back up the highway
into the darkness, therefore, and was rewarded with a distant
glimpse of headlights. Wracked with indecision, she hesitated as
her mind raced. The only land transport she had even dreamed
about during the last twenty-four hours and more belonged to
the Army of Christ the Infant. But they were on the far side of
the river and there were no bridges standing and no ferries
running. Moses Nlong and his men simply could not have got
their trucks over to this side of the river. But who else was out
there? Who was there who might be trusted?

Who?

Abruptly, Ado and Esan reappeared. Silently they doused the
fire, bringing a velvety, impenetrable darkness beneath the canopy
of banana leaves. Even so, they pulled the bivouac down to render
the sleeping Celine doubly invisible. Then they led the blind
Anastasia back into the thickest grove nearby, able to see much
more than she could, for their eyes had not been blinded by the
fire. 'All this will be useless if they have their windows open,'
whispered Esan as they crouched in the darkness at the farthest
point away from the road, which nevertheless allowed them to
see what was coming along it. 'Because they will smell the fire.'

'Then let's hope they are people we can ask for help,' said
Anastasia.

She felt Esan stir uneasily beside her and realized that anyone
wanting to help her would probably want to arrest him. But then
Anastasia's attention switched. Headlight beams, seeming to
shatter and scatter in the night, seeming to light up both sides
of the roadway at once. Then she understood. There were two
sets of headlights. Two trucks. And as the first came into view
at last, the headlights of the one behind it illuminated it quite
clearly. Its cab was white-painted with a wire grille over the
windscreen. The back was canvas-covered. But just discernible
on the front beneath its headlights were the bold black letters 'U
N', and on the canvas side under the lights of the second truck
there was stencilled the familiar white on blue logo with the
words 'United Nations Peacekeepers'.

Anastasia was in motion at once, running forward, shouting wildly, before she realized that she was still holding the AK. She pulled the trigger. The gun bellowed and the trucks accelerated. 'No!' she screamed, pounding forward wildly into the headlights of the second truck. She held up the rifle to show she was not going to fire again. The trucks stopped. She put down the AK on the warm tarmac of the road surface and backed away a little, her hands in the air. It must look so suspicious, she thought. A half-naked woman alone in the jungle with an AK. It could so easily be some kind of trap. Would they risk talking to her – let alone coming out and helping her?

After a few moments more, the door of the second truck opened and a man in combat fatigues and a blue helmet got down. He was wearing blue-coloured body armour with 'UN Peacekeeper' stencilled on it in white. He was carrying a gun which was pointed at her. 'Who are you?' he asked in Afrikaans accented English.

Anastasia's story came tumbling out. The truth, but not the whole truth. Not the part about Esan. As she spoke, she heard the door of the first truck open behind her. A burning between her shoulder blades told her that she was also being covered with at least one gun from there as well.

'And there are two more women out there?' asked the UN soldier at last. 'Just two women?'

'A student and another teacher. She is wounded. We need your help . . .'

The UN soldier was sceptical, guarded. But at last he stepped forward far enough to pick up the AK. He stepped back and passed it up to someone in the second truck's cab. 'Cover me,' he said, still speaking English. He turned to Anastasia. The headlight at last allowed her to recognize what he was carrying. It was an M16A4 that was becoming almost as ubiquitous as the AK. But it was a much more modern and powerful piece of kit. She didn't want to imagine what it would do to her if he pulled the trigger he kept caressing. 'Show me,' he said.

She followed her nose into the darkness, but after a few steps he told her to stop. 'Take this,' he ordered gruffly and handed her a narrow-beam torch that gave enough light to guide them without making whoever was holding it too much of a target. He kept back, keeping her covered as carefully as she had kept Esan covered that afternoon.

But the telltale torch beam at last helped her see the pale figure of Ado who was kneeling beside the body of Celine. 'Just the three of you?' he confirmed again.

'Just the three of us,' confirmed Anastasia desperately. 'We need help. We need to tell someone what has happened.'

'You'd better come with us,' said the soldier.

But as Anastasia and Ado carried Celine to the truck, he kept the three of them covered just in case. And, in spite of the fact that Anastasia insisted that Celine really ought to lie down in the back, he simply squashed the three of them on the bench seat between himself and the massive man driving the truck. Then the driver blinked his lights as a signal to the truck waiting up ahead. And they were off.

# TEN
## Zoo

Minister for the Outer Delta Bala Ngama was clearly not a happy man. Richard hated to imagine the conversation between the minister and his defeated corvette captain while the guests were being taken home in one helicopter after another. But, politician to his fingertips, he was equally clearly striving not to display the fact now, the better part of six hours later. Especially before guests from whom he was hoping to charm a considerable fortune. And with whom he was planning to complete a series of extremely lucrative deals.

'Captain Mariner.' Minister Ngama's broad hand carefully encompassed both Richard and Robin, courteously but casually, because they happened to be at the front of the crowd of dignitaries. 'Madame and Monsieur Lagrande, Mr Asov, Ma'm'selle Lavrov, Dr Holliday. Everybody . . . Welcome to the Zoo!' He hesitated, beaming around their expectant faces, with a smile that reached from ear to ear but somehow didn't quite climb to his eyes. Then he continued as he had begun, in English, 'Except, of course, it is not a zoo in the old-fashioned sense of the word. Let us rather call it a game park-in-waiting. A nascent Masai

Mara. Not even Zimbabwe's Lower Zambezi or Uganda's Impenetrable Forest game reserves and world heritage sites will rival the Benin la Bas Lower Delta wildlife sanctuary. It is – and will be – like much that you have seen on your visit so far, symbolic of my country and its vision for the future. What you will observe as we proceed is a collection culled regardless of expense from institutions all around the world, of animals, birds, insects, reptiles, amphibians and fishes that were once indigenous to the delta. Or the beginnings of an exhaustive collection at any rate: our pockets are not infinitely deep!'

Ngama turned, leading the group out of the considerable waiting area behind the big gates which said – in spite of his assurances – 'ZOO'. 'Here we have gathered together specimens of creatures which were driven to extinction in the hungry decades of the seventies, eighties and nineties but which we plan to reintroduce – in a controlled environment at first, but then more generally.' He continued, striding purposefully forward between the first few cages. 'And in the meantime, of course, the sanctuary will form the centrepiece of one of the most important industries of the early twenty-first century. One in which Benin la Bas will become a world-leader, like Florida, like Indonesia, like Egypt and the Sinai. Tourism. *Eco-friendly* tourism.'

Typically of life in a hot tropical climate, Richard, Robin and the rest had taken something of a siesta after their return from the disastrous war-game. The ebullient Max had choppered them to the hotel's helipad, leaving the disgruntled, deflated – defeated – Captain Caleb Maina to oversee the towage of his crippled command to the naval dock for repairs, after a debriefing with the minister. Typically of his boundless energy, however, Richard had used the quiet lunchtime for a lengthy meeting with his team rather than for a rest, but that had been in the air-conditioned comfort of the Nelson Mandela Suite with a light buffet supplied by room service. Now, in the cool of the evening, more general business was resumed.

The visit to the zoo was unscheduled and unexpected. Richard soon worked out that it was simply a delaying tactic by which the minister – with the connivance of President Chaka no doubt – was hoping to buy time. And he needed a bit of time, unless he was happy to give in to Max's almost overpowering demand that the Benin la Bas navy should purchase his Zubr – and several more like it – to replace the corvettes they currently relied upon. 'But this is still part of what we were discussing at lunch,' said Robin under her breath, as she and Richard followed Minister Ngama into the massive compound mazed with cages in a bewildering range of shapes and sizes. 'If we want to keep the business, then we have to grease the wheels. But this time it's not the president or his family we have to sweeten. It's the whole country's future. Is that going to be so bad?'

'You mean is there much of a difference between being asked to help support a wildlife park that might one day become a massive tourist attraction and being asked to buy the president's son a Rolls Royce or a private jet?' asked Richard thoughtfully. 'I don't know.' He shrugged. 'I guess it all depends on where the profits from the wildlife park are going to go in the end.'

'You mean, if the president still creams off the proceeds from the tourist industry we help to set up as the price of carrying on with the contracts to ship his oil, then it doesn't make much difference?' probed Robin thoughtfully.

'That's about the size of it,' said Richard. 'I still remember a story told by a friend who had dealt with the previous administration here. Hoping to finalize a contract after months of head-to-head negotiations with a Russian rival, he sent the minister in question a case of ruinously expensive vintage champagne. Only to receive an email saying, "Thank you for the case of champagne. It fits neatly into the back of the American limousine your competitors have just given me." This kind of game's not just illegal under UK law, it could be expensively stupid in all sorts of ways.' As if to echo his thoughts, a big cat of some kind started roaring in one of the cages, setting off a wild cacophony of hooting, screeching, howling and flapping. The stench of the place suddenly overwhelmed him, recalling at once visits to zoos and circuses in the days of his childhood, when the inherent cruelty of such institutions had been unknown to him, or to his parents. The feral stench of the jungle might indeed be symbolic of Benin la Bas and its future – in ways the minister had not yet considered. He looked into the first cage and was met by the burning golden gaze of a black panther that really and truly for a heart-stopping moment seemed to be eyeing him up for supper. Bonnie Holliday suddenly inserted her slim form between him and Robin, also unsettled, perhaps, by the sheer naked threat of the atmosphere.

'This is good sport, eh?' demanded Max, throwing his arm round Robin's shoulder at that moment and letting his fingers drift apparently accidentally across the cinnamon flesh of Bonnie's bare upper arm, while Irina Lavrov fell in beside the all too susceptible minister. 'It is like shopping in Chechnya, eh? All that bargaining! All those mind games! I love it!'

'I'm not so sure, Max,' said Richard simply, as the panther was replaced by a pair of equally lean and hungry-looking leopards. 'Heritage Mariner's relationship with this place is quite complicated enough already. And do we really need to get involved in all this internal horse-trading and double-dealing just to get President Chaka's OK over the fact that I want to move *your* oil from *your* wells – which just happen to be off *his* coastline – to *our* refineries in Europe.'

'It's not such a big deal for you, I know,' Max allowed cheerfully. 'Or not directly. But don't forget, for us at Bashnev-Sevmash it's the difference between keeping our full concession out there on the continental shelf and maybe having to share it with some nationalizing consortium set up by the minister for the outer delta – or pulling up sticks and walking away altogether. Then that *would* affect Heritage Mariner, would it not? At the very least you'd have to come back here hat in hand, trying to renegotiate your rates.'

The four of them followed the minister and his oh-so-charming companion past a cage full of mandrills, the cheeks of whose backsides were almost as colourful as those of their faces. 'And anyway, as you know, we also want to make a sale with the Zubrs,' Max continued. 'Not to mention the fact that we want back into the gold business in the delta. You remember we were getting such good returns from our placer system there before the president's people closed us down. He may be more amenable now – especially with the price of gold up at nearly two thousand US dollars an ounce.'

The minster had halted, and so they all stopped behind him and found themselves looking into a cage full of chimpanzees. The primates watched the people watching them and it was hard to tell which group was the more curious – or intelligent. Dr Holliday walked towards the cage as though hypnotized by the dozen or so pairs of round brown eyes regarding her. But then the biggest of the chimps suddenly exploded into action, hurling himself forward to grab the bars and shake them, screaming and spitting, as though he wanted to tear her limb from limb. She jumped back, colliding with the minister himself. He immediately swept her into his ambit and proceeded with a beautiful woman on each arm. Followed by Robin sandwiched between Richard and Max.

The whole group moved hurriedly on, past friendlier, less threatening colobus and blue monkeys. Without Dr Holliday kibitzing, Max became even more expansive. Suspiciously so, thought Richard, who was beginning to see that all this innocent intimacy was just another way of manipulating Robin and himself. But, to be frank, Richard enjoyed the mind games too. And Robin was a past master of almost Olympic standing.

'*Because*, of course, we want to get back into the business of finding the Holy Grail of modern metals,' Max continued over the fading shrieking and howling of the warlike primates. 'Coltan. It's fetching nearly one hundred dollars a kilo at the moment and the price is set to rise by more than a thousand percent over the next few years. You know it rose by nearly three hundred percentage points in three months alone back at the beginning of 2011? And the rise shows no sign of slowing. Especially as no one seems all that keen to give up their latest generation mobile phones, new generation BlackBerries, iPads, their laptops and their flat-screen, 3D television sets. We want *in* there – our people had found wolfram and cassiterite before President Chaka asked us so nicely to leave. And now he's asked us equally nicely back. And we just know there's coltan in *them thar hills*, as my American friends might say. And access to that might well be our bottom line if the opposition don't get there first. And if we can get at it, we will, no matter what the price. Irons in the fire, old chap.'

'Opposition?' asked Robin. Aptly enough, it seemed to Richard, they were now walking past a series of glass-fronted containers not unlike aquaria. But these contained snakes rather than fish. Huge jungle pythons, mambas, cobras.

'Everyone from the marauding armies like General Nlong's outfit to smugglers, gunrunners, local land-grabbers,' answered Max, also looking thoughtfully at the largest of the pythons.

'They live out there beyond anyone's control, like feudal tsars, princes and barons. Anyone who can find a decent source and motivate some slave labour into getting it out of the ground for them.'

'Motivate?' asked Robin dangerously.

'Threaten, torture, rape . . .' Max might have been listing reasonable business practices available to anyone.

'Not *legitimate* businesses, then?' asked Richard, intrigued in spite of himself.

'Precious few of those left in this neck of the woods, old man,' said Max airily. 'Am I right, Dr Holliday, or am I right?' he called forward suddenly, breaking the cosy little group apart for a moment. But the doctor did not appear to hear him, her horrified gaze riveted on a brightly banded giant centipede, the better part of twenty centimetres long, and which, like the alpha male chimp, seemed set on getting out of its vivarium at her. Beyond it, Richard could see a monstrous yellow scorpion. Ever the gentleman, he moved Robin sideways so that they could give the creatures the widest possible berth.

Max repeated his question sufficiently loudly to catch Dr Holliday's attention at last. 'Precious few legitimate businesses left in this particular section of the world,' he shouted. 'Present company excepted, of course . . .'

'Certainly,' the African expert replied, from the height of her Harvard degrees, 'the collapse of legitimate business in areas like this has inevitably followed the failure of settled, central government – and any real form of local government, of course.'

Richard realized with an inward smile – a small and wry smile – that the World Bank representative's reply had easily reached the ears of the IMF contingent just behind them. A neat point neatly driven home: Max at the top of his game.

'And that's what the Zubrs are about, isn't it?' Robin demanded suddenly, stopping dead as she made one of those leaps of association that often left Richard absolutely breathless. 'You don't just want to supply General Chaka's navy with vessels that are better suited to coastal and river work than the corvettes he already has. You want to control them.'

Max ruthlessly steered the three of them into the quiet, empty space just beside the glass-fronted containers that didn't seem quite large or strong enough to contain the huge forest, trapdoor, bird-eating and tarantula spiders that would soon be let loose in the jungle once again. 'It's nothing to do with a little short-term profit Sevmash might make supplying them and guaranteeing the spares and whatnot,' Robin continued, enraptured by her own thought processes. 'You know you'll have to crew them at first with Sevmash men like Captain Zhukov – and then take time to train up any local officers and crew. So for the foreseeable future you'll have a fleet of massive craft that you – and effectively *you alone* – control. Vessels that won't just be confined to the bay like these poor creatures locked up in the cages here. They'll be able to go upriver, into the delta – all over the place. Wherever they want to go. Wherever you *tell* them to go.'

Max stopped dead and simply gaped at her. In a fenced-off pit beside them, the spiders had been replaced by a range of reptiles that made Nile crocodiles look like baby salamanders. 'What the fuck?' he said at last. 'Where did you get her, Richard? I want one. Oh God, I want one of those! Can you actually read minds, Robin? Or are you some kind of *Ved'ma* witch? Richard's little blonde *Baba Yaga*?'

'I know you of old, Maximilian Asov,' riposted Robin, not a bit put out – flattered, if anything. 'All this bullshit and persiflage means I've hit the nail on the head, doesn't it? You're really hoping to pull the wool over these people's eyes and actually get them to buy the things that will allow you to sneak in behind their backs and get at their most valuable assets?'

'It worked for the Greeks at Troy!' Max's voice wavered between the offended and the amused as he moved them forward once again. 'My partner Felix Makarov thought it was pretty smart.'

'Yeah,' she snapped. 'But you're no Odysseus – and Felix Makarov's no Achilles.'

'You think it'll work?' asked Richard soberly. 'You think they'll buy it? In all senses of the phrase . . .'

'We sold them the Zubr pretty effectively this morning, didn't we?' demanded Max. 'And by the way, Captain Zhukov was able to scoot the better part of three kilometres upriver as part of that little game. The only government boats that have been that far before are the little Shaldag fast patrol craft, and compared to the Zubr they're nothing more than rowing boats. Man, if I can get them to buy just one Zubr I will fucking *rule* the delta!'

Dr Bonnie Holliday broke up the conversation just then by returning to confront Max, her face stricken. 'The minister says Captain Maina has been relieved of his command! Because of that fiasco you put on this morning the poor man has lost his corvette. The biggest vessel he's likely to command for the foreseeable future is one of those fast patrol craft. And it's all your fault!' She raised her hand in outrage and would have slapped the Russian round the face had Robin not caught her arm.

But Robin caught more than her arm. She caught some of the woman's outrage too. 'Have you done that?' she snarled at Max. 'Have you ruined this poor man's career over some grubby little business deal?'

Suddenly Irina Lavrov was there too, a thunderous frown making her face much less lovely than usual. More Lady Macbeth of Mtsensk than lovely Layla the Vampire Slayer, thought Richard. And he was suddenly almost sorry for Max. Almost.

Max looked at the three outraged women and shrugged. 'Come,' was all he said. 'I have something to show you. But I'll buy us dinner first, OK?'

What Max had to show them was a club and bar called OTI down by the docks. They arrived there just before ten, after a quick, light, nearly silent, nouvelle cuisine dinner whose gastronomic perfection was largely wasted on them. Max gestured at the sign: 'OTI'. 'It's supposed to be Yoruba for "drink",' he explained as they stood outside, listening to the raucous noises from within.

It was like being back at the zoo, thought Richard, intrigued.

'Is it the kind of a place you should be taking ladies to?' demanded Dr Holliday a little nervously.

'I wouldn't bring my mother here if that's what you mean,' laughed Max. 'At least not unless she insisted. It's where the sailors go. Especially the *navy men*.' He pushed the door open and ushered his four guests in.

It was a bar like any other, thought Richard. And surprisingly civilized – upmarket even. Better suited to officers, perhaps. The room was a big, low-ceilinged, smoke-filled square. Sweat-inducingly humid. Heady with alcohol fumes. Down one side ran a bar the better part of twenty metres long. Behind it were ceiling-high racks packed with bottles of all sorts. Along the back wall at right angles to the bar there was a stage – a proper one, with a proscenium arch and curtains. At the moment, there was only one person on the stage, an elderly man playing a grand piano – whose music was completely lost in the cheerful din. Opposite the bar was a series of boxes such as one might find in a theatre, and these too had curtains to ensure privacy. But the main area was a simple plain wooden floor crowded with tables of all shapes and sizes. Like the boxes, they were simply packed with customers. And a team of girls in revealing costumes, which owed more to Tarzan movies than ethnic accuracy, moved cheerfully from behind the bar and through the tables dispensing drinks.

The first familiar faces Richard saw belonged to Caleb Maina and First Lieutenant Sanda. Who, he suspected, would be equally deep in trouble with Minister Ngama. The two men were seated at a big table surrounded by a larger group that Richard did not know. He recognized their uniforms, and realized at once who they were. But he did not recognize the faces. Max did, however, and he bellowed, 'Hi guys!' and started pushing towards them. Irina also recognized them and followed immediately in his wake. Richard grabbed Robin's arm and – more gently – Dr Holliday's, and followed Irina's shapely back. As soon as the men with Captain Maina saw Max, they started cheering and pounding on the table. When they saw Irina, the noise redoubled.

A big bear of a man with a grey crew cut and a steel-coloured Zapata moustache stood up. He had piercing blue eyes beneath black, shaggy eyebrows and he had captain's rank badges sewn on his collar. 'Good evening, Captain Zhukov,' shouted Max. 'I trust the celebration is going well?'

'As you see, Mr Asov,' rumbled the Zubr's captain. 'At the moment we are trying to solve the age-old problem of whether the fact that Stolichnaya, which is bottled in Latvia, is any less genuine than Russian Standard.'

Richard counted a dozen bottles of each on the table. Clearly the men were taking the comparison very seriously indeed.

'It's probably all shipped down in tanks and bottled in Granville Harbour in any case,' said Max as the Zubr's crew made room for the new arrivals. Somehow Irina ended up between Captain Zhukov and Max. And Bonnie Holliday was squeezed between

Caleb Maina and Lieutenant Sanda. It was obviously Caleb's lucky night – he got Robin on the other side. But his interest was spoken for the moment Bonnie sat down.

'So,' said Richard, looking narrowly across at Max and Zhukov, 'you had an ace in the hole?'

Max shrugged. 'Let's say that I was impressed by Captain Caleb and Lieutenant Sanda. More so than Minister Ngama. At the very least Captain Zhukov and I feel obliged to ensure that when President Chaka finally capitulates and buys our Zubrs, the good captain will already be trained in how to handle them. Even if he has to waste his talents on Shaldag patrol craft in the meantime.'

It was Caleb Maina's lucky night in more ways than one. His quarters were only a short walk from OTI. And it was a walk a man could safely take, drunk or sober, in company or alone, because most of it was through the secure area of the naval base. The guard at the security gate nodded him through without comment – but raised his eyebrows in surprise when the captain's back was turned. Caleb was famous throughout the base – throughout the service, in fact – for being utterly faithful to one mistress alone. The lovely corvette *Otobo*. But tonight, for the first time, he did not return to his quarters alone.

As a senior captain, Caleb rated a small detached cottage with sufficient facilities to house a wife and family – which in his case did not exist. So Caleb lived alone.

'This is lovely,' purred Dr Holliday as he followed her into the neat little living room, which was suffused with golden brightness from the security lighting.

'As are you,' he said gallantly if unoriginally, closing the door behind him and crossing to stand beside her.

She was waiting at the window looking down the slope into the harbour where his ex-command sat with her riding lights ablaze, waiting to be pulled into dry dock for repairs sometime in a future that was far too distant to worry about.

He towered behind her and slid his arm around her waist, allowing his hand to rest gently on the swell of her stomach immediately below the belt line. She moaned a little, pushing sensuously back against him, and rubbed the shadow-dark fall of her hair against his cheek, filling his nostrils with the scent of her shampoo and perfume. Coconut and Chanel. She felt burningly hot to him. He tightened his grip, lowering his hands.

She turned, pushing her breasts against his chest and allowing him to cup the full cheeks of her bottom. 'I wanted you the moment I saw you,' she whispered, sliding her cinnamon arms around his neck like snakes.

'And you're going to get me. Over and over and over . . .'

'Aren't I the lucky girl?' she growled as their mouths closed together.

# ELEVEN
## Cite

C onversation died stillborn as the trucks ground through the night and Anastasia soon found herself fearfully calculating their chances of escaping rape and murder at the hands of the taciturn soldiers. As a distraction from thoughts that were likely to incapacitate her with simple terror if she wasn't careful, she started trying to work out what she could about the men she was suddenly surrounded by and the vehicles they were driving.

The truck ahead seemed to be a five ton six-wheeler and she assumed this one was the same, though she hadn't got too good a look at either of them. The back section of the lead truck was canvas over some kind of high frame. It was tightly secured at the sides. It looked to have been laced up tight at the back, but it had been opened sometime recently and it flapped open a little now. The canvas had been pulled almost closed, even if the laces were hanging untidily free, so there was no way of working out what the load was, short of simple guesswork. And she really didn't have enough data even to bother with that.

This truck contained more clues, though Anastasia was careful to hide the fact that she was taking such a detailed look around. The huge soldier beside her was a smoker – as was his driver. The atmosphere in the cab told her that much at once. Though neither man seemed to be smoking at the moment. And, now she thought of it, there was a smell beneath the tobacco reek that she had recognized. A whiff of cordite? Probably coming from her own AK, she decided at last – she had fired it to light the fire Esan had set and again to attract their attention. The soldier was also either still nervous or was unwilling to reveal his identity, because he kept his body armour on in spite of the fact that the truck seemed to have no air con and it was soon swelteringly hot. But his combat uniform and the UN trappings – badges, helmet and armour – all looked authentic. As did the big M16 he kept cradled between his knees beside the relatively puny AK.

The grim soldier's profile was chiselled and lean, especially in the reflected brightness of the headlights and the uplighting from the illuminated dash. He had high cheekbones and a hook of a nose. His chin was square and dark-stubbled. His mouth looked cruel to her – certainly it was thin-lipped and turned down. His eyes were narrow and it was impossible to tell their colour. His body seemed muscular beneath the armour. His shoulder was as solid as teak and his forearm was forested with hair like the gorilla's tattooed on her back. A gorilla which also nursed a gun. He smelt of sweat and metal. Gunmetal, she thought. When he moved his arm, there was a long dark stain reaching down from his armpit. But she was slick with sweat too – even though she was only wearing a bra. And, she reckoned, she probably smelt worse herself – especially as she still had a pocket full of oysters.

Anastasia looked across at Ado, who was crushed against the driver on the far side of the unconscious Celine, and the instant she looked away from the soldier she seemed to feel his eyes on her. Their eyes met, and Ado's were suddenly those of a woman rather than those of a child. She had grown up a lot in the last day or so, what with one thing and another. Anastasia hoped she would get the chance to grow up some more.

The driver's face was that of a prizefighter who has lost too many bouts. It was almost formless. The blue beret pulled down to the brow could not disguise the lack of forehead. The brows themselves seemed to be deepened with scar tissue and overhung cavernous eye sockets, with tiny eyes lost in pools of shadow. Shadows deepened by the uplighting from the dashboard. Fat cheeks and bulbous cheekbones. Flat nose, squashed slightly out of line. Swollen mouth overhanging a receding chin. Barrel chest falling to fat, solid-looking paunch. It strained the material of his uniform, making the openings between the buttons gape. What looked like a frayed-edged hole on the far side of the massive chest. The whole thing stained, like the soldier's beside her, with great dark gouts of perspiration. Arms even hairier than the other man's, muscles and sinews moving smoothly beneath the forested skin as he shifted what looked like a ten-gear gearbox. Sleeves so tight that they were beginning to come apart at the seams. It suddenly struck her that here indeed was what Simian Artillery had all been about. This really was an ape with a gun.

The trucks ground on, never seeming to exceed forty kph. Up a gathering slope, which was almost exciting, in that it broke the threatening monotony of the ride. Over a crest which suddenly really was exciting, for the jungle fell back from the roadway to reveal that the down-slope led into the great natural bowl that contained the huge ruin of Citematadi. Anastasia had never seen it from this angle and she blinked, hardly able to believe what her eyes were showing her. It could not be real, she thought. It looked more like the set from some post-apocalyptic sci-fi film.

Under a bright, fat moon, the whole lifeless metropolis lay stark and mouldering beneath her, like a rotting corpse sculpted in silver and ebony. The skeletal outline of it reaching in great square city blocks back towards the rim of the circular ridge. Like a war-zone in the middle of an air raid caught mid-blitz. On her left, the strange-shaped ruins of buildings that had once soared five or six storeys high now sagged, bursting with huge black explosions of bougainvillea and rhododendron frozen like bomb blasts fixed for ever in a monochrome snapshot. On her right, the great municipal buildings stood gutted, as though their violent destruction had also entered a state of suspended anima-tion, with trees erupting stilly from within them, with creepers, lianas and ivies stopped dead in the act of tearing their crumbling walls asunder. And, further to the right again, beyond the bright line of an embankment topped by the highway they were following, the broad quicksilver stream of the river itself was shattered into writhing motion by the cataract that hurled itself over and between the great stone and concrete boulders which were all that remained of the bridge.

The soldier with the M16 spoke at last. 'Home sweet home,' he said.

She knew then; knew with a certainty that reached deep inside her – as deep as her clenching womb which twisted in a contraction almost reminiscent of childbirth. What UN soldier would claim such a place as his home? Suddenly her mind was ice cold, running through the information she and Celine had gathered from their radio, satellite TV and Internet access about the current UN contingents in and near the borders of Benin la Bas; adding it to what she had observed here in the cab. There were currently French, Greek, Dutch and African Union troops, including Nigerians and a few from Burundi and Uganda, all in the West Africa area, doing everything from peacekeeping in Congo-Brazzaville and the CDR to chasing the Army of Christ the Infant, The Lord's Resistance Army and Boko Haram out of Uganda and Nigeria and through the jungles further north and west.

The South Africans were all over in Somalia and Sudan, trying to hold things together there. Almost against her better judgement, she looked back at the soldier sitting next to her. The metallic smell was, if anything, stronger. The humid heat in the cab had certainly intensified, and all the odours had strengthened with it. It must be touching forty-five degrees Celsius in here, she thought. But the dark patch she had assumed to be sweat beneath his armpit had not grown any larger. And she realized it wasn't sweat. She glanced across at the driver, at the frayed material round what suddenly looked like a bullet hole; at the great dark gouts that weren't sweat after all. It was blood, she was certain. And not the soldier's blood. Someone else's blood. Blood that belonged to the original owner of the uniform.

The lead truck suddenly turned off the road and the second one followed it. They were rolling off the causeway and on to the beginning of the bridge whose central spans lay at the bottom of the river. For a wild moment Anastasia wondered whether they were just going to drive off the edge and plunge into the roiling river below. But no. The truck turned left almost immediately and followed a track down the face of a steep embankment towards a wide flat bank side area below. They would clearly be arriving at their destination any moment now. Anastasia almost screamed, '*Stop! I still haven't worked out what the hell I'm going to do!*' But she suddenly found the atmosphere was too thick to breathe properly. And if she couldn't breathe, she certainly couldn't speak. She would have given anything for a comfort break, overwhelmed by the need to pee. She knew it was only panic. She had panicked plenty of times before. She planned to panic plenty more times in the future, too, come to that. On the assumption that she had a future. Once again she found herself wishing she'd had the good sense to blow her brains out beneath Father Antoine's chapel the night before last. Dear God in heaven, was it only the night before last?

The lead truck lurched to a stop. This one pulled up beside it. The four headlight beams shone on the back of a sizeable riverside building and on the wildly writhing water downstream of the shattered bridge behind it. The whole place looked as deserted as the city they had just come past. But, unlike the buildings in the city above, this one looked well cared for. Like the roadway. Used. In the middle of the building's back wall there was a sizeable entrance closed by a roll-down door. Beside this there was a normal door. Like the roll-down, it was closed. The motors died. Silence, disturbed only by the roaring of the cataract.

'Keep an eye on the bitches,' said the man wearing the dead soldier's body armour after a moment. He handed the huge driver the AK and climbed down, holding the M16 casually under one arm. Immediately, the driver flicked the select lever down to automatic, wound down the window and held the AK ready to fire like a handgun. He reached under the dash with his left hand and pulled out a square-looking automatic. Anastasia reckoned it was a Smith & Wesson M&P 9mm. The man in the flak-jacket glanced back up. 'If they make a move or a sound, kill them,' he said.

The driver nodded. 'I'm on it.'

The man with the M16 slammed the truck's door, then turned and walked forward slowly. The door ahead of him opened cautiously inwards. He vanished into the big building.

Anastasia looked across at Ado. The young woman's eyes were huge, but her mouth was set and her jaw was square, determined. Pretty good for someone with a gun jabbed into the soft bit under her rib. I hope I look like that, thought Anastasia, but she doubted it. The driver's piggy little eyes kept flicking from the women to the building.

The noise made by the roll-down door opening up was so loud and unexpected that they all jumped and Ado was lucky not to get shot.

'Here we go,' growled the driver and pulled the AK back in through the window and slipped it into the footwell between his knee and the door. One-handed, with the S&W still firmly in Ado's side, he switched on the motor. He reached across and put the forward gear shift into first, then reached down and released the brake. He put his hand back on the wheel and engaged the clutch. While he was doing all this, the truck that had taken the lead so far did so once again, rolling forward through the wide portal in the building's wall. The truck with the women in it moved slowly forward into the building behind it and stopped. The roll-down door behind them rattled loudly once again and slammed shut with a noise like a pistol shot.

Anastasia numbly looked around. They were in an open-fronted building overlooking the river. It was part warehouse, part dock. There was plenty of room for the two trucks to sit side by side on a floor made of concrete slabs – but there was also room for a sizeable if battered-looking vessel at an internal dock topped with wooden planks. The whole place was dimly lit, but the boat itself was dark. With a lurch that actually felt like a kick in the belly, Anastasia recognized the boat. It was the *Nellie*. She was looking wildly around for the superannuated Captain Christophe and his crew, when the driver ordered, 'Out!' and pushed Ado sideways with the gun. Carrying Celine between them, Anastasia and Ado climbed out on to the concrete. The driver followed them, carefully sliding across the bench seat so that he could keep them covered with his Smith & Wesson. The two men from their truck had been joined by three others from the lead truck. The soldier who had taken them aboard was clearly the leader. He was pulling off the body armour as they arrived, revealing a range of black-rimmed holes across the breast of his uniform. He crossed towards the three women. 'Time to wake up,' he said to Celine and slapped her round the face.

'Stop!' said Anastasia, outraged. 'You can't do that! She's hurt!'

'You don't get it yet, do you?' he asked. 'We can do whatever we want. And we will. And whether or not you all get hurt depends on how you cooperate.'

As he spoke, he continued to slap Celine. The blows weren't hard, but he kept repeating them until Celine's eyes flickered and opened.

Anastasia looked around the big building desperately, hoping against hope to see *Nellie*'s captain or a member of his crew. But whoever had been on the boat – whoever had let the soldier in and raised the roll-down door – was now inspecting the contents of the trucks. The noise they were making and the movements of the dusty canvas sides made that clear enough. Anastasia's whole mind seemed suddenly to be focussed on the immediacy of each vivid instant as it ticked past. She did not want to think about the future. Except for the faint, faint hope that the men currently inspecting the trucks' contents would indeed turn out to be the kindly old captain and his elderly, gentle crew.

But when at last they came back into the light and confronted the five soldiers, they proved to be half a dozen unfamiliar young men. Well armed and arrogant-looking.

'We have a deal, Van,' one of them said. He spoke in accented English to the lead soldier, but his eyes were raking over the three women.

'Money first, Captain' said Van. 'Party later.'

'OK. The money's aboard this floating shit-pile. You set up the party over in the office while I get it.'

The five soldiers and *Nellie*'s new crew dragged the women across to a sizeable lean-to built in a corner of the warehouse. There was a generator room just beside this, Anastasia noted inconsequentially, the pounding motor there providing the light. In the warehouse the light was dim and flickering. In the lean-to it was brighter. The place was more than an office, she noted numbly. It apparently doubled as a nightwatchman's shelter. There was a table, chairs, a Primus stove – as well as a desk, filing cabinets, bookcases full of mouldering ledgers.

There were several cases of drink on the table – beer, whisky, vodka by the look of things.

And there was a bed.

'You want to make a game of it?' Van asked the others. 'Or just go for broke?'

'Fuck it,' said the prizefighter. 'Let's just get our wicks dipped. We can maybe play some games later. Before we say *goodnight, ladies*.'

'OK,' agreed Van. He began unbuttoning his bullet-riddled shirt. 'I'll take the sleepy bitch on the table. I got some really excellent ways to wake her up.'

*Nellie*'s new crew took the alcohol over to the desk and began pulling out bottles, twisting them open and sucking it down, watching proceedings with every sign of enjoyment. Van lifted the dopey, disorientated Celine on to the table, laid the faintly protesting woman on her back. Pulled her knees apart. He leaned forward between her splayed thighs, tore open her blouse and reached back to lift her skirt.

Ado gave a whimper as one of the three men from the lead truck pulled her towards the bed.

The physical absence of her two companions washed over Anastasia like a douche of iced water. But it didn't chill her as much as the overwhelming need to do something. To do anything. To somehow take control of the situation and give her friends a breathing space. Buy them some time if nothing else . . .

There were only ten of them, she thought suddenly. Ten men. She had pulled a train of ten the night Simian Artillery's lead singer Boris had done a Kurt Cobain and blown his brains out in the toilet at the Petrovka Hotel after that last, disastrous concert in Red Square. But Simian Artillery were no Nirvana – and nobody but Anastasia had noticed that his brains were all over the washroom ceiling. She had pulled a train of ten that night and lived to tell the tale.

'What are you,' she suddenly heard herself demanding. 'Country and Western fans? Choirboys? Haven't you ever had a real *rock chick*?'

She tore her bra free as they turned, wide-eyed to watch her. Undid her belt and pulled down her jeans and panties to her knees in one brutal motion, then straightened as they fell to her ankles, flaunting the leopard tattoo at them.

'You haven't *lived* until you've pulled a train with a heavy metal maiden!' she snarled.

As she challenged them, she stood on the heels of her trainers one at a time, squeezing them off her feet while the man simply gaped. She stepped out of the left leg. Kicked the left shoe at the prizefighter. Working on reflex, he dropped his Smith & Wesson on the bed and caught it. Stepped out of the right one. Kicked that with the last of her clothing at the man who called himself Van. The bundle sailed past his naked shoulder and hit *Nellie*'s new captain as he came in through the office door.

'Fuck!' said Van, and swept Celine off the table into a bundle on the floor. 'You want it? Let's go for it!'

'All right,' shouted Anastasia. 'There's plenty for all of you. Just form an orderly queue . . .'

Van reached for her. Caught her under her arms. Lifted her off her feet. Slammed her down on the table and . . .

'Wait!' called the captain. 'Wait just a goddamn minute!'

Van swung round with a snarl that belonged in a zoo. 'What the fuck . . .'

As the jeans had wrapped themselves round the captain's face, so the oysters had fallen out of the pocket. He came past Van now and looked down at her, his eyes ablaze with something beyond simple lust. He brandished the oysters in her face so wildly that the huge black pearl fell out and rolled across the table like an eyeball.

'Where did you get these?' snarled the captain. 'Tell me where you got these!'

Events were going too fast for Anastasia now. She blinked up at the two faces hovering like a pair of moons above her. She opened her mouth to ask '*What?*' But she never said the word.

Van's naked torso exploded, spraying her bare body with boiling blood. He toppled sideways. A brutal hammering sound filled the room, beating on her ears as though someone were driving spikes into her skull. The captain span away into a sudden cloud of grey smoke. His face appeared to have fallen off. Anastasia rolled sideways, dropped on to the floor beside Celine. Clutched the shaking woman's head and shoulders to her like a mother protecting her baby. Looked up, her eyes wide with horror and wonder. The noise stopped as abruptly as it had begun.

Esan stood in the doorway. The AK was smoking in one hand, its butt in his armpit. The M16 was in the other, also steadied under his arm. His lips were moving but Anastasia couldn't hear what he was saying. A hand fell on her shoulder and she jumped, screaming with shock. The sound of her own distress seemed to unblock her ears, unfreeze her mind. She looked up. It was Ado.

'The boat,' said Ado, decisively. 'Run for the boat.'

# TWELVE
## Kingfisher

'This is a waste of my time,' said Robin quietly to Richard. 'I don't even know why I'm here.'

'In the room or in the country?' he breathed back with a wry, lopsided grin.

'Take your pick,' she mouthed, failing to see the funny side.

The pair of them looked around the table, with Minister Ngama at the head. They were in one of the conference rooms beside his breathtaking office in the new complex of buildings that stood where the shanty town had stood, three years earlier, on the south-east outskirts of the city.

The tall window behind Ngama showed the delta and the sea beyond it outlined against a hard blue early-morning sky. Shipping came and went busily across the bay. Only Caleb Maina's ex-command was immobile, tethered to the dockside, waiting to be towed into dry dock for repair, sitting oddly just behind the shoulder of the man who sacked its commander. Its slim grey bows like the point of a dagger waiting to stab him in the back.

In the room, the ministers' team of lawyers, geologists, oil men, shipping experts and civil servants sat down the long table to their right. Max, Richard, Robin and their teams of geologists, oil experts, lawyers and shipping men sat down the other. On the glassy mahogany board in front of them lay the contracts they were negotiating for the extraction and shipping of the Benin Light crude oil which was one of the country's greatest assets. In another room, no doubt – or in this room at another time – the men on the Heritage Mariner/Bashnev-Sevmash side would be replaced by teams from Shell, BP, Total, Texas Oil, Exxon or Chevron Conoco to name but a few.

But Robin's point held good. Richard and the others from Heritage Mariner understood the negotiations as well as she did. Richard's signature as CEO carried as much weight as hers did. She did not need to countersign anything. She did not need to add anything. She did not need to be here at all.

She was beginning to wonder why Julius Chaka had included her in his invitation in the first place. For he was not a man given to pointless courtesies or empty gestures. He knew the Mariners well enough to realize she did not have to be included – like Irina Lavrov – as a necessary extra to keep Richard happy. And yet he had specifically invited her.

Why?

'Excuse me, Minister,' she said. She stood up, smiled winningly as he nodded and smiled back. Then she walked out.

By the time she reached the main door of the building she was feeling listless and bored. She had moved on impulse, as though she could just drive up to the president's office and ask the man himself. But the instant the door to the conference room closed behind her, she saw the impossibility of such a course of action. What she had managed to achieve was to get herself smartly to a loose end. She was not used to having nothing to do, and she wondered briefly whether she should turn round. Even a tedious meeting where she was merely an observer was preferable to being at a loose end.

But the feeling was only fleeting. She changed mental gear, brought out her feminine side, and began to plan a day of relaxation, with a little sightseeing, perhaps. And shopping. But she was dressed for business, not pleasure, so when her car arrived, summoned by the security man at the door, she asked to be taken back to her hotel first.

Changed from her formal two-piece suit into a light dress and re-accessorized from head to toe, Robin was standing in the reception of the Granville Royal Lodge an hour later when Bonnie Holliday appeared. If anything, the doctor of African Studies looked more lovely than ever. Her cinnamon skin was positively glowing. Her eyes were sparkling. She seemed to be dancing rather than walking as she swept across towards the security gate and the huge glass doors that led outside. When she saw Robin, she hesitated, then crossed towards her. 'Hi,' she said. 'Just off somewhere? I thought you were stuck in meetings all day with Richard.'

'I walked out,' said Robin. 'They don't need me. I thought I'd try some retail therapy. Sightseeing maybe.'

'I'm off on an adventure,' Bonnie whispered as though sharing a wicked secret. 'Want to come along for the ride?'

'An adventure, huh?' Robin was amused. Intrigued.

'Surely. Captain Caleb is going to give me a ride in his command. There'll be a car here in a moment. I guess he wouldn't mind if you came too.'

'I thought Caleb's command was tied up waiting to go in for repair,' said Robin, surprised.

'His *other* command. Not his corvette, his Kingfisher,' said Bonnie, as though this explained everything.

'What's that?' Robin's eyebrows rose.

'It's a fast patrol vessel. Folks have been calling it Shaldag?' Bonnie raised her intonation as though asking a question. 'But it's also called a Kingfisher which I reckon is prettier. I don't know if that's a translation or just another designation. But it's the floating equivalent of an American Corvette. The General Motors Stingray roadster Corvette. And I for one would kill for a ride in one of those!'

Robin laughed and gave in. How could she resist? She looked across at the reception desk but it was empty. She fleetingly wondered whether she should leave a message telling Richard where she was off to, but Bonnie's ride pulled up outside and she stopped hesitating. The two girls left arm in arm, chatting excitedly, bound for the riverside docking facility where Caleb kept his other command.

Ten minutes after their car pulled away from outside the big glass double doors, another smart staff car pulled up and Colonel Laurent Kebila climbed out of it. He came in through the doors, setting off the security alarm without raising an eyebrow. Andre Wanago, the hotel manager, answered his peremptory ring on the service bell in person.

'Captain Robin Mariner,' the Colonel rapped impatiently. 'I understand she is here. Please inform her that I want her at once. I have orders to take her directly to the president himself.'

'I'm sorry,' said Andre. 'She's just gone out with Dr Holliday. I saw them leave on the security monitor but I have no idea where they were heading.'

Colonel Kebila slapped his hand on to the desk top with a sound like a pistol shot, turned on his heel and set off the security alarm once more as he strode angrily out to his car.

Bonnie's Kingfisher fast patrol boat, known to the others as the Shaldag, was considerably larger than a Corvette Stingray sports car – to begin with it was nearly thirty metres long – but it was just as sleek and pretty to look at. Maybe five metres in the beam – slim-hipped and racy. Caleb Maina did not raise an eyebrow when not one woman but two climbed out of the limo he had sent for Bonnie. His main purpose was to show off his baby, and as far as he was concerned, the bigger the audience the better. Furthermore, he thought with a secret smile, having two such lovely guests aboard would go a long way towards restoring his reputation in the place that mattered most to him – in the eyes of his crew. He met Bonnie and Robin at the head of the gang-plank, therefore, and showed them up to the flying bridge at once.

Robin, a little disorientated, found herself back to within a hundred yards of the place she had left less than ninety minutes earlier. But what a difference the passage of time and the slight change in location made! The wind came fragrantly off the bay, waves chuckled and tumbled. Lines tapped in the gathering breeze. In the distance ships hooted, their motors grumbling. The sun beat down like molten copper. She stood, drinking it all in, with her back to the little helm and engine telegraph, looking up at the tall window behind which Richard was poring over the contract. In which, weirdly, was reflected the very point of the crippled corvette Otobo's forecastle head. She stepped back, looking across the restless water to the real thing. There was a bustle of activity all over the crippled vessel. 'Shouldn't you be aboard her when they tow her into dry dock?' she asked without thinking.

'Apparently not,' answered Caleb shortly. 'Minister Ngama has more competent officers available . . .'

'His nephew, for instance,' chimed in Bonnie, her knowledge unexpectedly far-reaching; her tone tinged with contempt.

'Besides,' added Caleb easily. 'Mr Asov is expediting matters, supplying spares and experts – and footing the bill into the bargain. His people will almost certainly be aboard when she gets under way. And in any case, Lieutenant Jonah Ngama is quite competent, Bonnie . . . I told you . . .' Caleb's voice sank to an intimate whisper. Robin turned in time to see a look pass between them that suddenly made her feel, in the telling French phrase, *de trop. De trop* and then some, in fact. But only for a moment. For this was a bridge, not a bedroom. Lieutenant Sanda stuck his head up from the command bridge below. 'All in order, Captain.'

'Thank you, Mr Sanda. Cast off fore and aft. I'll take her out. Warn the men that we'll be going to full speed as soon as we're clear.'

A moment later, Captain Caleb was steering the sleek, powerful vessel out of her berth and into the broad, brown outflow of the river. 'Hold on tight, ladies,' he ordered, and opened the throttles full.

Robin had never come across acceleration like it in a vessel this size. Richard kept a blood-red cigarette go-faster launch called *Marilyn* down in the HM experimental shipyard near Southampton, along with the *Katapult* multihulls with which they regularly won the Fastnet yacht race – and *Marilyn* could go from idle to full ahead in a matter of minutes. But the Kingfisher simply flew. From slow ahead to fifty knots in fifty seconds, she calculated wonderingly. It was astonishing – she was glad she had taken Caleb at his word and got a firm hold of the guard rail.

Caleb took the patrol boat racing in a wide arc across the mouth of the river. 'We'll follow a normal patrol pattern,' he shouted. 'Don't want to be accused of joyriding . . .' Within ten minutes she was skimming beside the southern swell of the delta, then he took her on down towards the oil platforms and out towards the ocean proper, before swinging back and racing in towards the river mouth once again. The wind battered them, counteracting the fierceness of the noonday sun, but other than that it was a smooth ride. And surprisingly free of spray. The Kingfisher sat high and steady. She seemed to slide through both the outwash of the river and the waves it generated as it battled the incoming tide. Not to mention the bigger surfs that came in off the Atlantic to the south of the river, where the continental shelf placed a wall in front of the deep-ocean swells and drove them to heights that might have flattered Hawaii. The hull sat so high in the water that Caleb was also able to disregard the shallows that had proved fatal to *Otobo* yesterday, and skim across the waters that the Zubr had floated above.

Something about these thoughts made Robin turn and look

back. She squinted to see more clearly as the Kingfisher flashed up into the mouth of the river. It was hard to be sure at this distance, but she was suddenly certain. In the hour or so of the voyage so far, Caleb's old command *Otobo* had started moving. That's quick, she thought, even for Max and his people. As she watched, *Otobo* limped forward and began to swing unhandily out into the bay. As the corvette's long, slim hull came round it was possible to see a couple of tugs working her head with long tow-ropes to her forecastle, and a hump of dirty white water at her stern which showed where her one propeller was churning, trying to hold her stern steady. 'Hey, Captain,' she called without thinking. 'Your *Otobo*'s under way . . .'

Caleb reacted by bringing the Kingfisher round in a tight loop, swinging through 180 degrees in an arc of less than a hundred metres. 'Worried?' she called.

'Interested,' he said. 'And this way I can get a look at what's happening.'

The Kingfisher ran back across the bay at the better part of a mile a minute. Robin walked forward to stand at Caleb's right shoulder – Bonnie had already appropriated his left. The three of them watched through the low windshield as *Otobo* continued to swing out from the dockside. Caleb spoke into a microphone stalk above the basic slave monitors beside the helm. 'You see that, Sanda?' he asked in English.

'I see it, Captain,' the lieutenant answered in the same language. 'Whoever's in command is swinging her out far too tight and fast. The tide's making pretty powerfully now and it'll be pushing her back like nobody's business. They'd have been far better to leave her safe and snug in her berth. She certainly won't have liked that tight a turn from a standing start even with both shafts functioning. And God knows what the captain of that starboard tug thinks he's doing.'

'You'd think the chief engineer would have something to say . . .' mused Caleb, frowning. 'He must have pushed the engines right up into the red. Look at that mountain of foam at her stern.'

He was talking to himself, but Sanda still answered, 'Not if Ngama's boy Jonah's on the bridge. No one'll say a word. Not after what happened to us.'

'I agree. But even so . . .'

If Caleb had a further point to make, thought Robin, he never stated it. For just at that moment, disaster overtook the corvette. The starboard towline parted, allowing the tug to jump free. The bow swung left at once, threatening to collide with the tug on that side – perhaps even crush it between the corvette and the dock – it was hard to be certain from this angle. Whoever was on the bridge must have panicked, Robin reckoned, and pushed the engines further still into the red, trying to power his way out of disaster, while in the terrible grip of the inrushing tide. And it wasn't the shaft that gave way this time. It was the engines themselves. A jet of black smoke billowed out of the rear exhaust system, making it look for a terrible instant as though the whole of the aft section had simply blown open. Robin shouted with shock. A flat detonation like a distant bomb blast echoed across the water. Caleb spat something in Matadi. A curse of some kind. The wind snatched the smoke away, revealing that the hull was still intact – but showing a range of figures simply leaping overboard. More smoke billowed.

'What's happening?' breathed Bonnie.

Caleb was too preoccupied to answer so Robin explained. 'The engines are on fire. The smoke is coming out of the sides because of the ship's heat-reduction system – no more hot funnels, you see? But she's out of control. She must be badly ablaze for the crew to be jumping overboard like that. And, given what Captain Caleb and Lieutenant Sanda were saying about the tide, she's likely to drift back into the jetty pretty quickly.'

'Which,' said Caleb, 'could set the whole of the new wooden frontage on fire. Everywhere from the deep-water port to the new marina, in fact. Including the minister's new office and the whole of the complex it's in. Including the zoo, if the wind increases. And that's even before you start calculating what damage she could do if all of the armaments she has aboard start detonating because of the heat.' He spoke into the microphone stalk again. 'Put me on *Otobo*'s hailing frequency.' A moment later the open channel hissed. '*Otobo*, can you hear me? Is there anyone there? It's Captain Caleb.'

'Captain. It's the Chief. I think I'm the only one left aboard. That puppy Jonah Ngama screwed the motors then abandoned. He ordered everyone over the side. The tide's got her and there's nothing I can do on my own. We're going to drift back on to the jetty. It'll be bad.'

'I'm in the Shaldag, Chief. I can be there in a few minutes. What's the tug on your port side doing?'

'Keeping us off as best he can. The starboard tug's trying to retrieve its line. If they work together they might slow the drift. But I'm not hopeful.'

'Are the armaments at risk? Have you activated the safety equipment?'

'I've activated everything I can. But I wouldn't rely on it. We need help.'

'I'm on my way. Hang on. Radio Officer, I want the general frequency . . . All shipping in Granville Harbour, this is Captain Caleb Maina aboard Shaldag FPB004. Please be aware that the Corvette *Otobo* is drifting out of control, on fire and in a dangerous condition . . .'

Out of the confused babble of concern, one voice came loud and clear. 'Captain Maina, this is Captain Zhukov aboard Zubr *Stalingrad*. We see you and we see *Otobo*. We are five minutes distant. Please advise how we can assist . . .'

'Could we?' said Caleb. 'Could a Shaldag and a Zubr tug her out of trouble?'

He was thinking aloud, but Robin answered. 'All you have to do immediately is turn her head into the incoming tide. Her hull's so slim almost all the pressure would disappear at once. Then you could maybe pull her clear.'

'It's worth a try . . . Captain Zhukov. Thank you. See you there in five.'

The Shaldag FPB004 sped across the bay like an arrow. After four minutes she was beside the starboard tug, which had retrieved the broken towline and was trying to re-secure it. 'Think you could share that line?' asked Robin, surveying the situation, narrow-eyed as the burning corvette's forecastle head towered dangerously above them. 'I'm not sure about the physics – you have almost no mass, but you have power. Those big motors of yours should certainly help . . .'

'What about the Zubr? She'll be here in a minute. Could she link up with us?'

'Same problem. But compounded now I think of it. Those big fans of hers would do more damage than good – they'd effectively set up a hurricane wind blowing *Otobo*'s forecastle head back shorewards, just adding extra power to the push of the tide. No.

The Zubr will have to go on the port side and push outwards. She'll probably blow some windows out of the minister's office and conference rooms, but – wow! – she should be able to exert one hell of a lot of force.'

'How do you know all this?' whispered Bonnie as Caleb negotiated matters with Zhukov and the two tug skippers. Contacted the chief and got Sanda working.

'I'm a full ship's captain. I've commanded supertankers . . .'

'Not just a pretty face then,' said Bonnie with a nervous smile.

'Let's hope we both still have pretty faces when this lot's over,' said Robin and instantly regretted her words. Bonnie frowned, tried to look brave, but failed dismally. 'Only joking,' said Robin, but this time she couldn't even fool herself.

The captain of the starboard tug jury-rigged a double towline and, as the Zubr cruised majestically past, Shaldag FPB004 took it aboard. All Sanda had to secure it was the two stern bitts used to moor the Shaldag. There was no guarantee how much pressure these would take before they were ripped out. But they were big enough to secure the hawser so that was good enough to begin with. The Zubr vanished round the corvette's forecastle, and after that Robin could only make out its position by looking for the whip-antenna that topped its radio mast. But everything was ready surprisingly quickly and, with Caleb coordinating, the four disparate vessels carefully powered up until they could feel *Otobo*'s head beginning to swing across the tide, turning away from the shore.

Ten minutes became twenty as the tugs tugged, the Shaldag pulled and the Zubr pushed. Until, quite suddenly, the corvette's long grey hull settled and stopped fighting. 'We have her now, Captain,' said the skipper of the starboard tug through the static of the open channel. 'Where shall we put her?'

'She still represents a considerable hazard,' prompted Robin. 'And she will do until the fire is under control and the armaments are made safe. Have you a firefighting ship that you can call on to get things under control?'

'On its way. Should be here by sunset.'

'Then put her somewhere safe where the firefighters can get at her when they arrive, but where she'll do a minimum of damage if she goes up after all,' advised Robin briskly. 'Your chief engineer left everything as safe as possible before he went down into the lead tug. There's nothing more anyone can do until the firemen arrive. Why not beach her on one of those sandbars down by the south bank that started her problems yesterday in the first place?'

When the Shaldag FPB004 came back to its dock an hour later still, *Otobo* was a distant column of smoke heading for the minister's proposed wildlife park – or the silk-smooth mudbank nearest to it. The huge Zubr *Stalingrad* was back out in the bay. And, thought Robin, looking warily around, that was probably just as well. The damage the hovercraft's huge fans had caused looked even worse than she had feared. The whole of the government area appeared to have been hit by a tornado. Trees were uprooted and flower-beds simply decimated. Plasterboard, bricks and wooden beams lay piled on ruined lawns. Roof tiles lay scattered like autumn leaves. The entire top of the minister's panoramic office was sitting askew and the wide face of the building gaped as though horrified by it all. There was shattered glass everywhere.

Richard was waiting at the dockside. 'I don't know who thought of using the Zubr to push the corvette round,' he observed as Robin stepped unsteadily ashore and took his arm. 'But it was a stroke of genius. Blew us all away, you might say . . .'

Richard was not alone. Colonel Kabila was standing just behind him. 'You are all to come with me,' he said shortly. 'You too, Captain Maina.'

President Chaka received Captain Caleb's report in thoughtful silence. 'You appear to have resolved a potentially fatal situation through some inspired quick thinking,' he said at last. 'The damage to the government facilities is considerable but, I understand, repairable. And nothing compared to what would have happened if you had not taken action. There will be a Board of Inquiry of course, but I foresee a favourable outcome. For you, at least.'

'Much of the credit must go to Captain Mariner,' said Caleb. 'It was her quick thinking . . .'

'Indeed,' said the President thoughtfully. He looked at the faces ranged in front of him. 'It is upon Captain Mariner's quick thinking that I wish to call. And I am pleased to see that you and she work so well together, Captain Maina.'

'Me?' said Robin frowning. 'You want to call on me?'

'Yes I do. You will have realized, I am sure, that I did not invite you to my country simply so that you could accompany your husband on his business mission here. No. I have a request to make of you. A personal request that I believe I could not make to anyone else. Certainly no one else I can readily think of.'

Robin looked at Richard, then at Captain Caleb. Her frown deepened as her mind raced. Richard shrugged, apparently at a loss. Caleb echoed the gesture. Laurent Kabila cleared his throat and shuffled, but it seemed that even he had been excluded from President Chaka's plans for Robin. And for once in her life Robin herself simply could not guess what was going to be asked of her. 'What do you want, Mr President?' she asked.

'Celine,' he said at last. 'Celine, my daughter. You are one of the few people alive who might take her a message from me and make her listen to reason. I want Celine to come back; we have been at each other's throats too long. I want you to go upriver into the delta to the GPS coordinates of the school and orphanage she runs up there – coincidentally with Mr Asov's daughter Anastasia. I want you to go there with Captain Maina aboard his fast patrol boat and I want you to bring my daughter back to me.'

# THIRTEEN

## *Nellie*

Even with Celine draped across her shoulder, Anastasia managed to stoop and grab her jeans off the floor. Her panties were nowhere to be seen, however, so she forgot about them. It looked as though she was going topless for the moment – she might as well go commando too. With the black cloth wadded in one hand and the other around Celine's slim waist, she staggered forward. As soon as she stepped out on to the rough concrete of the warehouse floor she stubbed her toe and instantly regretted her trainers. Tears of pain flooded her eyes only to be blinked fiercely away. The trainers were long gone with her underwear. The price of being a drama queen, she thought wryly.

But then Ado swung in beside her, taking some of Celine's weight, and they rushed her forward towards the wooden dock and the vessel the dead captain had called a floating shit-pile. She looked pretty good to Anastasia at that moment, though. The most beautiful White Sea cruise liner could have hardly looked better, to be fair. Only a battleship might have pipped her at the post. A battleship full of marines with some chopper back-up and heavy armour support. But even that dream might not have come out on top.

Because Anastasia knew how to drive *Nellie*.

'You don't drive a boat,' Captain Christophe used to tell her, frowning with seriousness bordering on outrage. 'You *steer* her. If you are in charge of the power too then you *con* her. *Con*. Manoeuvre. Navigate.'

'If I'm holding a wheel and turning up the juice, then I'm driving,' she used to tease him, never quite sure how many of these games were really getting through her Matadi dialect's terrible Russian/American accent. But on their trips up and down the river, Christophe had taught her how to con his *Nellie* almost as well as he could himself. Had shown her how the whole battered vessel functioned, from the searchlight on top of the wheelhouse to the churning propeller below the square stern. And he had taught her something about the great River Gir, too. But the wise old teacher was probably dead now, she thought bitterly, floating face down in the water somewhere downstream of Malebo. Her eyes stung at the thought.

The dead captain's ex-command was sitting tightly beside the dock, one small step down from the level of the jetty itself. Anastasia heaved Celine aboard, letting her full weight fall on Ado. The two women went sprawling and the boat heaved jerkily, straining against her moorings. She slung her jeans down on to the deck and ran for the bollard where the forward line was tied. Her mind, still skittering everywhere like spit on a hotplate, knocked loose by shock and relief, suddenly gave her an image of what she must look like – stark naked and liberally spattered with blood. She stooped to pull the line free wondering who was getting an eyeful this time.

The all too familiar hammering filled the warehouse once again, seeming to detonate like a line of firecrackers inside Anastasia's head. Her white buttocks clenched as though they were the target. But it was the windows of *Nellie*'s bridge house that exploded, showering her like crystalline hail. The hammering was answered more loudly. Esan, firing back. She leaped down on to the foredeck, trying to avoid the still-dancing carpet of shattered glass, but needing to be quick, for the current coming down from the cataract of the ruined bridge had taken the river-boat's head at once and was swinging it away from the dockside pretty quickly. 'Esan,' she shouted. 'Get aboard.' Then she crouched in the shelter of the wheelhouse, hoping it would protect her from any more shooting. Got to cover your ass, girl, she thought. *Literally*.

*Nellie* dipped as someone – Esan, prayed Anastasia – jumped aboard, then the sturdy little vessel was loose of the jetty, drifting rapidly out on to the river, in the firm grip of the relentless current. Anastasia risked a glance back round the wheelhouse's wooden wall and caught a glimpse of Esan frozen in the act of throwing the rowboat's petrol can back on to the dock, wrapped in blazing rags like a massive Molotov cocktail. 'I hope he hasn't used my jeans,' she thought. But then she started calculating what he must have done to help them: heaved himself into the back of the second truck, ridden down here with them unsuspected, stolen the AK left in the footwell by the prizefighter and come to rescue them after all. Her eyes filled with tears of gratitude.

The can hit the wooden jetty and exploded into a wall of flame that spread right across the opening – on the wood, on the concrete, on the water in between. Anastasia risked a dash back and round into the raised wheelhouse, three steps up from the deck where Esan was helping Ado pull Celine to her feet. She glanced around the familiar little space in the flickering dazzle of the flames behind her. The windows were gone. So was most of the equipment. It looked as though the radio was defunct. Its guts lay scattered everywhere; and so did those of the venerable GPS. But the wheel was intact. So were the levers controlling the diesel. All she had to do was turn the key in the dashboard and pray. She did – and, not for the first time that night, her prayers were answered.

Anastasia held *Nellie*'s head as far across the current as she could while she eased the grumbling motor up to speed, feeling the single shaft shaking in its tubular bedding beneath the deck with the soles of her bare feet, feeling the propeller grip with all the vividness of a fisherman sensing a bite on his line, and finally feeling the battered, flat-bottomed hull attain steerage way. Without the GPS for positioning and the radio for help, she would find it hard to get *Nellie* to the dock at Malebo. But that had to be her immediate destination. There was at the very least a clinic in the little riverside township where Celine's condition could be assessed. Then it would be downriver to Granville Harbour, get some help, tool up and get back upstream to kick some serious butt. And, talking of butt . . .

'Esan,' called Anastasia. 'Can somebody bring me my jeans? I want to give you a great big thank-you hug, but I'll be damned if I'll do it like this. You've earned quite a lot, boy, but there are limits.'

Ado came in a moment later, her feet crunching on the shattered glass, and handed Anastasia her jeans. 'Thanks,' she said. 'Could you hold the wheel for a moment while I climb into these?' As Ado did what she asked and Anastasia slid on her jeans, she asked, gently, 'Are you OK, Ado?'

'Thanks to you,' said the young woman quietly. 'Thanks to you and to Esan.'

'Don't do yourself down, girl,' said Anastasia, buttoning her fly and tightening her belt. 'You were doing a real good job yourself. Wasn't it here or hereabouts they had an army of women warriors? Only women? Wiped the floor with the French for years. Amazons for real?'

'I have never heard of such a thing,' Ado answered.

'Well I'm pretty sure I'm right. And I'll bet some ancestor of yours was at least a sergeant in that army! Hell –' she laughed, looking out into the velvety, tree-lined darkness of the south bank – 'I bet she's still out there, with the rest of your ancestors in the forest.'

Ado smiled.

'How's Celine?' asked Anastasia, taking back the wheel.

'Nowhere near better yet.'

'I'm planning to get her to the clinic in Malebo. I'd be happier if it was me that was wounded and Celine was doing the tending. She's one hell of a doctor.'

Ado said, 'If you had been the one who was wounded and Celine had been the one who was well, then we'd all be dead now. Or still being raped in that *place*. Celine would never have done what you did. You saved us. It was not your ancestors who were warriors. It is you. *You* are a warrior.' And she walked out.

Anastasia was still crying like a baby when Esan came in five minutes later. 'Are you all right?' he asked. 'Are you hurt? Is it shock?'

'It's just a girl thing,' answered Anastasia. 'Nothing a soldier-boy like you would understand. Climb up on the top of the wheelhouse and see if you can get the searchlight working, will you? I'll need to see where I'm going if we're ever to have any chance of making Malebo. And the moon's just not up to the job tonight.'

For the rest of the night, Anastasia followed the big pool of brightness the searchlight cast on the river's surface downstream and across the river to the north bank. Every now and then she sent Esan clambering aloft to swing the golden beam from side to side until she managed to make out some half-familiar land-mark, then she knew where to make for next. As the dawn slowly gathered behind them and the sun came up over the jagged peaks of the volcanoes far inland, so she at last let the exhausted boy join Ado and Celine where they lay asleep in the cramped little cabin below.

It was only when at long last Anastasia saw the familiar jetty reaching out from Malebo and steered towards it, shaking with a potent combination of exhaustion, relief and early-morning chill, that she realized she was still naked from the waist up. Naked and thickly coated with congealed blood. She called to the others but they made no response, so she ended up easing *Nellie* forward until her bow just kissed the pier's outer end, then she quickly moored her in place and let her swing with the current while she ran lightly to the stern where she knew there was a bucket on a rope.

She looked around, but it was too early for the township to be stirring yet. The little boats and occasional pirogues tethered to the lower sections of the jetty were all empty – there had been no fish here since the nineties. There was no one about. She stripped off, glorying in the warm caress of the early sunlight, in the golden veil of mist it raised along the shoreline and in the fragrant breath of the dawn wind, flowing gently down towards the sea. She dropped the bucket overboard and pulled up clear, clean water. It took half a dozen chilly bucketfuls to get her anywhere near clean. Then she stood, with her arms raised, letting the sun and the warm breeze dry her.

She had no sensation of being watched at all.

After a few moments, she stepped back into her jeans – noticing for the first time how bad they smelt, then she ran light-footed below, searching for something to put on. It was close to a miracle that the shattered glass hadn't cut her feet to ribbons – but it was a miracle she could no longer rely on. She found an old pair of flip-flops that only stayed on when she clenched her toes round the piece of rubber between them and a *My People* T-shirt with an outline of Africa on the front, the familiar shape of the conti-nent framing the frowning face of a boy who looked a lot like Esan. She slipped it on without registering that it was many sizes too big for her and turned to wake the other three.

'What's the plan?' asked Esan, blinking himself awake and nudging Ado who was wrapped around him.

'Get Celine to the clinic and call for all the help we can raise.' Anastasia looked across at the woman sleeping restlessly in the other bunk. Through the semi-transparent cloth of her blouse it was clear that the makeshift T-shirt bandage was stained with more than just blood from her wound.

Esan frowned. 'What about me?' he asked. 'Anyone you call up to help you is likely to come after me too. I am Army of Christ the Infant.'

'We have to think of a way round that,' said Ado forcefully, untangling herself and sitting up, her face as fearsome as his. 'Esan saved us.'

'You're both right,' agreed Anastasia. 'But I don't think you need to worry yet. There's no police station or military camp in Malebo. Even so, I think you should stay aboard, Esan, while Ado and I take Celine to the clinic. All I'm planning on doing after we check her in is trying to get hold of a cellphone or a radio that will get me in contact with Granville Harbour. I want to warn them about what's happened. Tell someone where Celine is and how she is. I suppose there's an outside chance the author-ities would send a chopper up for us but I wouldn't bet on it.

Even though Celine's the president's daughter she says she and her father don't talk. Haven't talked for years. He wouldn't lift a finger to help her any more than my father would help me. No. I plan that we'll stick together and go on downriver if we can. There may even be someone in town who can help us with *Nellie* so we don't have to do all the driving. Does that sound like a plan?'

The little township was beginning to stir as Anastasia and Ado helped Celine stagger inland from the river through the dilapidated white-walled buildings that lined the main street. Behind them, the town spread out into more traditional round, mud-walled dwellings, better suited to the climate and situation. Families were at their early-morning chores, fetching water, stoking fires, preparing food. The road the three women were following was metalled through the township, but it became little more than a red mud track in the distance. However, it curved away into the jungle and ran right the way down to Granville Harbour. Ten miles north of the city, in fact, it opened out again to became, suddenly and unexpectedly, an eight-lane highway even larger than the one they had travelled last night into Citematadi. There was a gas station here, whose diesel powered *Nellie* as well as local trucks, and whose petrol fired up generators, occasional four-by-fours, battered saloons and ubiquitous motorcycles. There was post office and sometimes mail came and went. It had an old-fashioned exchange. Sometimes the phones worked. There had once been reliable landlines but they were long gone. Now communication from the post office relied – as was stated on the big poster in its window – on Benincom. There was a cellphone mast standing tall behind the post office on the edge of the jungle. And where there was communication, there was commerce: palm oil going down from local groves; bananas, plantains, dates, kola nuts, coconuts, okra on occasion – more than subsistence crops, grown on local smallholdings and gathered from the jungle. Up from the city came fish, meat and domestic utensils. There was a hardware store. There was a food shop. There was a bank, which opened occasionally.

And there was a clinic. It was just about the last of the square, white-painted, flat-roofed buildings in town. It was air-conditioned, blessedly quiet. The sister on reception took one look at Celine and called for the doctor. The doctor took one look at her and called for a bed. 'I'll fill in the necessary paperwork,' said Anastasia. 'You find the nearest phone, laptop or two-way radio.'

By the time Anastasia had filled out the paperwork – several sheets of it – Ado was back. 'The post office says everything's gone down,' she reported. 'Seems like bad luck. Benincom cell-phones were working fine until earlier this morning. Then it all went down. Probably something to do with the mast. That's it. No one has a laptop with Internet access either – that piggybacked on the Benincom signal apparently. The people at the post office think there might be someone with a satellite phone, but they don't know who. Nor does anyone at the garage. Or at the hard-ware shop.'

'That's it then,' said Anastasia. 'Looks like *Nellie* and plan B.'

The doctor arrived then and picked up the paperwork, frowning. Anastasia read the name 'Dr Chukwu' on the pocket of his white coat. 'I have cleaned the bullet wound,' he said, 'and bandaged it properly. Given her antibiotics and painkillers. She is sleeping now. Please explain how she came to be wounded.'

As Anastasia told her story, Dr Chukwu reached into his pocket and pulled out a bulky Benincom cellphone. Switched it on, frowned again. 'No signal,' he said. 'But this must be reported to the authorities at the earliest possible opportunity!'

'That's our plan,' said Anastasia.

'Why, Malebo itself could be at risk! The Army of Christ the Infant is notorious!'

'It doesn't normally attack towns,' countered Anastasia. 'But you're right. Is there a mayor, a chief, someone local in charge? Someone we could warn before we go downstream for help?'

'There is Mr Obada. He runs the hardware store. He's the man to tell.'

'Right. We'll do that on our way out, then. But Celine will be safe here?'

'As safe as we can make her,' said Dr Chukwu.

On their way back to the *Nellie*, Anastasia and Ado went into the hardware store and told their story to Mr Obada. Malebo's mayor frowned. 'I will call a council meeting,' he decided. 'Warn everyone. Set up armed defences as soon as possible. You are going for help, you say?'

'In the *Nellie*. It might take a day or two . . .'

'The *Nellie*? But where is Captain Christophe?'
'I wish I could tell you,' said Anastasia sadly.

The man who had watched Anastasia washing and drying herself
in naked splendour was called Odem. Esan knew him well but
had no idea he was here – any more than Odem knew the boy
was aboard the boat. Anastasia herself might have recognized
him as one of the phalanx of older men who had stood around
General Moses Nlong when he ate Sister Faith's heart. For he was
a captain in the Army of Christ the Infant and one of the general's
most trusted officers.

Odem watched the women now, still from the fringes of the
jungle, hidden with the little squad he had brought through
the delta downriver with him; moving, he had thought, at almost
incredible speed along the north bank through the all but track-
less jungle. Especially as they had brought with them a pair of
four-by-fours and a pair of Toyota 'Technical' trucks with
machine guns and rocket launchers on the back of them. And
yet three women – scarcely more than children – had beaten him
to his goal. It was incredible. It might be enough to change the
game – make him depart from the detail of his orders – a very
dangerous thing to do. So Captain Odem sat and thoughtfully
surveyed his target. Unsuspected still – in spite of the fact that
they had already disabled the Benincom cellphone mast and cut
the town off from the outside world.

Odem sucked his teeth in thought and indecision. His orders
were specific and clear. They had not included the *Nellie*. But
the general had not known about the *Nellie*. What would his
orders have been if he had realized that the boat and the escaped
women would be here? Odem's indecision was acute. His hesitation crucial. The women climbed aboard the boat, slipped the
mooring and were beyond his reach almost before he knew it.
That taught the soldier the dangers of hesitation if nothing else.
He gestured, silently. The little squad he had brought with him
detached themselves from the invisibility of the undergrowth and
followed him to the clinic.

It took only a moment for the six men and one terrified woman
to break into the white-painted building. They were experts at
this kind of thing. Dr Chukwu and his staff never stood a chance
of resisting. They didn't even get the chance to raise the alarm.

Captain Odem surveyed the terrified medical team as they stood under the guns of his men. 'You will come with us,' he said shortly. 'You will bring all the medicines and equipment you can carry. This woman is a nun with some medical training. Her name is Sister Hope. She will advise on what you will need to bring and ensure that you bring the best. Hurry! There is little time. I am sure you don't want to find yourselves in the middle of a firefight or a hostage negotiation.'

As the terrified clinic staff did what he ordered, with the help of Sister Hope, under the guns of his command, Odem went through the neat little ward. There were four patients. He looked at three of them with no interest whatsoever. He looked at the fourth and smiled.

Ten minutes later, Captain Odem surveyed his command and their prisoners. 'Bring the patients too,' he ordered. 'Leave the place empty. It will sow confusion. Give us extra time – for the women must have told them we are somewhere near. We will not take the sick ones far, as they will slow us.' He looked down. His smile lingered. Ngoboi had been kind. The capture of this woman would outweigh the escape of the other two. 'Except for this one. This one is Celine Chaka, the daughter of the president. General Nlong wants her specifically, so she will be coming all the way back upriver with us.'

# FOURTEEN
## Burning

'Dangerous?' laughed Robin. 'How could it be dangerous? Weren't you paying attention to anything Chaka said?' She pushed a plate of *apon* and *iresi* – meat stew and rice – to one side and looked up with a frown. 'The President's sending me upriver to take a message to his daughter. She's in a combination orphanage, kindergarten and religious retreat on the bank of a quiet river in the middle of a deserted jungle. She's surrounded by nuns and school kids. The scariest person anywhere near her is Anastasia Asov – and she's a friend of ours.'

Richard sipped his sparkling water; his expression said he was unconvinced.

'The only complication anyone can see is the fact that their communications have gone down,' Robin persisted, tapping on the tablecloth with her unused pudding fork to emphasize her points. 'But that's nothing unusual; they're in the back of beyond and even the nearest town, Malebo, keeps going off-air on a regular basis. It's par for the course. So they need a messenger to go up there in person and Chaka's chosen me. He thinks Celine will listen to me. If I can, I'm to bring Celine back to him. If not, then I'm just to wash my hands of it and come straight home.' She threw down her fork with a little more force than she meant to, and sat back. 'What could be easier?'

In the face of Richard's continued silence, she leaned forward again and continued, 'And what's he given me to back me up? In case Anastasia's antsy or the nuns turn nasty? Shaldag FPB004. A fast patrol boat that is just about the speediest thing afloat. A crew of ten commandos commanded by the best captain available. A boat that is, Captain Caleb assures me, armed with a stabilized 20 millimetre gun, and two 0.5 millimetre machine guns. Not to mention hand-held and shoulder-launched weapons systems, and, of course, standard issue personal armaments for each man. Semi-automatic, handgun, commando knife, whatever. And this kit isn't special issue if that's what you're thinking. It's standard. It's what the Shaldags carry.'

'It's not the weaponry,' said Richard at last. 'The last time you were up in the delta you and Anastasia had been kidnapped. Celine and I were coming after you, fair enough, but it was the fact that all we heard from you – all we heard about you – was the kidnappers' messages, threats and demands. It was you I needed to talk to – and you were out of contact . . .'

Robin's expression softened. She remembered how stressful the incident had been – oddly, it had been worse for him than it had been for her. She could understand why he wanted to avoid any chance at all that the nightmare might be repeated. But she was going to go for all that; the president's mission was simply too good to miss. 'FPB004 has broadband, satellite, GPS, radar, sonar. She has better navigation equipment than your precious top-of-the-range *Katapults*. She can sail at fifty knots for seven hundred nautical miles – more than enough for the round trip, especially as we will be carrying an extra six tons of spare fuel, which should get us another five hundred nautical miles or so. If we halve our speed – when coming back downriver, say – we double our range. And we are talking nautical miles here. That's twelve hundred and sixty klicks at full speed and twenty-five hundred if we're careful. God! I bet we could sail right up to those famous volcanoes – Mount Karisoke and the rest – if we wanted.'

She could see him wavering. So she pushed home her advantage ruthlessly. 'Jesus, Richard, it's like I was taking a walk from Nelson's Column to Buckingham Palace, wrapped in cotton wool with an armed guard from the household cavalry! It'll be a walk in the park . . .'

'Yes,' he acknowledged. 'St James's Park, in fact.' But there was still that lingering scepticism in his voice as he sought to puncture her grandiose comparison.

'Oh, Richard,' she challenged him directly at last. '*What on earth could go wrong*?'

Richard threw up his hands in defeat. 'I just wish I was coming with you,' he said. And that, she knew. was the crux of the matter.

'In case I need someone to hold my hand, wipe my nose or change my nappy?' she teased, lightening the atmosphere. 'Come on, darling! You've got enough to keep you occupied here. And the upside from the Heritage Mariner point of view is that while I'm doing my Mary Poppins act upriver, Chaka himself promises to head up the negotiations. That'll short-cut Minister Ngama and his cohorts. Maybe even outmanoeuvre BP, Shell, Exxon, Conoco and the rest!'

'OK,' he acquiesced. 'I give in. So what's the plan now?'

'I get my Jungle Jane kit on, throw one or two necessaries in a grip, and go down to what little Captain Zhukov's fans left of the new docks.' She was on her feet already, unable to contain herself any longer, heading from the reception room into the bedroom. 'You, my darling, get the team together and get ready to go and kick some presidential bottom.'

The conversation took place over the remains of a late lunch in the Nelson Mandela Suite. It had been a busy day so far and it looked like getting busier, if anything. While the Mariners had been lunching, the venue of the morning's meeting was being moved to the president's own offices for the afternoon session and everyone was due to reassemble there in the cool of the afternoon at four. Caleb's Shaldag was being refuelled and prepared to undertake the president's mission with a night-run upriver which should get them to Celine's school sometime the next morning.

For Richard the prospect was of another boring meeting, a quick change, another formal dinner, a lonely night and yet another lengthy meeting tomorrow. The only positive element to his day so far had been the adventure of the burning corvette and the awesome experience of Captain Zhukov's private hurricane. It was all clearly going to be downhill from there. He could not begin to express his boredom and depression.

Robin on the other hand could scarcely contain her excitement, he thought, with pure, simple jealousy. In about a tenth of the time it usually took her to change – only just giving him time to contact his negotiating team – she had slipped into a pair of jeans and solid-looking boots. She was tucking a seemingly indestructible plum-coloured brushed silk blouse into a solid leather belt and catching up a safari jacket he didn't even know she possessed. Then she was off, with Richard almost sullenly in tow.

'Get my bag for me, would you?' she asked winningly as she reached for the door handle. And so he followed her down to reception with a surprisingly heavy Louis Vuitton Canvas Keepall in one hand and his black leather briefcase in the other. When Andre Wanago gallantly relieved him of the Keepall in the lobby as they swept out towards the car, the pained look in the elegant manager's eyes showed that he realized he had made the wrong choice.

They settled into the back of the hotel limousine. 'Docks first?' said Richard. 'So I can kiss you farewell and wish you Godspeed like a good sailor's spouse?' The gentle irony at least showed he was beginning to come to terms with her plans, thought Robin.

'In a pig's eye, matey,' she answered shortly, but with a dazzling smile. 'President's offices first. And I'll go on downhill from there. You've had your kiss for the day. You'll have to save up for the rest. I want you glad to see me when I get back, sailor. *Very* glad!'

Half an hour later, just after 16:30 local time, Lieutenant Sanda found himself unknowingly sharing Andre Wanago's feelings as he shouldered the Louis Vuitton Keepall and directed Captain Robin Mariner towards the Shaldag's accommodation ladder. Bonnie Holliday was already aboard and the two women greeted each other like excited schoolgirls in the crew's mess and accommodation area. Bonnie had been aboard a while and, bubbling with enthusiasm, she gave Robin a quick orientation tour. Right in the bow at the forward end of the mess, there was a secure storage area. Its door was locked, but it was where their bags would go when their necessaries were unpacked. The mess and accommodation area, where they were now, was immediately below the main command area and bridge – above which was the open flying bridge they had shared with Caleb that morning. Aft of the mess there were the heads and then the ship's small galley before the engine sections. The placing of the galley raised Robin's eyebrow until she saw the logic of its access to fresh water from the ablutions and heat from the engines. The whole area below deck was more than six feet high – so both women could stand upright. It was also the better part of fifteen feet across at its widest, though the walls sloped inwards as dictated by the curve of the hull, and, reckoned Robin, nearly forty feet long, so there was plenty of room for the table – which was suspended from the ceiling and would be raised when the comfortable seats around it folded out into bunks. It was all so neat and practical. And, thought Robin, *air-conditioned*. Bliss!

Of course, the two women were not alone as they enjoyed their little tour. There was an engineering officer with a team of three looking after propulsion in the twenty-five feet of engine room. Caleb and Sanda had their junior navigators – two of them working up in the forty odd feet of command bridge, which was also nearly twenty feet wide and six feet high. There was a communications officer. And, just in case – in spite of Robin's overstated confidence that this would be a walk in the park – there was a gunnery officer.

Immediately before leaving, Caleb crowded everyone around the mess table for a quick briefing. He laid out a map of the delta on which a series of notes and GPS coordinates had been pencilled. 'We're due to depart at seventeen hundred hours,' he said. 'That'll give us an hour of daylight to get well upstream. We're going to follow standard river procedure and keep to the south bank on the way in. That will take us past the sandbank where *Otobo* is beached and let me assess the progress of the firefighting. Then we'll head upstream keeping to this channel here, south of the chain of small islands that split the main stream into two from here to here. We'll have to keep a good watch out for mats of floating water hyacinth – they're the main hazard for shipping there. We should keep a lookout for small vessels too – but that's the proposed site of the minister's wildlife sanctuary so there aren't any villages there. No people at all as far as we know. We'll pass the township of Malebo on the far side of the river, and keep to the south side as we shoot the rapids left by the fallen bridge beside Citematadi.'

'I'd like to see Citematadi, if possible,' said Robin. 'Richard's told me it's a spectacular sight – if rather creepy and depressing. I missed it on my last visit.'

'If there's time and opportunity,' said Caleb. 'But we won't be hanging around there.' He turned back to the others. 'Then it'll be the long haul upriver and across the stream to these coordinates here, which are the GPS location of the settlement where the president's daughter is currently located. Are we all clear about this? It's further upriver than I've ever been and further than anyone else aboard has been—'

'I've been up that far – past Citematadi at least,' Robin interrupted him again. 'I was a guest of General Chaka's revolutionary army just before he took the power and the presidency from ex-President Banda. It won't,' she added looking round them all and thinking, suddenly, that Richard might have had a point after all . . . 'It won't be a walk in the park.'

'No, indeed,' countered Captain Caleb with a smile. 'It'll be a cruise in the delta. So, ladies and gentlemen, let's get to it.'

Shaldag FPB004 eased away from the jetty at 17:00 local time on the dot. Once again, Caleb took control in the flying bridge while Robin and Bonnie stood at his shoulders. The evening was vast and sultry at first, the darkening sky high, the horizons far, the wind laden with a humidity that seemed to intensify the odd mixture of sea smells and river odours. The sun was setting away out to sea on their right as the Shaldag sat up and swept southward in that long arc designed to take her to the sandbar where *Otobo* was beached. Beached and still burning. Even from a couple of kilometres away it was possible to see the tall arches of white water that the two firefighting ships in attendance were pouring on to her. As the speeding patrol boat drew near, so the droplets began to catch the light from the westering sun, and the white water shattered into solid rainbows tinged with gold.

'Looks like your armaments are safe,' shouted Robin.

'Will they still be serviceable?' wondered Bonnie.

'It looks as though you'll still have a hull when this is all over,' persisted Robin thoughtfully. 'Everything else can be fixed when she gets into dry dock.'

'I guess so,' said Caleb less than happily, and he swung the wheel to bring the crippled vessel round on their right and the sunset directly behind them as he sped FPB004 due eastwards up the river, into the delta and the gathering darkness.

The sun set at 18:00 with military precision. It turned the delta on either side of the speeding boat into a slaughterhouse of red leaves, dripping like huge gouts of blood into the hyacinth-clotted artery ahead of them. The first of the midstream islands hulked on their left, making what had seemed a wide, inviting channel suddenly threatening and overgrown. The tall super-structure cast a huge shadow forward which camouflaged the floating islands of vegetation, making it hard for even the most experienced eye to distinguish clearly. Caleb kept up a muttered conversation with the man on the radar as he eased the vessel forward, its motors scarcely rising above a grumble. Even so, the beds of water hyacinth scraped eerily along the sides, like something out of a horror movie. Robin found herself shivering in spite of the humid heat. Richard's worries were suddenly looking more and more real. The narrow, arterial channel with its thrombosis of matted plants even smelt foetid, as though the whole blood-soaked place was rotting around them. She noticed Bonnie sliding ever closer to Caleb as the atmosphere got to her as well. And then, with a suddenness only the tropics can supply, it was dark.

'Searchlight!' ordered Caleb, and a great beam of brightness probed the channel ahead of them. But all it seemed to do, as far as Robin was concerned, was to emphasize how close the overhanging bank had become on their starboard quarter. How close the mid-river island was on their port. She looked across at the low, shrub-covered mudbank, wondering whether there were after all any of the huge crocodiles she had seen in the zoo yesterday evening still lurking hidden there. The thought was disturbing enough to shorten her breath and add to the sweat beading her upper lip.

But then something distracted her. A trick of the light, she thought. The shaggy overgrowth crowning the nearest island seemed suddenly to be illuminated from inside, as though not crocodiles but the strange local dancing deity Ngoboi and his ghostly lieutenants were about some supernatural business in there.

Robin drew in a breath to tell Bonnie and Caleb about her strange vision, when the most unexpected thing happened. Someone started shooting at them. A long rattle of automatic fire rang out across the silence of the river. Silence she hadn't even registered until the gunshots shattered it. She ducked, flinching.

'Get below,' ordered Caleb. 'Hurry! Kill the light!' And he shepherded them to the ladder down to the deck. 'Into the cabin,' he said as they reached the deck – then he strode through into the bridge.

'What on earth was that?' asked Bonnie, shaken, as they stepped down into the cool of the mess.

'Someone took a potshot at us,' said Robin briefly.

As Bonnie sat, shaken, on one of the padded benches that would later fold out into bunks, Robin stationed herself at the foot of the companionway leading up into the command bridge. She could hear the creak of Caleb and his bridge watch sitting in the big pilot's seats she had seen as she went past. She could hear the pinging of the sonar and the occasional contact from the collision alarm radar as a particularly solid raft of water hyacinth washed downstream towards them. The motors were grumbling away behind her at the stern, and those floating mats of water hyacinth were still whispering past the outside of the hull. But none of the noises around her were loud enough to drown out the quiet conversation the captain was having with his navigators and communications officer. Some of the technical language tested her understanding of Matadi to the utmost, but she filled in the gaps easily enough by assessing what she would be asking and answering under the circumstances.

'No contact?' Caleb asked quietly.

'No, Captain. I've tried every channel. There's no radio signal anywhere nearby.' That would be the radio officer.

'OK,' decided Caleb. 'Contact base, report that shots were

fired near to us – perhaps at us. No damage or casualties to report. But maybe they should be aware downriver. Sanda, anything?'

'The light beyond the island seems to have gone out. I guess there was some kind of vessel there and that's most likely where the shots came from. But she seems to have gone now. Do you want to pursue, Captain?'

'No. It's not really an option,' said Caleb. 'Navigator, where do you estimate the nearest big break in the island chain on our port side is?'

'Seven klicks ahead.'

'Five minutes at full speed. Twenty-five given the current situation. No. We'll carry on with the mission. But we'll keep a careful watch. And put the searchlight on again.'

'Man the gun, just in case?' asked the lieutenant.

'No, Sanda. Nor the machine guns. Let's keep everyone inside where it's nice and safe. For the time being, at least. Now, who's on galley duty? Let's get back to routine as soon as possible. You have the con, Sanda. And I want to know the instant we get free of this garbage blocking our way. I want a fast run up to Citematadi if humanly possible.'

'Yes, Captain.'

Robin didn't recognize the man who served dinner, but she decided that when the opportunity arose she would get his recipe for fish pepper soup and Jollof rice. The fish pepper soup wasn't a soup and it wasn't made with fish. It was a thick stew of huge delta prawns and a range of peppers – sweet and hot – and tomatoes. It was heavenly and it complemented the rice and mixed vegetables perfectly. She would have gone for seconds – but the seconds were gone before she finished her huge first serving. 'You'll have to be quicker than that Captain Mariner,' said Caleb in English, his deep voice rumbling with amusement. 'Seaman Erelu's *obe eja tutu* is famous throughout the fleet. Don't despair, though, there's Rocky Road for dessert.'

Robin and Bonnie dragged the meal out a little and Caleb's crew indulged them, for there were no entertainment facilities aboard. They were politely refused permission to help with the washing-up, but they were permitted back up on deck as the boat's evening routine proceeded in unhurried efficiency. Once cleared, the table was elevated and bunks folded down. The heads were tiny, but big enough to allow more than mere functionality – there would have been room to change into night-things had either woman wanted to. But they were both still too excited, and so they wandered around, above-decks and below, trying not to get in the way.

The next excitement came when the Shaldag finally broke free of the hyacinth-clogged channel between the islands and the southern shore. As soon as he was clear, Caleb pushed the throttles forward and his command sat up on the water again as her speed climbed. But from what Robin remembered of the notes on the map he had shown them at the briefing, they were badly behind schedule now. It came as no surprise, therefore, when they sped past the lights of Malebo township which glittered briefly on the far, northern, bank just before midnight.

Neither Robin nor Bonnie had any intention of sleeping, even though bunks had been prepared for them below with courtesy and care. The adventure had been quite exciting enough before the ingredients of unexplained gunfire, water-hyacinth clots and long fast runs up black, benighted river were added to the mix. And, to make the temptation of deck over bunk quite irresistible, there was a low, full moon dead ahead, magnified by some trick of the heavy, humid atmosphere, rising like a fat pendulous silver sun, while the stars lay scattered overhead like huge pearls across the black velvet of the lightless interstellar sky. The amazing moon lit their way so brightly that Caleb ordered the searchlight off again and let his command cut like a shadow through the shimmering majesty of the night.

Where the atmosphere at sunset had seemed threatening, almost horrific, thought Robin dreamily, now it was the opposite. The curve of the river with its overhanging forest-buttressed bank, the occasional tall palm tree soaring high against the Milky Way, was something out of every jungle romance ever written or filmed. And the figures standing so close together at the helm seemed almost to be outlined in a pearly luminescence. The air on the broader reach was cooler. It carried out to the speeding vessel the odours of the jungle so close at hand. Sometimes the rich stench of rotting detritus left high after the recent floods. Sometimes the clear crisp smell of fresh green vegetation, reminding Robin irresistibly of fresh cut grass. But the jungle was secondary; overgrowing what had in many places been civilized into gardens before the wildness reclaimed it. So once in a while – and more often as they approached Citematadi in the small hours – there were scents familiar from Robin's own garden: bougainvillea, buddleia, magnolia, myrtle and, 'Is that night-flowering jasmine I can smell?' asked Bonnie.

The breeze also seemed to carry sounds out of the vast near-silence that stretched out beyond the grumble of the engines. The whispering of the wavelets beneath the sharp bows and square back in the wake, the rustling of the millions upon millions of leaves. The occasional creaking of more substantial branches. Strange, formless sounds that made Robin think of wild animals – panthers and crocodiles – again, and also brought Ngoboi and his whirling acolytes to mind once more. But then, quite suddenly, very much more precisely placed, just round the wide right-hand bend dead ahead, there was a muted thunder that was more than fanciful imagination. 'What's that noise?' asked Robin.

Right at the same instant as Bonnie asked, 'Is that woodsmoke I can smell?'

Caleb stirred himself. 'That's the cataract caused by the collapsed bridge at Citematadi,' he said to Robin. 'Citematadi is just round that bend ahead – you see how the bank is higher and squarer coming up to the curve? That must be the embankment. And, yes,' he answered Bonnie, 'I smell burning too. I think we'd better have the light on.'

# FIFTEEN
## Punch

Anastasia brought *Nellie* round a bend to face due west – and sailed straight into the blinding impact of a blood-red sunset. 'I can't see!' she shouted, throttling back. 'Esan, is there anything up ahead? It's as though someone just punched me in the face! I feel like my eyes are full of blood!'

Thank God, she thought, that she had placed Esan up in the very point of the bows where he could keep watch for hazards that might be invisible to her. Tree trunks floating waterlogged just beneath the surface, unsuspected mudbanks, dead bodies and so forth. And, most particularly as they came downstream, mats of floating water hyacinth that could all too easily pile up against the blunt cutwater and slow the vessel from dead slow to stop. Or, worse, get tangled round the propeller and cripple her altogether.

'There's something in the middle of the river,' sang back Esan. 'It's big. An island I think. Go right.'

'There's a string of islands down near the river mouth, I remember,' Anastasia called as she shook her head and tried to clear her streaming eyes. 'When we're past them we're almost out of the river – then it's not that far to the jetty at the new dock facilities they put in place of the old shanty town.'

'How long will it take us to get past them? Come further right. Straighten up on that. Good.'

'Six, maybe eight hours. It depends on tide and current. And whether we get caught up in that filthy water hyacinth stuff. God, I'd like to get my hands on whoever brought it on to the river.' Anastasia slitted her eyes as they began to clear of tears and looked doggedly ahead. The channel which had been so wide and welcoming was closed in now by the tousle-headed islands in midstream and by the flats and shallows that spread out from them, causing the water hyacinth to clot the already narrowed waterway. Even with her flat bottom and almost negligible draft, *Nellie* had to stay in the deepest available channel. But that was by no means easy to settle on. Certainly she couldn't just put the wheel hard over to starboard and hug the north shore. The trees and bushes overhanging the northern bank stretched out into treacherous mangroves once again – but saltwater ones this time, as the river became tidal and prone to flooding-back with saltwater from the bay. The old captain, Christophe, had warned her that this was the most difficult part of the river. He had rarely let her con *Nellie* through here. And never unless he was standing at her shoulder as anxious as a parent taking their child for their first driving practice in the family saloon. He had had some tide tables, too, now she came to think of it. If Ado or Esan could find them, maybe she could work out how to use them to *Nellie*'s advantage.

'Ado, could you look for a book of tide tables?' she asked. 'Start in the drawers in here. It'll be quite a small book with columns of figures showing dates and times . . .' She stopped, almost ready to curse herself. There were probably charts and everything up in these drawers. Why hadn't she thought to search through them earlier? But then she gave a shrug. *Nellie* and she had made it this far. Nothing they were likely to find aboard could have helped them do any better. Thanks to Esan, they were even well supplied with guns.

But Ado's search revealed nothing. The whole of *Nellie* seemed to have been cleaned out – to such an extent, Anastasia at last decided, that the flip-flops and T-shirt she was wearing must have belonged to the new crew and not the old one.

While Ado searched and Esan stayed as watchkeeper in the bow, the sun set straight ahead, seeming to quench itself in the watery vista like a hot coal in a bucket. And night came. It was as sudden as that. Anastasia was struck by the speed of it yet again. Particularly as it robbed her of vital vision just when she needed it most. 'Stay where you are, Esan' she called.

'But I can see nothing . . .'

'We'll fix that. Ado, can you climb up and switch the searchlight on. Then you can go on to the bow with Esan and help him keep watch.'

Ado scurried up aloft and the light came on in a flash. Then Anastasia was edified by the sight of the two teenagers sitting side by side, trying to keep their eyes peeled and their hands off each other. Young love, she thought. Isn't it just wonderful? She rolled her eyes in amused despair, suddenly feeling very old indeed.

And just on that very thought, she saw the brightness behind the island trees. The kids probably didn't see it because they were looking in the water dead ahead. It was a pale brightness, flickering because of the way the vegetation in front of it was moving. It might have seemed ethereal, almost ghostly to some. But not to Anastasia. She knew what it was at once. There was another boat on the river, somewhere just beyond the island. Probably heading upstream, judging by the light. But *another boat*. With a radio, no doubt – a way to get the news about the Army of Christ the Infant out even sooner than the people at Malebo could – if their fears about their cellphone and Internet access were true.

'Esan,' she called. 'There's a boat, over there, just beyond the island. See if you can attract their attention.'

'HOI!' bellowed Esan willingly enough.

'It's "Ahoy!"' Anastasia advised from the pinnacle of the nautical wisdom Captain Christophe had given her. '"Ahoy the boat!"'

'AHOY THE BOAT!' bellowed Esan like a bull being led to the slaughter.

But there was no reply.

'Keep trying. They're still coming closer, I think. Ado, come here and see if you can swing the searchlight round. Maybe we can signal with that.'

But as Esan bellowed and Ado scurried up on to the wheel-house roof, the trees on the island separating the two boats thickened and grew taller. The light from the southern channel came and went increasingly fitfully. The beam that Ado swung to port simply seemed to reflect back off wall after wall of foliage.

'This simply isn't getting through!' shouted Esan at last, and he vanished back into the aft section behind the wheelhouse.

She had no idea what he was doing until the AK gave its familiar ear-splitting rattle seemingly just behind her head. The reflective leaves flashed yellow and red back along with the steady white of the searchlight as he emptied a full clip into the air. 'Esan!' Anastasia shouted. 'Stop! They'll think we're shooting at them!'

'Fine!' Esan shouted back. 'So maybe they'll come looking for us! Then we'll make contact after all!'

But nothing happened. The light beyond the islands went out. Ado killed their own light and the three of them strained to see any sign of pursuit. But there was nothing. After five minutes, Anastasia's nerve broke. 'Ado, switch the searchlight back on and point it straight ahead. Then I want the pair of you back in the bow keeping watch.'

The incident did not quite have no effect or aftermath. It galvanized Anastasia into pushing the throttle forward and taking the next section of the river a good deal faster than she would otherwise have done. And she got Ado and Esan to take turns to stand up on the wheelhouse roof for five minutes every half hour or so, swinging the bright beam left and right. So she clearly saw one of the last landmarks on the northern shore – the burned-out ruin of a casino with the mouldering wreckage of an old sternwheeler paddle boat beached in front of it. This was the

point at which the single-track road from Malebo turned itself
into a multi-lane highway, she remembered. It was also, more
famously, the point from which General Julius Chaka had
launched the last stage of his attack on Granville Harbour. A
popular uprising led by T80 main battle tanks that had toppled
his opponent Liye Banda and established Celine's father as president. Was there any way at all that she could get to President
Chaka with news about the invasion of his country and the
wounding of his daughter?

Only an hour or so to go. Then, perhaps she would find out.

And so it was that *Nellie* came alongside the jetty at Granville
Harbour a little before midnight. A full fat moon had risen behind
her like a silver sun, so Anastasia had no trouble jumping on to
the deserted jetty and mooring *Nellie* safely. Then she leaped
back aboard and went below to discuss things with the other two,
suddenly a little hesitant, almost scared by the situation she now
found herself in. There was no official welcome to the inland
section of the port – no customs or registration formalities. If
there was a harbour master, he was asleep in bed. There was
probably a security team watching the gin-palaces in the private
marina, but a battered old riverboat with three youngsters aboard
was far beneath their notice. No one of authority seemed interested in them at all.

'I'll have to go into the city itself,' said Anastasia. 'Find
someone who can get the alert out to the authorities. You two
will have to stay here. Esan, you can't even dream of showing
your face, just in case. Ado, you'd be best to stay with him.
Neither of you have any papers or anything. You could get into
a world of trouble out there.'

'You've got no papers either,' countered Ado. 'What's to stop
you getting into trouble?'

Nothing, thought Anastasia. Nothing at all. 'I'll be fine,' she
said, with much more confidence than she felt. 'I'll just try and
find a police patrol or something. Once I get in contact with
anyone from the police, security or the army I should be able to
get some kind of alert out. All you two have to do is wait for
me to come back. But try and keep an eye out. If anyone you
don't know comes this way, then slip the mooring and head off.
Do not under any circumstances start using the guns again.'

As Anastasia walked warily along the jetty in the moonlight, she looked about her in shock and confusion. She remembered this place well – her last visit had been six months or so ago. What had happened in the meantime? It looked as though a hurricane had hit it. The buildings appeared to be little better than the ruins of Citematadi. Certainly all the street lighting was out. Had the moon and stars not been so bright tonight she would hardly have been able to find her way. But things improved at the inland end of the compound. There were occasional street lights here and, although she wasn't familiar with the city, it wasn't too hard to work out what was what. The long, quiet road leading along the rear of the wrecked office compound led eventually to a fenced-off area filled with yellow security lighting. She went straight towards this, reasoning that there must be some kind of a guard there – someone she could start with.

But before she managed to get to the security gate, however, she was distracted by something else. It was a bar called OTI. As she passed the door, there was a tremendous cheer and a cacophony of laughing and applause. Intrigued, she looked in. She saw a long bar down one side of a low-ceilinged, square room with a stage at the far end and a range of boxes opposite the bar. A woman wearing no clothes whatsoever was just leaving the stage. Between the door and the stage there was a floor packed with tables and chairs, all of which seemed to be filled with drunken men. Some of them were in naval whites. She stepped in, thinking that a naval officer – even a drunk one – might be a better place to start than a security guard.

She had only gone a few feet before she stopped, simply frozen with surprise. She knew the men sitting at the nearest table. It was *Nellie*'s old crew. And the man opposite her, his face clear and unmistakable even in the smoke-filled gloom, was the captain. 'Captain Christophe? Is that you?' she asked in simple, over-whelming relief. 'Captain Christophe?' she called. 'It's me, Anastasia Asov. I thought you were dead!'

'Dead?' he demanded, surging unsteadily to his feet. 'Who says I'm dead?'

'No one,' she answered shortly. 'But when we found *Nellie* . . .'

'*Nellie*.' He subsided sadly. 'Ah *Nellie*. My poor *Nellie*! Where is she now?'

'She's at the end of the jetty,' Anastasia answered matter-of-factly. 'I've just moored her there. Listen. Captain Christophe, you have to help me . . .' She stopped. The old man was staring at her simply horrified.

'*You* have her? *You* moored her? Then where are the men I sold her to? They were bad men, those ones! The sort who chop off hands like the Rwandan Interahamwe. They'll come after *Nellie*, mark my words. After you too, if you stole her. Maybe . . . Maybe they'll come after *me!*' He surged to his feet again, staring down at the horrified woman. '*After me!*' he repeated, and he punched her full in the face. 'What have you done?' he roared. 'What have you done?'

One of the navy men took him by the shoulder. 'What are you doing, old man?' he asked. 'You can't go round punching women like that . . .'

He would have said more, but the terrified Captain Christophe rounded on him with a wild haymaker that floored him at once. Then, before Anastasia could grasp what was really going on, she was in the middle of a full-blown punch-up.

After all she had been through, this seemed like the final straw. She crawled under a table, closed her eyes and curled into the smallest, tightest ball she could. Which is where she was when the police arrived. The drunken brawl was quelled in an instant and the main protagonists dragged off to a paddy wagon waiting outside. And Anastasia might have stayed hidden under her table, had the young officer who tried to protect her not asked, 'Hey! Where's the woman who started all this? The one the old guy punched in the face?'

Five minutes later, she was with the others in the back of the wagon. She fought the overwhelming desire to shout, scream, swear at the aggrieved naval lieutenant. To punch the comatose Captain Christophe in the face as he deserved. To try and get someone to listen to a story she knew was going to sound frankly unbelievable. She sat in silence and cudgelled her brains therefore, until the wagon stopped, the doors opened and she was swept on to the next level of helplessness.

Half an hour later, her next opportunity to sit and think things through arrived – she was alone in a cell in the nearest police station to OTI, which, as it happened was police headquarters. She was charged with affray. She was charged with having no

ID or papers. The others were slung in a communal holding area. She was photographed and led to a single cell deep in the cellars of the building. It was chilly, badly lit, very basic. There was a pallet bed to sit on or lie on, a stainless steel washstand and beside it a stainless steel toilet with no seat. She would have used the toilet but she couldn't get over the feeling that she was being watched. So she sat, stunned by the enormity of the misfortune that had overtaken her, praying that the men who chopped off hands had not yet noticed that *Nellie* was moored at the end of the jetty, when the door opened.

She was so stressed that she actually screamed. Screamed again, even as her reeling mind registered that she knew the man in army officer's uniform, with his clipped moustache and Denzel Washington good looks.

'Good evening, Miss Asov,' said Colonel Laurent Kabila quietly. 'Welcome to Granville Harbour. I'm sorry your reception has been so upsetting so far but I'm sure we can improve things for you very soon. I think you had better come with me . . .'

# SIXTEEN
## MANPADS

'No,' whispered Caleb. 'It is out of the question. I will simply not allow you to accompany us.' He, like the team assembled to go ashore, was wearing body armour and a tin helmet. He was armed with a sidearm – as was Sanda – while the others carried semi-automatic rifles. Both officers also carried massive flash lamps.

But Caleb was staying aboard for the moment – as was Robin. This wasn't a TV programme – the commander stayed aboard and in command; guests did not go running willy-nilly into dangerous situations. He had other officers whose job was to go ashore and other responsibilities beyond indulging the adventurous desires of his passengers. But he would be following them the instant it was safe for him to do so. He was a 'lead from the front' commander to his fingertips. The problem was, so was Robin.

'That seems sensible, Robin,' added Bonnie, nervously, her voice breathy and scarcely audible above the grumbling motor. 'This stretch of the river's supposed to be deserted and now suddenly we have folks shooting at us and setting fire to stuff. If the president had known about all this he would never have sent us, I'm sure. And I'm equally certain he wouldn't want us going ashore and nosing around in burned-out buildings.'

'I can handle myself,' persisted Robin. 'I proved that when we turned the corvette round and got her out of trouble. And I'm trained to Accident and Emergency standard in first aid – that makes me the closest to a medic you have.'

'Even so,' said Caleb, his quiet voice ringing with finality, 'I'm not going to let you go ashore now. It will almost certainly be dangerous – even if all we're doing is going into a smouldering boathouse – and I simply don't want to put you at risk.'

As they spoke, Lieutenant Sanda was watching the helmsman bring the Shaldag gingerly into the cavernous opening of the burned building. Her engines were running as close to silent as possible, just giving the vessel headway against the restless current downriver of the cataract. There was an order for silent running aboard – as though this were a submarine. FPB004 was also in darkness, as anonymous and nearly invisible as she was silent. For Caleb was correct, thought Robin grimly, scanning the boathouse they were approaching though narrow eyes. This all looked wrong on so many levels.

The front of the building was gone but the back of it remained relatively unscathed. There had once obviously been a covered wooden jetty along one side, reaching out into the river, but all that remained of it was the concrete posts it had stood on and one or two beams above, outlined against the starry sky. Behind the posts, the concrete floor of the main area was littered with chunks of charcoal. But the thick, rough slabs seemed solid still. The roof above them was burned back to a ragged line of timbers that stood above what seemed to be an internal lean-to. An office, perhaps, or a storeroom. But it was difficult to see details even under the moonlight.

Caleb turned away from Robin, his armour creaking, its Velcro fastenings rasping. 'Put on the searchlight and get ready to go ashore,' he ordered, and suddenly the interior of the place was lit by the stark white illumination of a hospital operating theatre.

'Can you put her against the concrete?' asked Caleb, no longer keeping his voice down – the need for stealth over as soon as the light went on.

'Yes sir,' answered the helmsman. 'But there's nothing to moor her to.'

'Use the engine to hold her in place. Mr Sanda, you and the men I've detailed will go on my order. I will follow on your all clear.' He turned back to Robin. 'If it's safe when I've checked it out for myself then I'll call you ashore for a quick look around,' he promised. 'Or if there's anyone needing tending in a secure location. In the meantime, stay aboard and inside, please.'

'Thanks a bunch,' she answered.

Richard would have known from her tone that she had no intention of doing what she was told. But Caleb's experience with women was relatively slight, so he took this as acquiescence. He turned away from her and signalled to Lieutenant Sanda, who ran silently out of the bridge, crossed the deck and leaped ashore with the four men detailed for the first recce.

Robin followed them out on to the deck, but stopped at the rail, looking after the little commando unit as they went forward in practised formation, scouting carefully ahead and moving from one secure firing position to the next. After a heartbeat she returned to stand by Caleb on the bridge, inside, as he had ordered, listening to Sanda reporting back to the captain at every step, even though he and the shore party were etched against the brightness like saints in a stained-glass window. Within three minutes they had crossed the concrete floor. Then Sanda hit the door to the lean-to office, and vanished inwards. After a second, his torch went on, its light varying the lambency in the mirror surface of the internal window. Shadows moved against the frosted glass like some kind of magic trick or theatrical effect. They stooped, twisted, turned. 'Men down,' came his terse report. 'Not ours. Strangers. Five here. Some uniforms. Look like UN but hard to say. Pretty torn-up. Something's not right. There's a back door half open. Checking further . . .' The light went out. The window became a flat mirror once again.

That was enough for Caleb. He ran out of the bridge and leaped nimbly ashore. Robin followed him to the deck rail and hesitated. She could still hear Sanda's voice coming quietly from the relay on the bridge behind her. 'Back of the building deserted.

But there's a truck. UN markings. Checking inside . . . *Oshi!*
What is *this*? . . .' The torchlight in the office deepened the
window once again as Caleb's shadow hurried through.

Robin slipped down the companionway and found her bag on
the bunk that had been prepared for her. She unzipped the exclusive Louis Vuitton Keepall, reached in and pulled out a torch.
Less than a minute later she was back on deck.

'Where are you going?' asked Bonnie from the bridge door.

'You know very well where I'm going,' she answered. 'But
from the sound of things you do not want to come along.'

She leaped out on to the concrete and ran forward, crouching
a little, even though she was almost certain there was nothing to
fear. Unlike the soldiers who preceded her, however, she added
the beam of her own torch to the brightness sweeping across the
floor. So, just outside the stage-set wall of the internal office, a
little way from the door itself, she found a trainer that they had
overlooked. She scooped it up on the run, one glance was enough
to tell her it belonged to a woman or a girl.

However, one glance around the charnel house of the office
was more than enough. The stench of blood and cordite turned
her stomach but she refused to let the swelling nausea distract
her. She straightened, flashing her torch beam around, letting its
bright light add to the square of illumination coming in through
the window behind her. The table caught her attention first, for
it was most brightly lit. It was oddly placed, too close to the
door. The man lying beside it, with his chest blown open, had
his trousers and pants round his ankles. Taken in conjunction
with a woman's shoe, that was immediately sinister. But not as
sinister as the fact that the spray of blood across the table – which
had clearly issued from the dead man's chest – formed a rough
outline round a clean space in the middle. A clean space that
might, at a stretch, have conformed to the shape of a woman's
torso. Robin's torch beam went down on to the floor once again.
She found the second trainer almost at once. And then, most
tellingly, a bundle of cotton that turned out to be a pair of panties.

'Whatever happened to you,' she told the dead man with his
trousers down, 'I think you probably deserved it.'

Then she turned her attention to the other corpses there.

Caleb re-entered from the back lot to find her on her knees
beside a dead man whose whole face seemed to be sitting at such

a very strange angle. She was wrestling something out of the dead man's hand.

'What on earth . . .' he began in English, feverishly reassessing his basic beliefs about the entire female sex.

'I don't know what else they were up to – what else you found outside,' she grated, 'but at the moment retribution caught up with them, these bastards were in the middle of a rape party. *Coitus interruptus* of the very best kind in my book.'

'How on earth do you know that?' Caleb looked around, his horror intensifying.

Robin explained her reasoning tersely, as she continued to wrestle with the dead fist she was trying to open. 'But that's just from a quick scout round,' she concluded. 'I'd probably be able to give you more details if I had more time.'

Caleb took a deep breath. 'You'll have at least half an hour. I have to report this in. And I have to put some heavy stuff aboard my vessel. That truck outside has half a dozen Chinese QW1M shoulder-launched missiles in it; they call them MANPADS – short for Man-portable air-defence system. Each one can blow the guts out of anything on the ground or in the air. From a tank to a cruise missile. From a train to a jumbo jet, come to that. Half the terrorist groups on earth have been trying to get their hands on stuff like this for years and here it turns up in the middle of a deserted jungle in a UN truck surrounded by dead men. If we were on anything other than a mission for the president, I'd probably turn round and head back to base at once.'

Had Caleb been Richard, Robin would have made a *Blues Brothers* joke, but she didn't think Caleb would understand or appreciate references to being on *a mission for God*. Suddenly she missed Richard. The bloody man had been right all along. This was no walk in the park. This was getting really flaming dangerous.

As the thought occurred to Robin, the dead man's fist came open. An oyster shell fell out of it. And a black pearl the size of a marble rolled across the floor. 'Now that,' said Robin, her voice awed, 'is something you don't see every day.'

'What?' said Caleb in simple wonder. 'What in God's name has gone on here?'

\*    \*    \*

'OK,' said Robin half an hour later. 'Hang on a minute longer and I'll walk you through this. I think I can give you some idea about everything except the pearl.'

'I'm listening,' said Caleb grudgingly.

'Good. Because what I'm going to tell you might well influence what you want to add to your final report to base – and what they want you to do as a result. Let's start at the beginning. Way back through the jungle, way, *way* back, beyond Mount Karisoke and the volcano chain beside it, back in the UN mission in Somalia, Sudan, Uganda or wherever, there are a couple of trucks gone missing. Almost certainly a good few UN soldiers dead in a ditch, stripped of all they possessed. There's a smuggling route through the horn of Africa that starts with the Somali pirates in the Indian Ocean – which in turn connects with China where the MANPADS originally came from. It's supposed to be a two-way trade. Weaponry in – conflict minerals out, especially coltan for all those mobile telephones and whatnot. You follow so far?'

Caleb nodded dumbly, his eyes and his mouth a little wider than usual.

'The guys who killed the UN soldiers and stole the trucks dressed in the dead men's uniforms and drove through the jungles to here. Good disguise, eh? Not the first time it's been done either – not by a long chalk. Certainly our smugglers seem to have been wearing the dead men's uniforms when they in turn died – that fat bloke on the bed for instance, his uniform has a bullet hole surrounded by dry blood over his heart. But he's not been shot in the heart, he's been shot through the head. They were using the trucks as a disguise. I guess they were doing the same with the uniforms. Somewhere along the line, not far back, they picked up some prisoners – at least one woman, maybe more. And another passenger perhaps they didn't know about, in the back of this truck here. The lashings have been cut, and I found a Victorinox knife there – no one in their right mind is going to leave one of those unless the going's got tough. At least one of the women seems to have been wounded – there's blood on the seat there where neither a driver nor a single passenger would sit. Certainly not big men like these.

'They drive the trucks down off the road back there leaving

two sets of tracks coming – and one set going. One pretty *uncontrolled* set going, come to that, as though the driver was drunk. Or terrified. Or wounded. Or all three. There's blood on the ground beside where the other truck was parked, and a bottle of vodka on the ground, still part full. So I guess there weren't many survivors fit to drive, which is why you have this truck left behind.

'Anyhow, going back in time a little, they arrive, with their MANPADS, their disguises, their women bleeding in the front and their unsuspected guest hiding in the back. They are met by the next link in the smuggling chain. Men with a boat, therefore, as the road ends here. Men, now I think of it, who might have taken those potshots at us earlier as they also escaped, terrified, drunk and bleeding. Because, like the guys on the truck, their numbers have been brutally diminished. You notice that only half of your corpses are in uniform – the rest are in jeans and T-shirts: city boys, I'd say. Or maybe it was not the boat's crew who shot at us; they may all be here or in the second truck, wherever that is – maybe it was the women and their rescuer escaping, hyped-up and terrified. Maybe *they* fired those shots. Anyway, the two groups got together – Uniform guys and T-shirt guys – and decided to seal their deal by having a rape party. There's booze. There's guys with their trousers down and their peckers out – and only deflated, one assumes, by the massive loss of blood. And there's underwear belonging to at least one woman.

'But, as I said earlier, the party was brutally interrupted, one assumes by the unsuspected guest who lost his Victorinox in the back of the truck out there. Lost his knife but found at least one gun. Party pooped. Woman or women run out, leaving trainers and underwear behind. Boat goes. Boathouse burns. Now I think of it, the intended rape victims *are* most likely to be the ones on the boat and therefore the ones who fired those shots. Burned the boathouse to cover their escape. Good planning by someone.

'But I am simply buggered if I can tell you anything at all about the black pearl. Except that there were three more oysters scattered across the floor which I have in my possession – just in case they too contain black pearls.'

'Is that it?' asked Caleb, not a little dazed.

'Not quite,' answered Robin, who, like Richard, loved to save the best for last. 'The girl on the table – the one who left her outline in her would-be rapist's blood. She left her shoes and knickers, at least I guess it was her. Now, I can't tell anything about her from the trainers. Nike. Could be anybody's. Anybody's with the right shoe size. She could have bought them anywhere. The underwear, however, is another kettle of fish. Look.' Robin held the less than pristine garment up so that Caleb could see the label sewn into the waistband.

It said 'Дикая орхидея'.

'What is that?' asked Caleb, still stunned.

'It's Russian. It says, if memory serves, "Wild Orchid". It's the name of one of the more upmarket lingerie boutiques in Moscow.'

'*Moscow*? What has that—'

'Got to do with anything?' interrupted Robin triumphantly. 'Well, Captain, I think you will find that the only person in this particular jungle likely to be caught wearing Russian underwear is Anastasia Asov. And it doesn't take Sherlock Holmes to see that if Anastasia Asov is in the middle of a rape party then some of her closest friends might also be at risk. And who is Anastasia Asov's closest friend?'

'Celine Chaka,' said Caleb, shaken to the core. 'Oh my God, *Celine Chaka*.'

It was the underwear that made the difference in the end. Had it not been for the Wild Orchid Russian lingerie, Caleb and his men would have been scouting the road into Citematadi looking for the second truck and – presumably – another load of MANPADS. Or at least trying to tidy up the charnel house in the office. But Naval HQ was very actively of Caleb's opinion that if Anastasia Asov was in trouble, Celine wasn't far behind, so he was ordered to proceed with his mission. At once.

The Shaldag ran the rapids created by the wreckage of what had once been a great bridge stretching across the river, half as high as the Golden Gate, and carrying an eight-lane highway on the top level, and a railway line on the lower. The massive piers, starlings and footings that had strode across the river carrying the massive weight of concrete still stood. But their carefully designed aqua-dynamic profile was utterly undone by the massive blocks of masonry that now lay on the river-bed between them. Getting past the Citematadi bridge was a little like shooting the first cataract on the Nile. The only real difference was that if you were very careful indeed, you didn't have to carry your boat around it.

Frustrated in her desire to look round Citematadi, Robin remained on the bridge with Caleb to see how he got the Shaldag through the maze of rapids, falls and whirlpools that lay across the river like a dirty white wall. Bonnie preferred to stay below. The simple sound of the monster was enough for her. But, after Caleb and Sanda conned their vessel safely through, Robin joined her friend – for a moment or two at least. Armed with the Victorinox, the women set about opening the stinking little pile of oysters, and the three they prized inexpertly apart yielded two more pearls as black and lustrous as great drops of oil. Robin looked at them thoughtfully, then climbed on to the bridge again.

The Shaldag was running rapidly eastwards, hugging the south bank. Above her starboard quarter, the causeway leading down to Citematadi still loomed up against the moon-bright sky like a black cliff. Robin stared at it, frowning, and was struck suddenly by a simple truth that she had not examined so far. If Anastasia Asov had got herself aboard a truck up there, how had she managed to get across the river? Robin knew as well as anyone that the church and school they were heading for was on the north bank. And the man-made rapids they had just come through established absolutely that there were no bridges still standing across the mighty flood. With her frown deepening, she asked Caleb, 'Captain, would it be possible for you stay as close to the south bank as you can – and to shine your searchlight on it as we pass?'

Still in the grip of something akin to awe in the face of Robin's reasoning abilities – not to mention her gritty intrepidity – Caleb was in no mood to refuse her anything. For the next half hour, the Shaldag hugged the south bank of the river and the starboard searchlight cast its great white beam ashore, while Robin stood out on the deck beside the bridge, straining her eyes as the jungly overhang flashed by. The land behind heaved up into a ridge and fell back again, the distant heave of it etched in shaggy outline against distant galaxies that shone more brightly than Robin had ever seen. But the near bank remained simply a boring, repetitive wall of unvarying foliage, flashing green under the searchlight and fading to black in the shadows behind it.

Until, all of a sudden, the bank itself fell back into a little bay

whose outer edge was a tumbled mess of red mud and green
foliage where a cliff had obviously collapsed. And there – seen
and gone in a flash – a little rowing boat was moored to a fallen
tree trunk.

'*Stop!*' shouted Robin, tearing her throat. 'Stop! Go back!'

The Shaldag slowed. Reversed, her movements aided by the
downward rush of the river beneath her. The little bay returned.
The tethered boat.

Caleb ordered the Shaldag to get as close in as possible and
to wait. A ladder went over the side and the captain himself
climbed down to a solid-looking mudbank and walked the
mooring rope ashore to secure his command as close to the
rowing boat as possible. Then Robin clambered down and
followed him, carrying her torch once again.

'You knew it was here,' he said as the pair of them stood
looking down into the little vessel.

'Had to be,' said Robin shortly. She looked up. 'I'll bet there's
something up there too. Other than the road,' she said, and handed
him her torch.

Caleb scrambled up, pulling out the sidearm he was still
carrying as soon as he reached the roadway she had known he
would find up there.

Robin crouched down, looking intently into the boat. It was
the blood she saw first, the black smears of it on the bench seat
beside the little outboard. Then the water in the bottom, with the
oars and the boathook. Like most boats, it stank and she supposed
the smell was coming from the bilge. But then she saw the handle
of a plastic bag sticking out from beneath the bloodstained seat.

When Caleb came scrambling back down the collapsed bank,
carrying a T-shirt and a camouflage jacket, he found her gazing
in wonder into the bag. She looked up at him, wide-eyed. 'There
must be thirty more oysters in here,' she said. 'Maybe more.
Looks as though whatever else happens, someone's going to get
a necklace out of this. A black pearl necklace.'

# SEVENTEEN
## Kebila

Colonel Laurent Kebila looked at Anastasia Asov in thoughtful silence. 'You have always had a reputation for resourcefulness,' he said at last in his beautifully modulated Sandhurst English. 'But you are beginning to stretch my credulity now.'

'But it's true. Every word! It's what has happened to me since the Army of Christ the Infant attacked.'

'The whole truth?' he probed gently.

'*Yes!*' Anastasia's eyes slid away from the colonel's steady gaze, however. A simple gesture that undermined his faith in her truthfulness almost fatally. And she knew it. But what could she do? She had never felt anything but trust and respect for the soldier sitting opposite her, leaning forward across his desk, his swagger stick resting beside the cooling coffee cups and empty plate of chocolate digestive biscuits, the CCTV monitor patched into his laptop still showing the picture of the cell they had held her in until he came down to fetch her. To rescue her.

But even Kebila could not be relied on to see that Esan was no longer a murderous child-soldier to be detained at once, or to be shot like a rabid dog if he resisted for a second. That, instead, he needed congratulating, helping and rewarding. So she had been very circumspect indeed in her version of how the young man had fallen in with them before he began to prove the valuable friend and helper he now was. And that one omission, that one flaw in her story, was in danger of undermining the whole thing.

'Well,' he said at last, 'we can start by checking some details that are closer to hand. Begin at the end of your story, so to speak, and then work our way back to the start of it, fact by fact. Captain Christophe is in our holding facility. We can talk to him immediately . . .'

But that eminently sensible course of action was another

problem for her. Not because of what Captain Christophe might say or do – but because of what he had said and done already. Specifically, what he had said about the men who might be coming after them. Who might be aboard *Nellie* now, asking about their absent friends and missing cargo. And chopping off hands while they did so.

'Please, Colonel,' she said. 'Check on the captain later. Check on *Nellie* first.'

Kebila looked at her thoughtfully for a moment longer, then he said, 'Very well. I will order a squad to accompany us,' sounding to the squirming Anastasia like a parent who knows his child is lying but is willing to give them enough rope to hang themselves. Been there, done that, she thought.

But once again Anastasia found herself with a problem. If Esan saw a squad of soldiers coming down the jetty he would either turn tail or open fire. 'Why do we need a squad?' she said, feeling her eyes sliding guiltily away from his once again and fighting to hold his gaze like an honest person would. 'Surely we can check on the existence of an ancient riverboat and a couple of youngsters without back-up.'

'Hmmm . . .' he said. 'Very well.' *More rope.* He picked up a phone handset and spoke into it without dialling. 'Car and driver,' he ordered. 'Sergeant Major Tchaba, I think.' He hung up, looked at her for a moment longer then said, 'Right. Let's go.' He picked up a cellphone, checked that it was on and slipped it into his uniform jacket pocket. Then he rose and led her across to the door of his office. Here he paused for a moment and lifted a Sam Browne off a coat stand. As he ushered her out and followed her down towards the front of the building, he slipped the wide belt and shoulder strap securely into place, and patted the leather holster that now sat snugly on his right hip.

The car was waiting for them beyond the security gates at the main entrance, its engine running. A huge soldier sat in the driver's seat and, as she followed Kebila into the back, Anastasia noticed that he had several powerful-looking weapons on the passenger's seat at his side. 'I don't think you've met Sergeant Major Tchaba before,' said Kebila easily. 'Though given the range of your adventures in my country I wouldn't be surprised if you had. He is the diplomatic solution to both our requirements, I think. A one-man army.'

Anastasia's irritation at having been outmanoeuvred vanished the instant Sergeant Major Tchaba pulled up behind the ruined office complex that led down to the jetty and the marina beyond. For a battered flat bed truck had appeared from nowhere and was sitting parked with arrogant disregard for the law half on and half off the pavement. Something about it made Anastasia fear the worst. 'I'd bring as many of those as you can carry,' she said to Tchaba, nodding to the guns. 'Just in case . . .'

Tchaba looked back at Kebila and the colonel nodded.

Suddenly full of the most terrifying premonitions, Anastasia hurried the two soldiers down the hill through the apparent hurricane damage, therefore, too focussed on *Nellie* to register properly the fact that Tchaba was limping. She did notice, however, that he was checking and preparing his considerable arsenal of weapons as he moved. But as she reached the landward end of the little jetty where the venerable riverboat was moored, she slowed, frowning. Kebila closed up behind her, and Tchaba stepped closer behind the pair of them, his hands at last still as the quiet clicking and cocking and sliding of metal on metal was done.

It was then that she realized two things. Firstly and most worryingly, there was the sound of moaning coming from *Nellie*. It wasn't all that loud, but it was enough to carry over the lapping of the waves and the stirring of the hulls and the tapping of the rigging nearby. Secondly and almost comically, she realized that Tchaba had a false foot. It hit the ground with a decided *thump* each time he took a limping step. Under almost every circumstance this would not have mattered. But Anastasia wanted more than anything to approach *Nellie* unsuspected, along a wooden jetty, its hollowness likely to amplify any sound made on the boards that made up its surface.

'The sergeant has to wait here!' she breathed. 'We have to get aboard as quietly as possible. Can't you hear?'

Kebila nodded once. Prepared to move forward.

'I need a gun,' she whispered.

Kebila paused. She could feel the weight of his speculative gaze on her. The moaning from *Nellie* intensified. Someone started counting in Matadi. Neither sound was pleasant.

'Ten . . . Nine . . .'

He nodded again. Tchaba passed her a boxy pistol. She

recognized it as a Browning BDM. The same as the one with which General Moses Nlong had shot Celine. How apt.

'Cocked,' whispered the sergeant. 'One in the chamber. Fourteen in the clip. Double action mode – just keep pulling the trigger.'

'. . . Eight . . .'

She nodded and was off. Imagining herself to be as light as Tania the Fairy Queen from long-past childhood stories, she ran on tiptoe along the thankfully silent planks, holding the Browning two-handed out in front of her, level with her groin, pointing downwards, at the end of her straight arms, completely unconscious of Sergeant Tchaba's approving, respectful nod.

'. . . Seven . . .'

She was aware of Kebila behind her, but only on an almost psychic level – he was making no more noise than she was. So she was able to hear the rough male Matadi voice saying, '. . . Six . . .'

At the seaward end of the jetty she paused again.

'. . . Five . . .'

The moon gave enough light for her to see that *Nellie*'s deck was stirring as the waves came in at the top of the tide. Her weight would not make much difference as she stepped aboard. Nor would Kebila's if they timed it right. And the deck boards were solid and unlikely to creak. Even so, she kicked off her flip-flops just in case. She looked across at Kebila and he nodded, understanding. They waited for a down-swoop . . .

'. . . Four . . .'

. . . and stepped aboard.

Steadying himself against the up-swoop of the next wave in, Kebila went for the bridge house and the companionway that would take him below, as Anastasia paused for a heartbeat and looked around the familiar deck.

'. . . Three . . .'

Anastasia was in motion, flitting like a moth towards the column of brightness that soared like a faint square searchlight up from the skylight that gave brightness to the cabin below. Both of them moved like ghosts and the good old planks of the deck did not let them down.

'. . . Two . . .'

Anastasia stood, spraddle-legged, looking down into the cabin

through the glass skylight. She could see Ado, her blouse gone,
sitting at the table with her hands stretched out before her, tied
by cord which pulled them tight. Beside her, foreshortened by
the fact that Anastasia was looking straight down from above his
head, stood the man who was counting. And he was holding a
matchet above Ado's wrists. Anastasia risked a quick glance
across at Kebila who was crouching ready to go down the companionway at double speed. She looked back. The man with the
matchet had a bald spot right at the top of his skull. She aimed
at that.

'. . . *One* . . .' said the man beside Ado, and raised the matchet,
two-handed.

Ado screamed.

Anastasia pulled the trigger. The Browning's bullet exploded
in through the skylight and hit the man on the top of the head
with all the force of a baseball bat. It went straight through his
skull and body, slamming into the deck between his feet. He sat
down as though a huge weight had suddenly landed on his
shoulders, dropping the matchet as he did so. He flopped back-
wards and lay still. It all happened so fast that glass was still
falling on his prone body.

Anastasia looked for Kebila but he was gone. She heard the
flat report of his gun, the thud of another body falling and then
silence. Except for the moaning. 'Come down,' he called.
'Quickly.'

She arrived in the cabin to see Kebila standing beside the body
of a second man, trying with limited success to untie something
that looked like fishing line hanging tautly from a hook in the
cabin ceiling. And she saw in a flash why it was important he
should do so. The lower end of the line was secured round Esan's
scrotum and the boy was half-hanging, bent like a bow, face-up,
with his trousers round his ankles, on the bunk below. His eyes
were rolled back so only the whites were showing and it was he
who was moaning. Which didn't surprise her at all. She crossed
the cabin in four swift steps and caught up the matchet that had
been destined one second later to have severed Ado's hands. She
stepped past Kebila and cut the line. Esan collapsed back on to
the bed. His moans became a howl of agony. He clutched himself
and rolled on to his side. Anastasia slammed the matchet blade
down again and Ado's hands were free. Ado was on top of Esan

immediately, covering him protectively with her body. Which, Anastasia noticed now, was battered, bruised, bleeding in one or two places, and also naked.

'You know, I'm beginning to find your story a little easier to believe,' Kebila admitted in a grimly conversational tone.

Sergeant Tchaba came stomping through the door like Long John Silver. 'Three for the hospital and one for the morgue,' said Kebila, 'and I think we'd better prepare the interrogation cell at headquarters.' And Anastasia registered for the first time that the man at the colonel's feet was still alive.

'So,' said Kebila twenty minutes later as the ambulance wailed off into the distance, while Tchaba engaged the gears and eased the colonel's staff car into motion. 'You managed to get away from those gentlemen's colleagues in the good ship *Nellie*, dropped Celine Chaka off at the clinic in Malebo and came straight back down here to alert the authorities about smugglers, rapists – mostly deceased – and secret armies overrunning sections of the jungle unsuspected.'

'Yes,' she said shortly. 'I told you. The same as I told you about the men who might be coming after *Nellie*. And I was right about that, wasn't I?'

'Indeed. However, there are still elements in your narrative I find hard to believe,' he said. 'Even making allowances for the fact that it is *you* who are at the heart of it all. Logic dictates that, if everything you say is true, I should wake up the president and get some sort of expeditionary force up there. But it is –' he consulted his watch – 'still two hours until dawn. And the president will not thank me for disturbing him at this time of night without absolutely incontrovertible proof. Especially as we happen to have a Shaldag fast patrol boat in the area and we haven't heard a whisper out of them about any of this so far. But we are conveniently situated to get an update on their latest contact. Naval headquarters, please, Sergeant.'

Kebila's presence was like a magic pass. The car was waved through the security gate and into the golden aura of the security lighting. As it passed, the guard slammed to attention and saluted. Tchaba parked in a bay marked 'Commanding Officer Only' and then waited while Kebila led Anastasia into a three-storey white-painted box of a building with a display of antennas and dishes on its roof that would have flattered GRU headquarters on Khoroshevskiy Highway in Moscow. The security guard on the door also slammed to attention and waved them through like his colleague on the gate. The twenty-four-hour communications room was on the third floor and the pair of them ran lightly up the stairs side by side. The officer in charge leaped to his feet and was halfway to attention when Kebila said, 'That will do, Lieutenant. I'm here to see the latest communication from Shaldag FPB004, not to hold some kind of an inspection.'

'Just in, sir,' said the lieutenant, relaxing infinitesimally. 'It's quite a long one. Here's the transcript . . .'

The lieutenant handed Kebila a long flimsy of white paper covered in dense writing. The colonel stood frowning over the report for some moments, then he said, 'All right. Captain Maina has found your boathouse and your bodies. And –' his eyes raked her from head to toe with a suddenly disturbing intimacy – 'Captain Mariner has found and recognized your underwear. Wild Orchid, from Moscow.'

Anastasia blushed from the pit of her throat to the roots of her hair. 'My underwear . . . *Richard* . . .'

'No. I understand your girlish embarrassment. It was *Robin* Mariner who found it. I sincerely trust that *Richard* would *never* have recognized your lingerie.'

It took the red-faced woman an instant to understand that she was being teased. But her mind was whirling away from her embarrassment. Richard and Robin Mariner were here. *Richard and Robin*. In Granville Harbour. In the delta. How could she not have known that?

'But as I must now accept the absolute truth of everything you have been telling me,' Kebila continued, at his most po-faced and urbane, 'I think it is time to send the Shaldag back to Malebo with orders to pick up Celine Chaka if she is in any fit state to be moved from the clinic there. I think I have the authority, even without referring to the president.'

He turned to the lieutenant and opened his mouth to issue the order. But before he could utter a word, his cellphone started ringing. 'Excuse me,' he said, frowning. 'That tone denotes a high priority call. I must take it at once.'

He put the cellphone to his ear and listened for a few minutes in silence. Then he broke contact and turned to Anastasia, his face folded into a frown. 'The mayor of Malebo . . .' he began slowly, as though trying to get his mind round something that lay just beyond his mental grasp.

'Mr Obada. He runs the hardware store. Yes . . .' she prompted him.

'And the garage evidently. And he owns a Ford Ranger Wildtrak which he has just driven down from Malebo himself – that must have taken some doing, even for a vehicle so aptly named. He has arrived at my headquarters to report two very disturbing developments. First, that the mast which carries all his town's communications has been sabotaged, leaving them absolutely cut off from the outside world. And, secondly, that everyone in Malebo's medical clinic has disappeared. Including Celine ·Chaka.' He paused for an instant. 'I think perhaps Captain Maina aboard Shaldag FPB004 should be alerted,' he said to the communications lieutenant. 'And I think it is at last time to inform the president . . .' he added, looking round at Anastasia.

'Sod the president,' said Anastasia roundly. 'If I were you I'd wake up Richard Mariner. And quickly.'

Richard often woke around four a.m. Aboard the ships he captained, this was the moment the middle watch became the morning watch, and he liked to be up and about then if possible. He had passed a restless night in any case, full of half-remembered nightmares, most of them involving Robin. He switched on the bedside light, rolled out from under the tangled duvet, straightened his blue silk pyjama jacket and ambled through into the reception room, intent on making a cup of tea. Which is what he was doing when someone started banging on his door.

Never a man to give in to premonitions of doom, he strolled across the room, teacup in hand, his mind automatically seeking ways in which a visit at this time of day could be a good thing, and opened the door without even checking the spyhole. 'Well I'll be damned,' he said. 'Anastasia.'

The night porter, hovering behind her in the little three-door lobby, said apologetically, 'Miss Asov was insistent, and as she was dropped off by Colonel Kebila himself . . .'

'That's fine,' said Richard. 'You did the right thing. Come in Anastasia and tell me what's on your mind. Did you know, by the way, that your father's in the suite next door?'

'My father?' Anastasia almost scurried into Richard's room. 'What's he doing here?' she demanded, closing the door with her shoulders and glaring at him as though her father was his fault.

'Trying to sell the government some massive hovercraft. And a brand new T80U main battle tank.' Richard's words were airily dismissive but his mind, like Kebila's under similar circumstances, was racing. 'You look dreadful,' he continued cheerily. 'You'd better tell me what's going on. Coffee or tea?'

Unlike Kebila, Richard had no trouble in believing Anastasia. 'It sounds as though Kebila will be able to get more intel on the smugglers,' he said. 'Especially as he has a suspect he can question. But it's what's going on along the north bank of the river and right in the heart of the delta that's really worrying. And the fact that Robin's in the middle of it now as well as Celine. I don't know how President Chaka will react – he sent Robin up there to bring Celine back for a family reconciliation. He's going to want to take action – and quickly. But he's disbanded most of the late President Banda's army. He's kept some of his own men – like Kebila and Captain Caleb – and the T80 tanks that helped him win the presidency. He has the rump of an air force, some choppers – but nothing big. Nor any special forces he could get upriver in sufficient numbers to find and confront General Nlong and his army.'

He stopped speaking for a moment, his eyes narrow.

'But I think I know a man who has,' he said. He rose to his full height, strode into his bedroom, grabbed his dressing gown and swung it on as he stepped into his slippers. 'Come with me,' he ordered, and Anastasia didn't dream of arguing.

Five minutes of knocking on Max Asov's door finally elicited a response. A tousled, heavy-eyed, less than happy Max opened up. 'Richard!' he spat. 'What—' Then he saw his daughter who had been hiding behind his friend and stopped speaking, winded by surprise.

'Sorry to disturb you, Max,' said Richard cheerfully. 'But it's important.'

# EIGHTEEN
## Compound

C aleb Maina had no real intention of excluding the women from his plans, Robin thought. But now that the going was getting tough, he was focussing on the elements aboard he was certain he could rely on. He turned to Lieutenant Sanda, therefore, and Robin was vaguely surprised that he didn't order her and Bonnie off the bridge while they talked.

'To sum up,' the captain said to his first lieutenant. 'The latest intel suggests that what we have discovered on the south bank at Citematadi is almost irrelevant in the face of what has been happening on the north bank . . .' He listed in terse militarese that strained Robin's understanding of the Matadi dialect the details that had just come in from Naval headquarters, with the further information added by Colonel Kebila. 'We have to decide our own priorities and report what action we propose,' he summed up. 'Keep HQ informed. But what should those priorities be?'

Sanda was a slow, methodical man, who weighed the odds and did not rush to judgement. 'As I see it, we have two conflicting calls on us,' he said. 'HQ needs us to check on the situation downriver in Malebo – has everyone including the president's daughter really vanished from the clinic there? If so, where have they gone? But HQ also wants us to see if we can find out what's happening upriver. Has the Army of Christ the Infant really hit the church and orphanage compound up there? If so, what state are the survivors in – if there are any? And what can we do to help them?'

'And where is the extremist army at the moment – and where is it headed next?' Caleb concluded. He sighed. So many priorities, so little time. And the president's daughter thrown in for good measure. Robin looked at the frowning man with lively sympathy. Then she thought that Richard dealt with conundrums like this on a regular basis and usually came out OK. Where was the bloody man when you really needed him?

In her husband's almost wilful absence, Robin opened her mouth to give some advice, but Bonnie beat her to it. 'This is my field of expertise,' she said quietly. 'My doctorate is not just on West African belief systems but also on social organization – including the phenomenon of armies such as the Army of Christ the Infant. Basically they are scavengers. They have such a high attrition rate that they need to keep topping themselves up constantly with new recruits, with supplies to feed them, with artefacts that let them keep their bank accounts full – even if they carry their currency around in trucks with them. They need to have enough wealth in barter goods, gold, blood diamonds or conflict minerals, as well as good hard cash to allow the purchase of transport, fuel, arms and ammunition, and drugs. They have to have drugs because that's how they keep the kids in line. Drugs and magic – Obi. Crack and Ngoboi.

'They isolate the kids they pick up from any hope of returning to their original adult communities by making them perform specifically targeted acts that look like random barbarism to us, but which are carefully designed to break the most basic . . . call them *taboos*. Once a kid has killed a relative, raped a cousin, eaten part of a body, they can never go back, even if there's anything or anyone left alive to go back to. From that point on there is only the army, except for a very lucky few. Very lucky. Very few. But of course there are problems of guilt and fear; the kids have committed the most terrible sins and they know it. Added terror in the build-up to battles and so forth. That's where the drugs come in. They dull a guilty conscience, stop the nightmares, give loads of Dutch courage as well as building dependency. Free sex with any of the girls they have along with them helps too of course; the soldiers are mostly teenage boys after all.

'And Obi, like I say. Magic far beyond the simple Poro jungle societies that a good few of the older kids have been inducted into, in any case. You'll all have read accounts of soldiers wearing wigs, make-up, outlandish costumes. They believe these make them bulletproof – because as often as not Ngoboi has told them so. But of course it's all lies. The kids aren't protected. They get killed and wounded. They get depressed and try to kill themselves. They get AIDS from the random sex. They get hurt in accidents. Whatever. But the drugs the army has are recreational, not medical. They don't have doctors of their own – that's why they've taken Malebo's, I guess. They don't look after their invalids like a regular army. Anyone who slows them down gets slaughtered and left behind – unless they get added to the food locker.' She paused for breath.

'So,' concluded Caleb. 'The army is like a shark. It keeps moving or it dies.'

'Unless there are circumstances that conspire to stop it. But that would have to be something quite unusual, because it would put the continued existence of the army itself at risk. And I have to say that where the Army of Christ has been, there's never anything left behind. Certainly no one needing any kind of help, apart from a decent burial.'

'So, we check on Malebo. Sounds like we'd be wasting our time heading upriver . . .'

'Not necessarily,' interjected Robin. 'Think it through. Who, apart from General Nlong or his men, would want to isolate Malebo and then take a clinic full of doctors, medical supplies and nurses? And why would they do that unless someone needed medical attention? Someone so powerful that they could command this to be done – someone so vital that they wouldn't just be left to die because they're slowing the others down, like Bonnie says.'

'So we do need to check upstream as well as down . . .'

'Look,' said Robin. 'How about this? You get back to Malebo as fast as you can and drop off a commando of half a dozen or so. Get them to check the clinic and see if they can follow whatever trail they've left and report back to you at regular intervals. If I'm right and the army has taken the missing people, then you'll have a direct line to wherever they are. And you're getting closer to wherever Celine is into the bargain. Meanwhile, on the off chance that something catastrophic has happened to them, something bad enough to cripple them, you run up to the compound and see what there is to see up there.'

'Now that,' said Bonnie with unexpected forcefulness, 'sounds like a plan.'

The run down to Malebo took an hour at full speed. With the river's current behind them adding another couple of knots, the banks flashed by at a mile a minute. Caleb didn't waste the time. He detailed Sanda to choose five more men and to prepare to go ashore and follow whatever trail was left behind by the clinic staff and the men who had kidnapped them. By the time they reached the jetty at Malebo, Sanda's little commando was ready to go ashore and start their mission. The radio man carried a SINCGARS kit using 25 kHz channels in the VHF FM band, from 30 to 87.975 MHz, and was set to FPB004's secure channel. The fighting men had an assortment of personal sidearms – Beretta M9, Glock, SIG. Sanda himself, Robin noticed, favoured a Heckler & Koch .45. But they all looked well supplied. As they did with clips for the Uzi each of the three had slung over his shoulder. All in all it was a wonder that there was room on their belts for the range of grenades that they also carried. Or for the lethal-looking unscabbarded matchet each man wore with its naked blade down his left thigh to the knee and beyond.

Sanda led them on to the jetty in the humid predawn greyness and they automatically went into full battle mode. Watching them jog into the early morning bustle of the town was unsettling to say the least. Inquisitive early-rising townsfolk fell back as if the soldiers were a group of plague carriers. The jetty itself emptied before them, and it was only when they vanished into the jungle like something out of *Apocalypse Now* that the citizens of Malebo seemed to regain their confidence, and tried to communicate with the patrol boat once again.

The surge of people coming towards the Shaldag was something neither Robin nor Caleb had counted on, but the quick-thinking young officer jumped up on to the end of the jetty and called, 'I am Captain Caleb Maina. My command and I have been sent to assess your situation but we cannot evacuate anyone as we are headed upriver into the delta, not downriver to Granville Harbour. We know from your mayor that your communications have been sabotaged and that everyone from your clinic has vanished. The soldiers you have just seen are going to search for your missing people. Meanwhile, I have another emergency upstream to check on so, unless anyone here has more information to give me, I must ask you to go back to your usual routines until the authorities send more substantial help to you.'

The speech did the trick. It was less than twenty-four hours since the *Nellie* had passed through after all. At first it seemed that no one had any new information, and the fact that their mayor had alerted the authorities who were taking such swift action seemed to settle everyone down.

Caleb took the opportunity to top up the tanks with the spare fuel from the jerry cans they had brought along then – and invested an extra half hour in refilling those at the petrol station. Then he swung Shaldag FPB004 in a wide U-turn and headed back upriver into the dazzle of the rising sun, while yet another crew member tried his hand in the galley and the depleted contingent occupied the empty time by filling their stomachs first, then checking their arms and equipment.

The run upstream took two hours, not just because of the distance or because they were now sailing against the current, but because Caleb became increasingly cautious the further east they got. Sanda's reports had something to do with this increasing caution. Every half hour – or sooner if he found something specific – he updated his commander on the little commando's progress. His reports described a trail wide and clear enough to show that whoever made it was not worried about pursuit. Certainly, they – and whoever was up ahead of them – had no trouble in following it.

And, as if the casual nature of the signs they left behind was not enough, there were the bodies left scattered in their wake. There had been half a dozen patients in various states of disrepair when the clinic was emptied. Five of them appeared one after another at the side of the trail, their throats cut as their particular ailments slowed their kidnappers down. There was no identification on any of them, but Sanda – like everyone else in Benin la Bas – knew what the Angel of Granville Harbour looked like from the days when she had so famously stood against President Liye Banda and the torturers of his secret police. So he was able to confirm that, whoever the corpses might be, none of them was Celine Chaka.

But then Sanda's men came to the side of a forest track wide enough to serve as a road. No more corpses – tyre tracks. Kidnappers, victims and equipment had all been loaded into two four-by-fours and a couple of heavier technicals according to the tracker. And they had taken off pretty quickly, heading east.

At last Caleb brought the Shaldag to an almost dead stop. The whispering engines just gave enough power for steerage way, holding them motionless against the bank, precisely balancing

the counter-thrust of the river's current. The vegetation dead
ahead seemed to be an outgrowth of freshwater mangroves, variously festooned with detritus from the recent floods, hanging
like crows' nests in the upper branches. The mangroves hid
the vessel from any casual upriver observer, but they also hid the
hillock with its chapel, school and compound from Caleb, Robin
and the rest. It was, Robin thought, accurately if unoriginally,
the moment of truth. They were within a few hundred metres
of the GPS coordinates that were their target.

Caleb couldn't just sit and wait. He either had to take the
Shaldag forward or try to get yet another little commando ashore
to spy out the land. The first course of action would alert anyone
at the compound that the authorities were nearby – a good thing
if there were survivors awaiting rescue; a bad thing if General
Nlong had left any of his army behind to keep an eye out for
just such an eventuality. A particularly bad thing if the men who
had kidnapped Celine belonged to his command; and who else
could they be? The second course of action would allow them
to make their final decision based on a clearer understanding of
what was going on. But of course the downside of that was the
fact that sending a spy ashore was in itself problematic – the
mangroves were pretty widespread – they must stretch back for
a kilometre or more – and although pretty matted, they did not
look all that strong. A fact made relevant because Caleb had
selected a range of the biggest, butchest – and, therefore, heaviest
– men available to him. And during the last ninety minutes or
so they had all been loading themselves with a range of kit and
weaponry that must almost have doubled their weight. 'Tell you
what,' Robin said to the cautiously calculating Caleb, 'why don't
I climb up into those mangroves there and see what I can see?
It's been a while since my tomboy days but I reckon I should
be able to find some kind of a secure vantage point up there and
take a good squint at the compound.'

That gave Caleb something else to hesitate over, so Robin
gave him the benefit of her assessment of the alternatives, and
that helped him to make up his mind. Five minutes later, already
beginning to regret her offer as sheer bloody madness, Robin
was easing herself through a springy tangle of branches which
took her straight back to childhood days creating secret dens in
the huge rhododendron bushes in the garden of Cold Fell, her

family home in the Scottish Borders. Eventually she found a kind of bed made out of a mat of water hyacinth that allowed her to look down past a fork in the branches where some kind of a flower lay crushed and dead. Her outlook was surprisingly good and she found herself speculating what a lethal field of fire she could lay down from here if she had any kind of automatic or semi-automatic weapon. But such thoughts were short-lived; crushed out of existence, like the flower at the branch junction, by simple, overwhelming surprise.

Robin had come here with an idea of what she was expecting to see. A burned chapel. Ruined buildings. Dead bodies in various states of disrepair and decomposition. She had steeled herself to observe all this. Observe and report, as was her mission. What she actually saw was not a ravaged compound, wrecked and burst open like a corpse picked over by vultures, but a stockade, almost a rudimentary fortress. Not by any means the leavings of an army eternally on the move, as Bonnie had described. But the defensive stronghold of a command with every intention of staying exactly where it was.

This was so precisely the opposite of what she had been expecting to see that she spent some extra time examining it, committing to mind the disposition of the rough palisade of wall – clearly chopped from the local jungle and carefully erected here. Of the stubby watchtowers – effective gun placements – providentially unoccupied at the moment. Of the long slope of naked mud that would allow whoever was defending the place a very effective killing field if anyone was mad enough to attack on foot from the river. Of the columns of smoke and hum of industry from within, which spoke of no fly-by-night group but of settled, steady, disciplined hard work.

And, as she looked and listened with all the fearsome concentration at her command, so she heard the revving of motors that grew louder and then stopped, as though several vehicles were pulling in from somewhere in the jungle and parking in the middle of the fort. And amid the shouts of welcome and enquiry that followed the arrival, she was certain that she heard the name of *Celine Chaka*.

# NINETEEN
## Zubr

'I am certain the president will see you at the earliest convenient moment,' Colonel Kebila told Richard firmly. 'But at present he is extremely busy.' The two men stood face to face in the anteroom to the president's office. They had met there, apparently by accident, but Richard was getting frankly suspicious about all these coincidental meetings. He had come from his meeting with Max Asov, full of ideas to help the situation upriver. He had paused only to change into an almost indestructible cotton shirt and a sturdy tropical suit and a pair of boots almost guaranteed to break the teeth of any crocodile. As he sped up to the president's compound in the hotel limousine, he knew that Max was contacting Captain Zhukov on the strength of Richard's assurance that he could get in to see The Man. Irina, meanwhile, was trying to clothe a mutinous Anastasia on the deeply mistaken assumption that she was still a child needing help or advice from anyone – least of all from yet another of her oversexed father's mistresses.

But Richard's progress – smooth as silk from the Nelson Mandela Suite to the president's anteroom – had been brought to an abrupt halt by the man who kept on turning up with such suspicious regularity that Richard was beginning to wonder if he had been slipped some kind of bug or tracking device.

'I bet he *is* busy, Colonel,' answered Richard with some asperity. 'One part of his country seems to be a conduit for unregulated arms smuggling while the other part of it is open to unopposed invasion by foreign armies. But I have a proposal to put to him which may help. In the short term at least.'

'I'm sure you do. To the benefit of Heritage Mariner or Bashnev-Sevmash also, no doubt. And I am sure he will wish to talk to you the moment he is free.'

But that moment came sooner than Colonel Kebila calculated, for the door of the president's office opened suddenly. Julius Chaka stood there himself, dressed in the military fatigues familiar from his soldiering days, his face thunderous. 'Laurent, there you are! Have you heard this report yet?' he demanded, waving a print-out covered with writing. 'It's just in from Naval HQ. Oh, good morning, Captain Mariner. Come through with the colonel please, this report will be of interest to you as well, I should imagine. Because it was your wife who sent it. She's apparently hanging in a mangrove tree up the delta even as we speak. She's overlooking the GPS coordinates we gave to Captain Maina, and this is what she can see . . .'

The president led the two men in, describing the detail of Robin's report as he did so. Richard looked around, distracted, but still paying close attention. Preferring to study the room rather than to start speculating what in God's name Robin was getting herself into now. Or, indeed, what the Doctor of African Studies Bonnie Holliday was getting up to at her side. At the thought of Bonnie, he frowned thoughtfully. But then the room he was entering distracted him again. The president's office, inherited unchanged like the rest of the compound from the more grandiose days of Liye Banda, was based on the White House Oval Office of the Bush administration, rather than the more conservative Obama makeover. The Great Seal of Benin la Bas lay at the centre of a carpet patterned with radiating lines in beige and brown. The desk was a double of the *Resolute* desk given to President Hayes by Queen Victoria in November 1880 and which had stood in the Oval Office through many administrations since.

Seated on the sofas flanking the long teak coffee table at right angles to the president's desk were senior officers from all of Benin la Bas's armed services. Richard recognized the uniforms, if not the men wearing them. With Kebila representing state security, it was the equivalent of a meeting of the British prime minister's emergency Cobra committee. There was nowhere to sit and nobody made any room, preferring to glare at both Kebila and himself with ill-concealed hostility. So, like the colonel, he stood, while the president paced restlessly, his movements reminiscent of the big black panther caged in the zoo.

'Well, I'll throw the question open,' said Julius Chaka, prowling around the seated officers and ministers as though sizing them up for dinner. 'What sort of force do we need up there to overwhelm an entrenched army in a simple but effective defensive position with the maximum speed and the minimum loss of life? Remember, independent of the fact that they have almost certainly got my daughter – a national heroine with a worldwide reputation – they also have a range of innocent bystanders, including doctors, nurses, priests and imams from a range of religions. And nuns. God knows how many nuns. Not to mention several hundred orphaned school children who were looking to us for help and protection.'

In the face of an uneasy silence, he began to get more specific and personally challenging. 'Air Marshal, how soon could you get planes or helicopters up there?' he demanded impatiently, stopping to tower over the slight figure in light blue serge and heavy gold braid.

'Planes within an hour, attack helicopters within two, troop transports within two hours of the troops being ready,' answered the air marshal unhesitatingly. 'We have the Chengdu Jian-7s which can get up there at twice the speed of sound. We have the Hip and Hind attack helicopters and the Eurocopter Super Puma transports. All armed, fuelled and ready to go. But I believe that air attack, while guaranteeing minimum time loss, will also guarantee maximum casualties; and unless you want troops para-chuting or abseiling into the battle zone, again with high levels of casualties guaranteed, then we will need to define a watertight safe landing zone first.'

'General?' snapped Chaka, turning to the next uncomfortable-looking officer whose beautifully pressed brown uniform – a tad less perfectly presented than Kebila's – was also festooned with gold.

'We have an emergency special forces command on standby. They can be ready to go within ninety minutes. But they are here in Granville Harbour. What would take the time is getting them up to the middle of the delta. You know the state of the roads and tracks in the jungle up there. You famously brought your tanks through it when you overthrew the tyrant Liye Banda five years ago, but you had to use the snorkel facility on the T80s and come downriver underwater for a good deal of the way, because there aren't any roads wide enough for tanks or troop carriers left up there. We could chopper them in on the Pumas as the air marshal has suggested – but they will only be effective if we can deliver them to the battle zone safely. No question of parachuting or abseiling into the middle of a battle, I'm afraid.

Always assuming the Army of Christ the Infant doesn't have anything that would bring the choppers down.' Like the six QW-1M shoulder-launched MANPADS being smuggled down the other bank, thought Richard. *I wonder what was in the other truck – and where it is now . . .*

'And ideally I would like some kind of artillery or armour in support,' the army man concluded. 'Especially if they are going against a fortification of any kind. Even a wooden stockade.'

'Admiral?' Chaka's voice betrayed frustration and anger mounting from volcanic to seismic, thought Richard sympathetically. The admiral's dress whites were at least less laden than those of his colleagues. But his words were only marginally more hopeful.

'We have five more Shaldag fast patrol boats. They could get up there within eight hours if they can proceed at full speed. But Captain Maina's reports of channels being all but blocked by water hyacinth make me wonder whether we could actually guarantee to get them there even within that time frame. Of course, anything larger, like the one corvette still functioning, couldn't even begin to get up there. Independently of blocked channels, she has far too deep a draft even to consider it. No. Only the Shaldags could make it. Like the FPB004 which is on site already, they could each carry ten commandos or Seals doubling as crew. But sixty men isn't much of an army, even though they'll have the back-up of a considerable artillery section of six 20 millimetre guns with twelve 0.5 millimetre machine guns, one pair per boat.'

President Chaka looked around the room, frowning, his anger and frustration erupting at last. 'That's the best we can do is it?' the ex-General, ex-tank commander snarled. 'Sixty men, half a dozen 20 millimetre cannon and a dozen or so light machine guns, sometime this afternoon or, perhaps, this evening *if we're lucky . . .*'

Richard cleared his throat and stepped forward, almost literally into the fray. 'Actually, Mr President, no. It's not the best you can do at all. I believe that, with your permission and with the cooperation of these gentlemen, I can deliver three hundred and fifty troops armed to your specifications, one T80U main battle tank with a 125 millimetre cannon, two RIM 116 missile systems, four 30 millimetre Gatlings, and two 140 millimetre Ogon rocket systems, to a point precisely beside FPB004's present position within six hours of the moment I get your go-ahead. And I can deliver them in a safe environment that will allow all the men and materiel to land on the slope of a bank which I believe lies downhill from the chapel – and which, therefore, will be within a couple of hundred yards of the stockade wall.'

'What!' spat Minister Ngama. 'Do you have some kind of Obi magic?'

'No, Minister,' answered Richard gently. 'I have a Zubr class air-cushioned landing craft called *Stalingrad*. And she is at your disposal, Mr President.'

'But she is not armed!' said President Chaka, his frown becoming less apoplectic and more calculating. 'She has aboard nothing more than the toys with which Mr Asov humiliated Captain Maina – paint-filled warheads, blank rounds. Even the T80U, the upgraded tank he has brought for me to look at, is very limited in the matter of arms and armament. Benin la Bas is not the sort of country that allows unregulated arms imports!'

Unless, of course, you're a smuggler disguised as a UN patrol, thought Richard. But for once in his life he kept his smart retort to himself. Instead, he said, 'I believe I have a way round that, Mr President, a way to arm her quickly and efficiently even as she proceeds upriver to her target. I believe I have a plan that will guarantee the best hope for General Nlong's prisoners. And for your daughter, of course. As long as I can count on your cooperation. And that of these gentlemen.'

The president looked round the oval office with eyes as hard as jet. 'Perhaps you would be good enough to wait outside, Captain Mariner,' he said, showing Richard to the door. 'I'm sure we won't keep you long!'

Half an hour later, Richard was sitting beside Colonel Kebila in a staff car heading for the docks. In the inside pocket of his jungle-proof jacket he carried a letter from the president which was almost the kind of commission familiar to him from the Hornblower novels he had loved in his younger days. 'To whom it may concern,' it said. 'You are hereby requested and required to furnish Captain Richard Mariner with any and all assistance he may demand . . .'

It was not so much that the document gave him

extra confidence – though there was no doubt that it added considerably to his clout – it was more that it rearranged his priorities by making him, albeit temporarily, an officer of the state. 'Have you put a tracking device on me, Colonel?' he asked, without giving the question much thought.

'Of course, Captain. It is in your Benincom phone. When Mr Bourne arranged for one to be sent to Heritage Mariner I had a bug put in as a matter of simple expediency. You are not the sort of man I wish to have running around my country unobserved. That is why I was tracking your movements personally right from the moment you deplaned at the international airport. Look at what you and Mrs Mariner became involved in on your last visit. What uncalculated consequences arose from a simple attempt to negotiate some oil concessions with the previous administration. A near civil war and a new president being perhaps the least of them. It is the way you seem to do things. Cause things. Do you remember Sergeant Major Tchaba, my driver here? All you did to him was to steal his boots. *Borrow* his boots, perhaps; *in a good cause* of course – that goes without saying. But now he has a false foot. Uncalculated consequences. This part of Africa is full of them after all, is it not? The uncalculated consequences of your ancestors setting up the slave trade. The uncalculated consequences of a European and American rush for ivory, rubber, copper, gold and diamonds. And oil, I need hardly add. And the new, wider, imperatives. Cassiterite and coltan; tin and tantalum. The western lust for things as innocent as baked beans and mobile phones – let alone for motor car tyres, petrol engines, jewellery and so forth – simply leads to my countrymen being enslaved and slaughtered. And crippled.'

'Perhaps it is you who should be running for president, Colonel,' said Richard stiffly.

'If I thought I could send the IMF, the World Bank, the CIA –' he paused meaningfully – 'the UN, the NGOs, the charities, Exxon, Shell, Mobil, De Beers, Bashnev-Sevmash and, yes, Heritage Mariner, and all they represent packing, then I might perhaps consider it. But alas, I, like you, live in the real world. In which it is necessary to employ a Russian hovercraft armed with American and European weaponry to transport one African army to confront another African army – in order to rescue several hundred African children, and, more importantly it appears, half a dozen *non-African* nuns and priests.'

'And the president's daughter,' added Richard shortly, his mind distracted by something of a revelation – the way Kebila had coupled the World Bank and the CIA – could that explain the delectable Dr Bonnie Holliday?

'Yes.' Kebila looked straight ahead, frowning. Richard remembered what Robin had said on the night of the white-tie reception. The colonel loved Celine Chaka more than anything and anyone else on earth. 'As you say,' whispered Laurent Kebila. 'And the president's daughter.'

As Kebila's staff car drew up at the slipway beside the mooring point occupied yesterday by the crippled *Otobo*, so Zhukov eased *Stalingrad* back to the place where his massive fans had all but destroyed the buildings through which the limousine was driving. This time, however, the three great motors were on near-idle, and the airstreams coming from them were pointing safely out to sea. The broad rounded bow of the Zubr slid ashore, the inflated skirts making no differentiation between sea and land, except that the metre-high wall of spray around them fell away to nothing. Then they slowly deflated and the massive vessel settled on to the ground. A fore-section opened and lowered itself on to the concrete with a *clang* and Richard found himself looking into a rectangle of darkness twenty metres wide and eight metres high, whose depth he could only guess at – though he reckoned fifty metres at least. Kebila gaped. 'And you expect to get this beast up the river?' he breathed.

'Its draft is less than a Shaldag's, even without the skirts inflated and fully laden. With the skirts up, it will ride over anything up to and including two metre walls. Irrespective of water hyacinth, shallows, sandbars and mud flats, of course. My only real worry is the ruined crossing at Citematadi. But we'll cross that bridge when we come to it, as they say.'

Richard stepped out of the staff car and closed the door. He looked in at Kebila's thoughtful profile for a moment, then he turned and walked swiftly and purposefully towards the Zubr. The Benincom phone in his jacket pocket tapped rhythmically against his thigh and for a moment he considered chucking it into the harbour. But then he thought better of the childish action. He would almost certainly need to use the local cellphone network

– and he really didn't give a damn if Kebila knew exactly where he was during the next twelve hours or so – because he was going to be as far upriver and as near to the heart of the delta as he could get, and it would probably be safer if his movements were known at all times.

Before he reached the huge hovercraft, however, he turned smartly right and crossed to the security barrier that protected the Naval HQ. 'I'd like to see the CO,' he said in his rough Matadi, making first use of his letter of authority. The presidential signature and stamp worked wonders and he was ushered into the camp commander's office five minutes later. 'What can I do for you, Captain?' asked the officer in flawless, if French accented, English.

'*Otobo*'s chief engineer. Is he available?' asked Richard.

'He is aboard at the moment, inspecting the fire damage and the water damage and preparing his report for the admiral's inquiry.'

'Is there any way I can communicate with him?' asked Richard, and five minutes later he found himself in the room that Kebila and Anastasia had been standing in last night when the first news from the Shaldag had arrived.

'The chief's name is Oganga,' the communications officer in smart lieutenant's whites told Richard. Redundantly, as it turned out.

'Chief engineer Oganga here,' barked the radio suddenly, in locally accented English. 'What is it now?'

'Chief Oganga, my name is Richard Mariner and I'm sorry to disturb you. I know you're doing vital work and it can't be any fun for you.'

'Well?' asked the chief, clearly somewhat mollified.

'I have to ask you a couple of things. They are vitally important. The first is about power aboard *Otobo*, and the second is about your own personal availability to participate in a little project that we're planning for later in the day . . .'

After his conversation with Chief Oganga, Richard went back to the CO's office. 'Chief Oganga needs half a dozen of his engineering crew out on *Otobo* as soon as you can get them there. And some equipment. Here's a list,' he said. 'It's an urgent matter or I wouldn't be bothering either of you.'

'It's no trouble at all, and I can get all of these men, I think,' said the officer affably enough after a quick glance at the list.

'And everything else. I also have Shaldag FPB002 immediately available. Everything and everyone will be there within the hour.'

Richard was hurrying back towards the Zubr when his Benincom cellphone rang. He slipped it out and answered it on the run. It was Anastasia. 'Are you going back up the river?' she asked without introducing herself or indulging in any pleasantries.

'Yes. How did you find out?'

'Kebila. I'm at the hospital with Esan and Ado. He came in to collect his smuggler for a question and answer session down in his torture chamber. I offered to help but he said no. We're coming with you. Don't go anywhere without us.'

Richard was silent for a heartbeat – two strides. On the one hand he was weighing what Max's reaction to his daughter's plan would be – especially as it was his vessel under the command of his men. On the other hand, here were the three people who knew the river, the situation, the compound and the Army of Christ the Infant best of all. 'Of course,' he said. 'Get to the dock as quickly as you can.'

'You took enough time making up your mind,' observed Anastasia icily.

'I must be getting old,' he countered. 'My reaction times are slowing down. I suggest you come via *Nellie* if there's anything aboard her that you want.'

'Nothing there,' she answered shortly. 'Kebila's men took all our guns. And we've all been supplied with everything else. Whether we wanted it or not. Everything except what we *really* wanted . . . Like children . . .'

'Don't worry about that. We'll have enough guns to satisfy even you.'

'Boy!' said Anastasia. 'Do you ever know the way to a girl's heart! Maybe you're the one with the Obi.'

And that was all it took to set something off in Richard's mind. After he broke contact with Anastasia he contacted the Granville Royal Lodge Hotel and asked for Andre Wanago in person. A few moments later, as he was slipping the mobile back into his pocket, the first of the army trucks came rumbling past at about ten miles per hour, its canvas rear section packed with well-armed men. He leaped up on to the footplate at the back, grabbed a handhold and was carried aboard *Stalingrad* with the first of the soldiers.

The space inside the Zubr was massive, echoing like a hangar. Twenty-five metres wide and fifty metres deep, the floor space was twelve hundred and fifty square metres. It stood eight metres high so the cubic capacity was just on ten thousand cubic metres. It was more like a level on a multi-storey car park than anything one would expect to find aboard a fighting vessel smaller than an aircraft carrier. The truck drew up beside a T80U main battle tank that was simply dwarfed by the size of the chamber it was parked in.

Richard jumped off as the vehicle slowed to a stop and ran across to the nearest companionway. The layout was not dissimilar to the big *Lionheart* series of car ferries Heritage Mariner ran across the English Channel, though the scale was far greater. Richard ran confidently upwards, counting off two deck levels in his head until he had no option but to cross inwards and climb more stairways up the centre of the bridge above the weather deck. Finally, he walked forward and found himself in a strange, almost circular command bridge, amid a bustle of officers and crewmen getting ready to set sail.

Max was standing beside Captain Zhukov, their heads close together as they went through some kind of manifest on a laptop. 'Ah, Richard,' said Max, looking up and seeing his friend. 'We're just checking the most vital elements aboard. Luckily, I interpreted the president's provisos pretty liberally, especially in the area of weaponry we couldn't access too easily down here. We have rockets for the Ogon system with the five point six kilo high-explosive warheads. We have more than mere paint in the warheads of the RIMs. But we don't have much else except the small arms we have brought for the crew – who are of course a pretty effective fifty-man fighting force on their own.'

'Hopefully we won't need them. But don't worry about the rest. I've already made provision to arm us to the teeth. Beyond that, my plan is simply to expedite the movement of men and materiel as supplied by Benin la Bas and let them sort their own problems out with a minimum of interference.'

'But what good will that do our businesses?' asked Max.

'You'll be surprised, Max. Remember, in all your negotiations with the president and his representatives during the next few days you want to emphasize that we are just here to offer help if it's asked for – we do not want to interfere. These people aren't children, Max. Don't come the heavy-handed parent with them.'

Richard's advice to Max – based on his conversation with Kebila, as well as on the not-so-hidden message of the white-tie dinner and everything that had happened since – was still in his mind half an hour later when the last of the Benin la Bas soldiers were safely aboard and Captain Zhukov was making restless noises about getting under way. Richard at last saw a pair of taxis draw up beside the slipway and three slight figures climbed out of the first, while the lone figure of Andre Wanago laden with a large box climbed out of the second and the four hurried aboard together. But it was only Anastasia who came up on to the bridge.

'Ready to go?' she asked as she strode up to Richard, still in defiant mode, clearly stuck in reaction to her shopping adventures with her father and his mistress.

'Ready as soon as Andre gets off again,' he said. 'Captain Zhukov?'

'We're ready,' growled the captain, clearly old-school, even compared to Max, and approving of none of this. Starting with women on his bridge.

'Then what are we waiting for? There he goes!' called Anastasia from beside the window. She put her hands on her hips and spread her legs, settling her feet solidly on the suddenly rising deck. She was wearing black boots that looked almost as indestructible as Richard's own; black jeans, skintight, with a thick black steel-buckled belt at their waist and their cuffs tucked into the boot-tops. And a T-shirt that was black as well – except for a phrase printed in blood red across the front. 'LOVE THY NEIGHBOUR' it said.

# TWENTY

## Scavengers

The Zubr *Stalingrad* eased past the Shaldag FPB002, which was secured to *Otobo*'s stern, and settled on to the mudbank where the crippled corvette's forecastle was securely beached. The hovercraft's wide front section opened with a semi-liquid *splash* and Richard ran down on to the slippery red surface, grateful for the fact that his boots were waterproof as well as nearly indestructible. 'Where are you going?' demanded Anastasia, materializing at his shoulder like a malevolent genie.

'Aboard,' he answered shortly, looking up the corvette's towering side, the top of which was outlined against the hard mid-morning sky.

'Why?' she demanded truculently.

'Come with me and you'll see.' He was enormously pleased with himself and was quite keen to have someone to show off to. Like the villain in a James Bond story with a compulsive desire to explain his plans for world domination to the one man able to stop them. It went far deeper than reason or logic; or sheer good sense, come to that. It was to do with the fact that he was missing Robin, his usual muse. He was Holmes without his Watson. And, besides, what she would see was bound to lighten her mood, he thought fondly and not a little paternally.

The pair of them ran across the surprisingly solid surface towards *Otobo*'s sloping side. Behind them, on Zhukov's orders, *Stalingrad*'s crew were already busy, and the soldiers were preparing to join them under the command of Colonel Leon Mako, Kebila's opposite number at field brigade rather than security.

'How are you with rope ladders?' Richard threw over his shoulder, as he grasped the bottom rung of a vertiginous Jacob's ladder reaching right up to the slight overhang of the gently tilted deck. 'At least there are rungs instead of ratlines,' he continued cheerfully. 'And chain rather than cable. But you'll find it easier if I hold it steady from the bottom.'

She gave him an old-fashioned look that bordered on the wifely. 'Thank God I didn't let Irina talk me into a skirt,' she said. 'Or yet another Mariner would be getting far too closely acquainted with my knickers.'

'Up you go,' he said severely. 'And don't be ridiculous. I'm old enough to be your father.'

'Now that,' she said, swinging nimbly upwards, 'never seems to make any difference to my *real* father, does it?'

When Richard joined her on the slightly sloping deck five minutes later, she had already made the acquaintance of Chief Engineering Lieutenant Oganga, who looked old and grizzled enough to be her grandfather but who, thought Richard, was looking at her in a way that was anything but paternal – or grandpaternal. Having read the front of her T-shirt, he obviously fancied himself head of the neighbourly queue. But thankfully Anastasia was amused rather than offended and proved happy to manipulate the impressionable officer. To manipulate him right round her little finger, thought Richard. But although Chief Oganga's eyes remained firmly on Anastasia's bust – greatly flattered, thought Richard, by precisely the kind of push-you-up-and-shove-you-out bra he would have expected the delectable Irina to favour – his attention had to focus on Richard. It was Richard's plan they were bringing to fruition here; his orders they were carrying out.

*Otobo*'s electrical circuitry was waterproof, but the fire in the engine room and the subsequent soaking from the firefighting ships had closed down her main power sources. Chief Oganga had been supplied with a powerful generator, therefore, and a team of his own electrical officers and men capable of using it to reawaken some of the corvette's power. In particular to the ammunition hoists.

Richard remembered all too clearly Max's boasts during the ill-fated war-game. The corvette and the Zubr shared so many systems it was uncanny – and all the Zubr lacked was the actual live ammunition to deliver her potential firepower in full measure. But there were no such problems aboard the crippled corvette. In every respect except propulsion, she was fully armed and battle ready. 'It's the exact opposite of *Stalingrad*,' he explained to Anastasia as he guided her below and showed her around the oddly angled arms lockers and ammunition movement systems. 'The Zubr has propulsion but no real armaments. So we're scavenging one for the benefit of the other. You see these? These are boxes of 30 millimetre rounds for the Gatlings. They're on their way up to the main deck. They will be followed by every shell they have aboard for the 125 millimetre gun on the forecastle head there. And finally by the RAM missiles and the eleven kilo blast and fragmentation warheads that go with the RIM116 system. All in all, when we have finished scavenging from the crippled corvette, almost all the weapons systems aboard the Zubr will be fully armed and battle ready.'

Richard and Anastasia accompanied Chief Oganga and his

team down the slanting companionways to the sloping decks and back again as Richard explained what he had caused to be done. 'It's lucky,' the engineering lieutenant told Anastasia's expensively enhanced bust, 'that the angle is no greater than it is or the lifts would not function. But we have performed miracles and everything is working well enough.' He dragged his eyes reluctantly towards Richard. 'However, we have not been able to power both the ammunition lifts *and* the cargo winches . . .'

'That's OK,' answered Richard easily. 'There's a plan B.' He reached for his telltale Benincom cellphone.

Anastasia watched closely as Richard ran her through all this – literally and figuratively. Frowning fiercely to conceal her wide-eyed astonishment, as the cases and crates of ammunition, explosive warheads, missiles and rockets were piled on to the after deck. Not piled randomly, she observed as she prowled restlessly and impatiently around them as he spoke forcefully into his Benincom cellphone – arranged carefully on flat wooden pallets. Even with his handset wedged between his shoulder and his ear, Richard was seemingly able to climb everywhere, assessing the piles of armaments, discussing with Chief Oganga – and whoever was on the other end of his phone call – obscure matters of weight and stability that seemed utterly arcane to her. Neither of them at the moment paying any attention to her at all. And it seemed to Anastasia that their overcareful preparations were something of an irrelevant waste of time – as though they were rearranging deckchairs on the *Titanic*. Until she heard the first distant throbbing and understood everything.

'The lift weight on these things is nine thousand kilos,' Richard explained to her, appearing at her shoulder as the Super Pumas appeared low in the sky behind them and pocketing his mobile as he spoke. 'The chief and I have had to be careful but the ammunition hoists have built in weight assessors and we've calculated how each load was added to each pallet. So we should be all right according to the experts at the helicopters' HQ. Two choppers, three lifts each. What do you reckon?'

'Not bad,' she said. 'For some ancient geezer old enough to be my father . . .'

'Ah, but there's more . . .' Richard pulled one specific box from the final pile the chief had sent up from the arms locker. He flipped the top and swung it back. 'Don't you ever tell your father,' he admonished her, but she hardly heard him. Nestled in the box's black foam interior three semi-automatic carbines sat side by side. 'They're special forces kit,' he said. 'SIG SG 453s. Folding skeleton stock. Curved clip like your AK. Special order – fifty rounds per clip instead of the usual thirty. Three settings: single shot, three tap or fully automatic. Fire rate: eight hundred rounds a minute on automatic. Happy now?'

'Yes,' she whispered. 'Oh yes.' She glanced almost coyly up at him as she stroked the nearest gun. 'My shrink used to say it was penis envy, my fascination with guns. But she was an old-school Freudian.'

'You had a shrink?'

'How do you think I got over Simian Artillery and their aftermath? And anyhow you should know. You paid for her. Or Robin did. My bastard father most certainly did not!'

She crouched forward possessively and, as he digested all this, Richard registered for the first time there was writing on the back of her T-shirt. The front said 'LOVE THY NEIGHBOUR'. The back said 'AND F*** YOUR FAMILY'.

The Pumas hovered over *Otobo*'s poop, and lowered ropes that split into four strands, each with a carabiner designed to clip to the corner of a loaded pallet, then they lifted them off the corvette and lowered them on to the mudbank in front of the Zubr, where they were unloaded by the crew and their passengers working smoothly together. It took less than half an hour for everything from the ship that might be useful to be moved over to the hovercraft, as Richard planned.

Richard and Anastasia rode the last pallet down, standing side by side on the clearest corner, holding on to the guy rope – with Richard's arm ready to reach round her waist if she slipped or panicked. Neither circumstance seemed likely to him. He knew that Max would find it hard to forgive him for giving his little girl a gun. But he would never *ever* forgive him for letting her get hurt. His Russian friend loved his petite *printyessa* – even if he still refused to talk to her. Or pay to fix her mental wounds, come to that. Too busy with his own penis – to the envy of most of his friends.

*Stalingrad* was a quiet bustle of activity as she lifted herself back on to her skirts and slid off the mudbank and back on to the surface of the water. The missiles, rockets, warheads, shells and ammunition were all taken to the places they would be needed most, and, where appropriate, loaded into the weapon systems that would use them. A burly sergeant took Anastasia's gun box to her quiet corner of the bustling area and she called Ado and Esan over to look at her new toys. It was coming up to midday and the Zubr's galley was preparing food designed to enhance the battlefield rations Colonel Mako's three hundred soldiers had brought aboard with them. Up on the bridge, Richard looked at his steel-cased Rolex Oyster Perpetual, calculating. He had promised to get up the river within six hours. And that was his plan. He wanted to arrive six hours from now, in fact, for the timing itself was a crucial element of his exhaustive calculations.

'Full ahead, Captain Zhukov,' he said quietly and the silver bear of a commander nodded. '*Pulniv piot,*' he said quietly – or something approximating to that; Richard's Russian was a little rusty and the captain's accent was thick and unfamiliar. The helmsman's hands pushed the throttles forward, however, so the message had got through well enough. The message was also immediately transferred to the engine room. The power to the three huge turbines behind the bridge house cranked up to maximum. With the whole of her massive hull vibrating gently, *Stalingrad* lifted up her skirts and flew.

The mouth of the main channel closed before her with shocking rapidity, in Richard's eyes. But Zhukov stood on spread feet, hands clasped behind him, relaxed. He spoke a word or two in his gruff Russian to the officers, ship-handlers and navigators around him. They answered equally tersely. What Richard's rusty Russian was too unpractised to follow, the situation made clear enough. There was no sonar because the vessel did not break the water's surface. But there was radar – wide band and collision alarm. All the captain seemed worried about was the width of the channels ahead. The radar would show him anything rising more than two metres above the water's surface – and, if it was solid enough to present a threat, the collision alarm would sound.

But the monosyllabic conversation established that although the bank was gathering in on their right, and although there were islands looming midstream on their left, these two stood more than fifty metres apart, and all that lay between them, except water, was a solid mat of water hyacinth. Richard could well understand how this would slow even the speedy Shaldags, but the Zubr soared across it at more than a mile a minute, leaving a wake of shattered vegetation behind it.

They reached Citematadi just after three. Richard knew all too well what lay behind the wide sweep of the bend at the apex of the embankments rising up like square escarpments on their right, so he called to the captain, 'Slow!'

'*Meadimna*,' said the gruff captain, and slowed his command for the first time since midday.

*Stalingrad* came round the wide bend below Citematadi with just a little more caution than she had showed coming upstream so far. The ruin of the bridge stretched across the river ahead of her, and even as the eyes aboard the command bridge registered it, so the collision alarms started sounding. The huge hovercraft sailed circumspectly forward, the 3D display of her Doppler radar calculating and displaying measurements – the heights of the piers still standing; the distances from one to the other. The massive blocks of masonry lay half submerged like boulders between the bridge's solid piers, their surfaces rearing three and four metres above the roiling wilderness of foam around them. There was simply no channel anywhere near thirty metres wide. 'It is a solid wall,' growled Zhukov at last in English. 'There is nowhere I can take her through.'

'I know there's no way *through*,' Richard answered confidently. 'But I'd thought of that. I believe there's a way *round*.'

'What do you mean?' The captain looked away from his displays and his fierce blue gaze rested like a weight on Richard.

'The south bank,' Richard explained. 'Look. Just beside that burned-out boathouse, the bank rises quite gently on the inward side of the curve. And, if you can get up on to the shore beneath the embankment there, the first span of the bridge is still intact, you see? The roadway actually projects out over the river like a huge ramp before the real destruction starts. But the bridge and the highway behind it are still intact. There's a roadway coming down off the embankment to the boathouse, so it's not too easy to see, but I think if you take it carefully, you'll just be able to squeeze her under that first span and slide back down the bank on the upriver side.'

'I see,' said Zhukov, grudgingly. 'That is very clever. We will give it a go. But take it one step at a time. Helmsman, come

right. Navigator, you see the slope of bank below that burned-out
boathouse with the truck parked behind it . . . ?'

Richard stiffened as the penny dropped. He had been so
focussed on his own plans he had forgotten what he had seen of
Caleb and Robin's reports from the Shaldag. What Anastasia had
told him of her adventures. 'Captain!' he said. 'Can you call
Anastasia Asov to the bridge, please?'

'For what reason?' Zhukov was still understandably nervous
at having his owner's daughter aboard without Asov's specific
directions.

'You see the boathouse?'

'Of course. We are swinging round towards it . . .'

'It was Anastasia and her friends who burned it. She was on
this bank a matter of hours ago. If anyone can give you updates
on current conditions then she can. And, come to think of it, you
might get in touch with Shaldag FPB004. Captain Caleb might
have some relevant intel for you.'

Anastasia was on the bridge four minutes later, as the Zubr
eased itself delicately ashore on to the long slope of bank behind
the burned boathouse. Ado and Esan came with her. She brought
her gun but they did not. Richard looked at her as she surveyed
the place. She was pale and seemed a little shaky. The three of
them crowded together for mutual support and the Russian woman
in her black jeans and childish T-shirt suddenly seemed hardly
older than the teenagers beside her. She held on to her SIG SG
carbine with an almost disturbing intensity. 'The parking area
where that truck is standing is just concrete slabs laid over the
mud of the bank,' she said quietly, her voice a lot steadier than
her hands. 'It was dark when they brought us down here, so I
can't be certain of the details, but I got the impression that the
road out on to the bridge was as solid as the road down here.'

'I got the impression there was lots of room behind me when
I climbed out of the back of the truck,' Esan added. 'I was looking
around for enemies and it was dark – but the moon was up and
I certainly thought there was a wide, deep space back there.'

'What was actually in the back of the truck you hid in?' asked
Richard, sidetracked. 'Did you notice that?'

'Crates and stuff. I really have no idea what was in them.'

'There were MANPADS in the other one,' said Richard.
'Shoulder-fired guided missiles. Nothing like that?'

'I've no idea,' said Esan. 'But I'm certain that there was something like a huge wide tunnel stretching away behind me when I got out . . .'

'OK, boy,' said Zhukov. 'We proceed. Into your tunnel, if it's really there.'

*Stalingrad* eased herself right up on to the bank and swung her face eastwards. The slope of the bank canted gently downwards from right to left, from bank to waterline, but nowhere near steeply enough to cause the hovercraft any trouble. The first span of the bridge reached out above them, soaring upwards a good twenty metres to the underside of the roadway. The first pier of the bridge, with its solid column of masonry towering to the shattered end of the road it had carried more than forty years ago, stood out on the water, leaving a gap on the shore side at least fifty metres wide. But the collision alarm continued to sound stridently. Because the second truck was parked in the middle of their path, in the shadow beneath the bridge.

'I blow it out of the way,' rumbled Zhukov. 'Now I have real munitions.'

But Richard shouted, 'No! Wait! Look. There's someone moving in the cab. And besides,' he emphasized, sensing that even Zhukov wasn't going to be slowed by one man any more than by one truck, 'anything big enough to blow the truck out of the way might bring the bridge down too. Especially if it has more missiles in it. Here's a chance for some of us to live up to your T-shirt,' he said to Anastasia. 'To the front of it at least.' And that seemed to settle things.

But he drew the line at letting her come with him. Instead, when the front of the hovercraft banged down on to the brick-hard mud of the bank, he was standing with Colonel Mako at the centre of a small contingent of his well-drilled, fearsomely armed and very impressive-looking soldiers. A point team fanned out ahead of them, running up on to any elevated sections, in case this was a trap. The colonel was clearly a strategist, thought Richard. The point team signalled the all clear and the command group strode forward. As they approached the truck, three men climbed out of the cab with their heads hanging and their hands high. Two were dressed in shorts and T-shirts, obviously from *Nellie*'s crew. The other wore a UN uniform and body armour. They were all staring past him at something which had clearly scared them. When Richard glanced over his shoulder, it became obvious why they had not even considered resistance – the presence of the Zubr was simply overpowering. It sat in the opening beneath the bridge like some massive crocodile, its mouth agape, lined with soldiers instead of teeth, a T80U main battle tank lurking in the dark throat of the thing instead of a tongue. It almost made Richard's hair stand on end – and the monster was on his side!

As Mako's soldiers disarmed and searched the frightened men, Richard went in hard with the first questions. In a moment or two he had established that there were no more of the smugglers left alive. That these three had not been part of the rape party; that the wound in one man's shoulder had come from a ricochet. That they had panicked and driven the truck into Citematadi when the shooting had started. But that the deserted city had offered very little in the way of shelter and nothing in the way of sustenance. And no hope at all for rescue. So they had come back here where there was at least water and shelter from both sun and rain beneath the bridge. They had simply hoped that someone would come past before they starved to death. In the absence of civil authorities, Mako placed them in military detention and his men led them aboard *Stalingrad*, while the colonel himself prepared to climb into the cab and move the truck.

'Colonel, have your men all got body armour?' asked Richard, watching the third prisoner walking up the ramp with his bright blue UN vest.

'Yes. It's standard issue.'

'Not for us or the Zubr's crew . . .' Richard's first thought was to scavenge body armour in case anyone on the Zubr had to get involved in the fighting, but soon enough he was thinking bigger than that. Mako drove the truck up beside its companion. Richard jumped down and glanced into the first truck. Caleb's men had arranged the dead men from the boathouse neatly and covered them with a respectfulness Richard suspected they did not really merit. They had simply piled the body armour on the bench seat in the cab. 'We should take that,' said Richard. 'And we should take a look in the back of this one too. Esan might not have recognized what was in the crates back here, but we might have a better idea.'

As it happened, they didn't. The marking on the crates meant nothing to them – even the sections of it that were written in English. But when Richard snapped the top of one open, it was immediately clear that they were looking at some kind of communications equipment rather than any actual weaponry. 'I'm not sure it's worth wasting much time over,' said Mako, but Richard's Scottish blood simply would not allow him to discard something so thoughtlessly. Ten minutes later *Stalingrad*'s communications officer was standing beside Mako's army man. And both of them were wide-eyed. 'It's the latest update of the Parakeet,' said the army man, his voice simply awed. 'It is state of the art.'

'Parakeet,' said Richard, disappointed. 'That doesn't sound like much.'

'It's the complete battlefield communication system,' breathed the soldier. 'Like the British Bowman – but it works better.'

'Battlefield communications?' said Richard. 'You mean from command vehicles to attack vehicles and so forth?'

'No,' said Mako, his light baritone voice decisive, authoritative. 'The Parakeet system is for use by dismounted personnel. On foot. Using this I can stay in detailed personal real-time contact with as many squad leaders as I want. Secure, encrypted, two-way, no matter where I am on the battlefield, or they are.'

'Well, I think we should take it aboard,' said Richard, impressed.

'So do I,' agreed Colonel Mako. 'I'll drive the truck straight up the ramp.'

'And I'll drive the other one,' said Richard. 'Waste not, want not. And at the very least it'll allow Anastasia and Ado to give us a complete list of the men who tried to rape them, living or dead.'

'And Celine Chaka, of course,' called Mako, slamming the truck door behind him. 'She's the reason we're here after all.'

Just at that very moment, four hours upriver, the stiff and aching Celine Chaka finally realized that Anastasia Asov had saved her life. Twice. The first time she had saved it was when she pulled Celine out of the compound, under the chapel, and got her down to the boat. She had saved her then, even though she had been wounded in the shoot-out with the pursuing Army of Christ the Infant. And she had saved it now. For the two shots Anastasia had fired from the AK47 had wounded the two men that the army could least afford to do without. Two men so severely wounded that even the young doctor kidnapped from the clinic at Malebo could not guarantee to save them. Only she, with her far wider and more painfully learned experience, could do that. Which was the reason that she was still alive, where all the other invalids from the clinic had been executed long since. Which was why she would stay alive – like the young doctor and his little medical team, like Sister Hope and Sister Charity, and Jacob, the useful handyman – for just as long as she could be of service to these brutal and terrible people.

The two wounded men lay in the chapel itself, where her own sickbed was, though the interchangeable places of learning and worship had been stripped out ages ago. Now it was, as closely as it was possible to make it, a hospital. Albeit a hospital with only two patients remaining, now that Celine was finally up. Celine called the man with the chest wound Ngoboi, for that was the costume he was wearing when Anastasia shot him, though she understood his real name was Ojogo. His responsibilities within the Army of Christ the Infant were for the oversight and maintenance of transport. And since his shooting, the transport section had all but closed down. Especially as one of his most trusted lieutenants – a boy called Esan, apparently – had vanished in the melee of that night three days since.

Moses Nlong himself had been coherent – although in great and increasing agony – for some time after his wounding. Just long enough to issue a whole string of orders, from the building of the stockade to the kidnapping of the nearest doctor from the clinic at Malebo. But he was delirious and helpless now. So much so that the men in charge at the moment, led by the man who had kidnapped her – the fearsome Captain Odem – had very pointedly allowed her to live as long as she tended him and kept him alive. But that was becoming increasingly hard to do.

The bullet from Anastasia's AK, beginning to tumble at the end of its flight, had hit the general directly on his left knee. It shattered the kneecap, spreading into a misshapen mushroom as it did so, and smashed the joint behind the patella – splintering both the big bones – the tibia shin bone and the femur thigh bone, before tearing the fibula free – thus destroying the ankle below as well. 'It was lucky for the general that Sister Hope was a competent first-aider,' said Celine to young doctor Chukwu.

'She managed to stem the blood loss from the popliteal artery and vein before he bled to death. But, in spite of her ministrations, Nlong will never walk properly again.'

'Indeed,' Dr Chukwu agreed, frowning. 'If I were a more confident surgeon I would have taken the leg off below the knee and tried to reconstruct the shattered end of the thigh. But surgery is not an option under these circumstances. Gangrene, however, is.'

A footfall behind Celine made her turn. It was Odem. He stood for a moment eyeing her as though he could see through all of her clothing, instead of just through the gossamer of the bloodstained blouse she had put on instead of the hospital robe from the clinic. Her flesh rose in goosebumps of revulsion at the thought of him doing to her what he apparently did to the harem of girls he kept with him each night. He crossed to the general's bed and looked down at him. 'I don't think he has long to live,' the soldier growled. 'He was growing weak in any case; wanting to settle down. To negotiate with your father. Become a *farmer* once again.' The full lips twisted in contempt.

'I'm sure that would be a wise move, Captain,' said Celine carefully.

'So are some of the others,' he sneered. 'They have given him until dawn. He either starts getting better soon or I assume command.' He shouldered the doctor aside and crossed to the second bed where the dying Ngoboi lay tossing restlessly, coughing and choking. 'His right-hand man, Captain Ojogo,' said Odem thoughtfully as he slid his matchet out. 'My greatest rival.' The blade rose and fell once. Twice. The sound was indescribable. Odem turned his back on the fountain of blood which burst from Ngoboi. 'You have 'til dawn,' he said, his red-rimmed eyes moving from Celine to the doctor and the nurses cowering with the two nuns on the raised platform that had once been an altar. 'All of you.'

He went to move away and then turned back.

'If you last past midnight,' he concluded.

# TWENTY-ONE
## Dark

Stalingrad whispered into position half an hour after sunset, just at the moment that the tropical darkness closed down most fiercely. Thunderheads massed in the west once more, blotting out the last vestiges of daylight and threatening the upper sky. During the final section of their approach, Richard had asked Captain Caleb to get Robin back aboard the Shaldag, to drift downstream to the western end of the mangroves and rendezvous with the larger vessel there. He calculated that this put a good solid kilometre of cover between the compound and the two craft set to attack it. While there seemed to be every chance that the Shaldag had gone unnoticed, it seemed very unlikely that the massive Zubr would. And the plan that Richard was discussing with Colonel Mako, Captain Zhukov and Captain Caleb relied on surprise. Intelligence and surprise.

Robin, who had climbed back down to give her initial report, had then returned when the heat was going out of the afternoon, just after four, to spend some time completing as detailed a survey as possible of the stockade, relaying what information she could. Inevitably, it went to *Stalingrad* via Caleb aboard FPB004. Richard and the men he was working with, therefore, had a clear idea of the section of the compound facing the river. The stockade wall stood about four metres tall. It was built of thick-looking tree trunks chopped bodily out the nearby forest, which had been well secured together and seemed to be invulnerable to anything smaller than artillery. The primary watch position was the bell-tower of the chapel immediately behind it which seemed to have a platform beside the bell itself, and Robin had seen men come up and down what seemed to her to be a ladder reaching up from the chapel – judging from the way they moved. Something that looked like a shoulder-launched missile stood there, ready.

Robin described a couple of other rudimentary watch positions at either end of the wall – or that section of it she could see clearly. There was one where it vanished into the jungle on her left and another where it turned to run parallel to the river on her right. That second watchtower was the next most frequently occupied for it overlooked the little jetty. There was what looked like a heavy machine gun there. It had been empty in the morning. Now it was manned. The watch routine had seemed to be desultory before she made her first report. Things had tightened up noticeably by the time she returned for her second tour of duty. It seemed to her that whoever had come back with the vehicles and with Celine had had a marked impact on the discipline and routines of the encampment.

'We need more intel,' said Mako thoughtfully, after an extended briefing, as 20:00 hours passed into 21:00.

'I agree,' nodded Richard. 'I mean, we can sail *Stalingrad* up to the jetty, all guns blazing, and send our troops ashore with a very high expectation of success. But during the time it takes us to get past that stockade and into the compound in any serious numbers, God alone knows what may have happened to the people we came up here to save.' He turned towards the microphone connecting him to the Shaldag's bridge. 'Caleb, any feedback from Sanda and the patrol you sent ashore?'

'Nothing of any use yet,' the captain's voice answered. 'But they're making good progress along a track cleared by the vehicles they've been following.'

'They'll be coming through the jungle on the other side,' mused Richard. 'They'll be able to give us a new perspective when they get into position. But what we really need before we attack is some kind of solid intel from inside the compound itself. Ideally, we need someone actually in there who can tell us when the optimum moment for attack arrives – and can then get to Celine and the others and try to protect them during the time it takes us to break in and rescue them.'

Nobody said 'dream on' or 'what planet are you from?', which surprised Richard, especially as Robin was listening. But the fact was that what he said was true. Unless they could actually smuggle some sort of fifth column into the compound, the chances of Celine and the others surviving were slim to negligible. So he went one step forward – the step that he had always known would take him on to the thinnest ice. 'So I have an idea,' he said. 'Something to be working on while we wait for the intel to firm up. I brought a disguise,' he explained. 'I got Andre Wanago to bring up some costumes from the Granville Royal Lodge.'

'What costumes?' asked Robin's voice over the radio-link from the Shaldag's bridge. She sounded genuinely intrigued.

'Ngoboi's costume,' answered Richard. 'From the white-tie dinner. Ngoboi's costume and his helpers'.'

'Ngoboi's costume,' said Robin. 'Clever. But we'd need to be desperate, surely, to take the risk . . .'

'Fair enough,' temporized Richard. 'But you never know. I noticed that Ngoboi's costume covered the dancer completely. There's no way to see through it. It's the perfect disguise. So I thought I could put it on and—'

'It might work if you know the dance,' said Robin. 'Do you know the dance?'

'Wait!' commanded Caleb, interrupting the conversation at that moment. 'Lieutenant Sanda and his men have just reported on the other radio. They have finally arrived at the inland perimeter of the camp. I'll patch Sanda through so he can make a more detailed report. Wait . . .'

'. . . technicals,' came Sanda's voice suddenly, clearly part-way through a sentence. 'Flatbed trucks – Toyotas – with heavy machine guns mounted on them. They are in a section of the compound that's quite well lit so I can see them pretty clearly. I count half a dozen. A couple look as though they have the relatively new Chinese 14.5 millimetre QJG 02 heavy machine guns on the back. The rest have the older W85s. That's quite a lot of firepower, if they get it deployed. And there are a couple of four-by-fours – the ones we've been tracking, I'd guess. They seem to have Russian Strela missiles aboard them. They're plane killers that will take out a tank too, of course. The whole lot is pretty well guarded by a serious-looking patrol. But I think that's just standard procedure. I don't think they suspect we're here.' There was a brief silence, then Sanda added the thought that had been on everybody else's mind during his terse report. 'I wonder what other nasty surprises they have hidden away in there . . .'

After a moment more of silence, Richard continued, 'Well, it seems that my idea is more important than ever.'

'Accepted,' answered Robin roundly. 'But by the same token, if we're sending someone in for a look around, it has to be

someone who fits the bill. Who knows what they're looking for
– and who knows how Ngoboi would behave?'

'Well, I'm pretty well up on modern weaponry,' persisted
Richard. 'And I thought I could improvise the soft-shoe shuffle,
you know? Make it up . . .'

'*Do you know the bloody dance, Richard?*'

Richard opened his mouth to admit, 'No . . .'

But Bonnie Holliday interrupted. 'I do. I know the weaponry.
And I know the dance.'

An hour later still, as 22:00 reached round to 23:00, Richard was
rowing the tiny cockleshell in which Anastasia, Ado, Esan and
Celine had escaped back under the jetty and along the eastern
bank behind it. The little rowboat carried Ado, Esan and Bonnie,
in Ngoboi's costume. A couple of things had changed since
Bonnie's declaration and the heated discussion that had followed
it – not least with some of Mako's Poro officers who saw even
the idea as a weird kind of sacrilege. Changed and progressed.
Sanda and his men were in position to contact and support the
undercover dancers. Sanda reported that there was no defensive
wall on the jungle side – indeed, that, apart from the vehicles,
the compound seemed open and undefended from the perimeter
section where the jungle met the river upstream east of the jetty.

The jungle section was the most sporadically patrolled, so it
seemed the most obvious point of entry into the compound, even
though there were the powerfully armed technicals nearby and
patrols were keeping a regular eye on them. Behind the little
cockleshell of a boat, three larger inflatables whispered through
the water, also being rowed, filled with a carefully selected
mixture of men from both the Shaldag and from *Stalingrad*
herself. Men and one insistent young woman who refused to take
'No' for an answer. If Bonnie was going into the camp, she was
not going in without support, and if Esan and Ado were going
with her as Ngoboi's companions to try and pull Celine and the
others out of the firefight, then Anastasia was going to be there
beside her friends no matter what. Unlike the others, she had not
needed to change in order to put on non-reflective black clothing.
And she had positively revelled in covering her face, arms and
hands in thick black camouflage paint. The only things about the
warlike Russian woman likely to catch the light, thought Richard,

were the whites of her eyes, the barrel of her SIG SG 453, or the teeth she kept baring in a truly unnerving tiger-smile. Perhaps there had been something in her psychoanalyst's Freudian diagnosis after all.

The three vessels eased under the ramshackle little jetty. The bow of Richard's cockleshell hissed on to the mud of the bank and his passengers eased themselves ashore. A lone dark figure detached itself from the blackness of the nearby bush and beckoned. Sanda's voice whispered in the earpieces of the headsets they were all now wearing. And even as it did so, the black inflatable bows of the other two vessels bumped ashore and black-dressed figures, armed to the teeth, started pouring silently on to the bank. As they whispered towards the treeline, the first glimpse of the rising moon shone downriver, reflecting weirdly off the bottoms of the roiling thunderclouds low overhead. It gave just enough light to define the vanishing commando. And to give Richard, as he eased the boat back into the stream, one last glimpse of Anastasia's unsettling tiger-smile as she went to rescue the friend she loved and the children she had nurtured and guarded for so long.

But the instant that Anastasia vanished, a strange and truly terrifying roaring sound began to echo out of the heart of the darkness ashore. He thought of the vuvuzelas at the 2010 Football World Cup. The sounds were a timeless and chillingly sinister reincarnation of the African bullhorns. By the time the river took him, sweeping him back downstream towards the Shaldag and *Stalingrad*, his mouth was dry and his heart was pounding; his palms were sweating and the hair on the back of his neck all astir.

At the sound of the bullhorns, Celine looked up, her face drawn with horror. She, Dr Chukwu, the nurses and Sisters Hope and Charity were all wide awake – and had in fact been praying; as close to midnight mass as they could come without Father Antoine. Until the distant, terrible roaring began, the little hospital chapel had become an almost sacred place. Even with a pagan mass-murdering butcher as the principal patient and a blood-soiled sheet concealing the chopped remains of his dead captain beside him. Even with a watchkeeper up in the little bell-tower above them, armed with semi-automatic rifle and MANPADS missiles.

But Celine knew all too well that the roaring of the bullhorns meant that Ngoboi had been reincarnated out in some terrible corner of the jungle. In his last incarnation the appalling Poro god had taken hearts for the general to eat. Celine knew in her own heart that this incarnation would be worse still. She came up off her knees as though some invisible hand had lifted her, and staggered to the door. The compound was unsettlingly empty under the dull yellow glare of the lighting. The buildings and shelters along its edges apparently shut tightly against the awful supernatural invasion. Above the misty outlines of the jungle treetops, the eastern sky was eerily pale with the promise of the rising moon, but its light refracted strangely and restlessly off the cloud cover rolling away towards the distant heights of Mount Karisoke. The doctor arrived at her shoulder. His hand fell on her upper arm, gripping her with almost painful intensity. 'Get back,' he hissed. 'It is death for a woman to look on Ngoboi!'

'I've looked on him before and survived,' grated Celine, 'which is more than I can say for poor Father Antoine and the others. And, in any case, the chances are that Ngoboi is coming for me!'

'More likely he's coming for Moses Nlong,' said the doctor, looking back at the general's bed where the restless body was beginning to writhe awake. The soldier's sharp-toothed face no longer looked so brutally powerful. It looked sick, agonized, terrified, almost childlike, as growing realization dragged him unwillingly up out of his coma, the louder the bullhorns brayed. 'Then he's still going to have to come through me,' said Celine, though in her current condition that wasn't much of a threat.

Shadows flooded into the compound, as though the edges of the place were filling with the black water that had given birth to the pearls Ado had found on the riverbank. Flashes of yellow light gleamed, strange, inhuman reflections of eyes and teeth. A weird hissing became a whispering as the shadows became the boys of the army, all agog with excitement, high on adrenalin as they had once been on cocaine. But over the top of the rushing murmur, the trumpeting roar of the bullhorns gathered. And into the light at the far edge of the compound, the ghastly figure of Ngoboi whirled, with two attendants stroking and smoothing the fluttering wildness of his raffia costume. And, as soon as he appeared, over the top of the bullhorns themselves, the first distant peal of thunder came echoing out of the strange, cavernous sky. The misty brightness smeared across the eastern firmament began to die. There was nothing but the blackness beyond the security lighting, the glittering shadows and the wildly whirling figure of Ngoboi coming relentlessly towards the little chapel and the defenceless folk within it.

Celine shrugged off the doctor's restraining hand. She stepped out through the door and staggered down the steps that were still stained with Father Antoine's blood. The whispering that had run round the edges of the compound became a growl. She walked unsteadily towards the whirling dervish in raffia, head held high, face set, nostrils flared. As she neared the capering figure, she was able to see that, like the steps behind her, the front of the dancer's costume was stained with blood. A bullet hole had been carefully mended but the dark spatter around it remained. Ngoboi's two assistants danced threateningly close to her, their task of keeping his costume smooth doubling with the need to keep her far enough away to avoid desecration of their god. It was bad enough that she looked upon him. What might happen if she touched him was incalculable. But, short of knocking her down or pulling her back, they could do nothing to turn the determined woman aside. So that, at last, Celine and Ngoboi were standing face to face in the middle of the compound.

Ngoboi stopped his dance and drew himself up to his full, towering height. Behind him, a great bolt of lightning smashed down the eastern sky, seeming to shatter on the top of distant Mount Karisoke. The bellow of thunder was overwhelming and instantaneous. In the instant that it died, a matchet appeared in Ngoboi's hand. Its disconcertingly hot blade stroked Celine's left cheek from cheekbone to ear lobe and beyond, razor-sharp enough to be shaving the hairs on her neck, and only the steadiness of the god's right hand kept her from disfigurement or death – for the moment. 'I had meant to keep you alive and trade you with your father,' said Ngoboi in Captain Odem's voice, so softly that only Celine could hear him. 'You would have been worth such a *fortune* . . .' There seemed to be genuine regret in his tone. 'But now I shall eat your heart instead.'

The matchet swooped upwards for the killing stroke.

But a second bellow of bullhorns made him hesitate. Over his monstrous shoulder, Celine's disbelieving eyes saw a second incarnation of the god come dancing out of the jungle's impenetrable shadows into the yellow security light. Also monstrously tall. Also swathed in restless raffia. Also attended by two dancing acolytes who kept the costume carefully in place. Also dancing the dance steps known only to the god himself. The man with the matchet swung round, his reed-straight victim forgotten for the moment. The roaring round the compound's edges lost its rhythm and faltered into uncertainty. Lightning ripped across the sky again. Thunder exploded with disorientating power. Rain came pounding down like doom. Odem shouted something Celine couldn't hear and threw the matchet aside. He tore the headdress off and reached into the raffia costume swathing him. Still shouting to his bemused followers, he tore out a handgun and ran towards the second figure. His shouts rising to screams of inarticulate rage, he began to shoot. The second Ngoboi staggered, blasted back as the bullets slammed into its chest. Staggered, stumbled and fell to the rain-washed mud of the compound.

Odem whirled back, levelling his gun at Celine, still close enough to be shooting almost at point-blank range. He would have killed her there and then – no matter what the damage to the prospective meal of her heart, had not several things happened to make him hesitate.

The army of his followers around the compound edge gave a collective gasp that was almost a groan of terror.

The second Ngoboi pulled itself up off the streaming mud and whirled into its dance again.

A rocket streaked in out of the jungle just behind the dancing figure to behead the chapel's bell-tower with an axe of white fire.

And a second explosion punched a great hole in the palisade wall between the burning chapel and the river.

# TWENTY-TWO

## Heart

Richard learned to drive a T80 main battle tank some years earlier on a virtual tutor halfway between a flight simulator and a video game. On the rare occasions he got to handle the machines for real, he was surprised that the actual controls were heavier, and the whole experience both noisier and jerkier than the training sessions had been. Especially when the 125mm gun in the turret almost immediately above his head was firing high explosive shells scavenged from *Otobo* at the stockade wall he could see through the screen immediately in front of him. In old-fashioned tanks, the driver had looked through a letter-box opening in the armour. Nowadays it was all done with miniature cameras giving electronic enhancement and sighting systems. But even so, what he could see was still framed by the widening aperture of the Zubr's gaping loading ramp, down which he was beginning to roll, even as the massive hovercraft shuddered to a standstill, rammed up hard against the shelving slope of streaming mudbank.

Like everyone else in a command or control situation, Richard was wearing one of the battlefield headsets attached to the system they scavenged from the second truck, and he was finding it hard to sort out the babble of overlapping reports from Bonnie, Sanda, Anastasia, Colonel Mako's men in the field, and Captains Caleb and Zhukov. He had offered Mako a ride so that the colonel could control his men from the heart of the battlefield, but the soldier had preferred to stay aboard *Stalingrad* and oversee his battle plan from there.

'Kudos to this UN body armour. Stopped half a clip of bullets at near point-blank. Stopped the bastard who fired them at me, too. I think he believes I'm the real deal. May have cracked a rib, though . . .' Bonnie's breathless voice echoed in Richard's ear. Winded with impact, shock and pain.

'Good shot.' Sanda was saying to whoever had fired the MANPADS scavenged from the first truck. 'The bell-tower's gone. Now get the watchtower nearest the jetty . . .'

'Bonnie!' came Anastasia's unmistakable accent. 'If Ngoboi's outside, where will my girls be?'

'Locked away,' came the strained reply.

'First squad!' Mako barked. 'Wait for the watchtower to go then get up to the compound as fast as you can. There's no one to protect the people inside yet . . .'

Except for Bonnie and Anastasia, thought Richard. 'I'm going in now, Colonel Mako,' he announced.

'Ladies and gentlemen,' rapped Robin suddenly, from her central position beside *Stalingrad*'s radio operator, in command of the whole system. 'Idents as you speak, as we agreed, please.'

'Sanda. This is Caleb. Have you a squad heading for the technicals?'

'Yes. Squad One . . .'

'Squad leader one here. Just getting there now . . .' The soldier's voice was lost beneath a rattle of automatic fire as battle proper was joined at last. Clearly someone else had got to the technicals with their heavy machine guns and their anti-aircraft missiles first.

'Captain Mariner,' the colonel rasped. 'Can you support Squad One? Things will get complex if the enemy regain and deploy those technicals . . .'

'On my way, Colonel . . .' Then the gun detonated again and his hearing seemed to close down for an instant, as though his ears could blink.

Richard's T80 was capable of seventy kph on a road. Even on the rain-slick bank of the Great River it could reach the better part of fifty. It was doing that when Richard, still half deafened, smashed it through the blazing hole his gunner had opened in the palisade, with the accelerator hard down and the GTD 1250 gas turbine screaming at full power.

He flicked a switch convenient to his thumb and the display in front of him adapted itself to include the targeting system for the remote 7.6mm coaxial machine guns he could control. The tank shrugged off the last of the blazing logs and Richard hurled it left, just missing the rear of the decapitated chapel. The back wall snatched itself magically out of his enhanced but proscribed view. The compound replaced it, showing figures scattering wildly into the shadows, even though the two Ngobois still stood facing each other in the withering downpour, with the quick-thinking Celine staggering away behind them, heading back towards the chapel. It was incredible how little time had passed since the first strike. Five seconds? Ten? Richard zeroed the machine guns as close to the outlandish figures as he dared and blasted the parade ground open, scattering the pair of them, even as the second missile streaked out of the jungle and blew away the watchtower by the jetty. Fifteen seconds and counting.

Richard swung left again, flicking another switch, enhancing his view still further with infrared, seeking hot targets in the darkness. He got his first close-up of the Toyota Hilux technicals. A mixture of Mako's and Caleb's men were fighting their way in out of the jungle. Though it looked as though the patrols around the technicals were putting up some stiff resistance – and some of the other fleeing army men were slowing down, forming up and joining in. The rest of Mako's men would now be following the path he had cleared up from the Zubr and into the compound. He ached to turn aside once more and try to protect the innocents caught unprotected in the middle. But he knew Mako was right, for they had discussed this in their battle plans. The T80 had to get to the technicals before the Army of Christ the Infant did, or there would be slaughter on a massive scale. Starting with Celine, Anastasia, the nuns, the nurses and the children they had come to save.

But even as the thought came to him, a missile sped out of the parking area where the army's technicals were and smeared itself across the front of the T80 with such power that only the reactive armour saved the tank and those inside it. That, and the fact that the missile had been hastily aimed and had hit at an extreme angle. Even so, this was no time to give whoever was out there leisure for a second try. He focussed on what lay dead ahead and forgot about the people in the buildings around the compound. 'Gunner!' he called in his rough Matadi. 'Fire as soon as you have a lock on where that came from!'

Anastasia hit the back door of the biggest hut and the flimsy wood yielded as easily as she had known it would. She had helped Brother Jacob hang the thing in the first place, seemingly aeons ago. She rolled into the hut, spraying warm rain all over the floor, her head filled immediately with shrieks of terror and shouts of rage. She pulled herself on to her knees, with the long SIG like a crutch beneath one arm, and looked around. In the dim light she saw the younger, smaller girls, huddled in terror against the back wall. And, in front of them, armed with bits of wood, chair legs, knives, forks, anything they could grab, a wall of older girls, Ado's friends, ready to do battle. 'It's me!' shouted Anastasia, just in time to stop them coming at her. Her voice halted them the instant they recognized it, she realized. But only her voice. For her clothes and blacked-up face would hardly be familiar – and she was certainly not the first person they had been expecting to see.

The plan had made no allowance for a potential squad of

young women ready to fight. But the best plans were the ones that adapted most quickly to changing circumstances, she thought, as she pushed herself to her feet, then eased between them to the front door and opened it. The moment her feet started moving, so did her lips. 'Robin. Anastasia. I have the girls,' she said into her headset. 'We're in the longest of the huts by the brick-built generator house. Do we have back-up?'

'Sanda? Squad One? Robin here. Can you spare anyone?'

'Yes,' answered Sanda. 'We have to fall back from the vehicle compound anyway because some maniac in a burning tank has just charged over here at the better part of seventy kph, and opened fire at point-blank range . . .'

'Very funny,' snapped Richard. 'I'll cease fire and let you mop it all up if you like. From where I'm sitting it looks as though the Army of Christ the Infant was coming at you mob-handed . . .'

'So you say. Maybe they were simply running for cover . . .'

'Enough!' snapped Robin. 'Sanda, leave Squad One to sort out things there. Get your men to Anastasia's location. That'll be target four on your battlefield GPS.'

'Sanda. Anastasia here,' said the Russian as she eased the door open a crack to get a good look across the compound towards the chapel with its blasted bell-tower and roof still well ablaze now in spite of the rain. 'Bring guns as well as men. We have some people here who want to get actively involved. It's starting to look like payback time . . .'

But now it was her turn to give a shout of shock. For no sooner had the door eased back an inch than Ngoboi himself burst in through it. The only thing that stopped absolute pandemonium was the fact that the familiar figure of Ado followed the weirdly dressed form inside. Then, even as Bonnie Holliday fought out of her soaking disguise – though not out of her life-saving blue body armour – Esan stepped in too. He stood shoulder to shoulder with Ado and the fact that she accepted him ensured the other girls did as well. The two of them started organizing the girls' escape at once, even as Sanda appeared with half a dozen men and twice as many extra guns.

'I may have spoken too soon,' he gasped. 'Things are hotting up out here. Squad One and Richard seem to have driven them back from the technicals but there's still a good deal of increasingly well-organized resistance. Some of these soldiers of Christ the Infant have been well trained and very well equipped. We may have to barricade ourselves in here, hunker down and wait for the colonel's men to follow Captain Mariner's T80 in.'

Bonnie joined Anastasia at the door. 'We need to get whoever's in charge. General Nlong or Ngoboi,' Anastasia calculated. 'Where did he go?' she asked. 'The other Ngoboi? He has to be someone powerful. Did you see where he went?'

'Into the chapel,' answered Bonnie.

'Shit!' spat Anastasia. 'That means he went after Celine. And from the look of things the chapel's not going to be a safe haven for long. Rain's easing but the roof's still burning. We have to get over there!'

But even as she spoke, the doorway of the distant chapel filled with figures. Wreathed in smoke, like something out of a nightmare, Ngoboi led a tight group down the steps and on to the level of the compound itself. The white coat of the doctor and the soiled white robes and coifs of the nuns caught the light behind the weird, raffia giant and the masked faces of the two helpers who had danced with him. It also gleamed against the blades of the matchets and the barrels of the guns that a number of them appeared to be carrying. The unmistakable figure of Moses Nlong stood at the heart of the group, taking Saddam Hussein's infamous 'wall of bodies' technique to new heights.

'I can take out that bastard Ngoboi,' grated Anastasia, raising the long SIG semi-automatic to her shoulder and taking aim. 'That'll be a start . . .'

'STOP! *Anastasia, hold your fire!*'

Mercifully, the Russian woman had broadcast her thoughts as she spoke them into the battlefield comms headset. And Richard's voice answered, shouting almost painfully in her earpiece. Then 'HOLD YOUR FIRE!' was bellowed in English and Matadi as Richard repeated the order over the T80's loudspeaker system.

Richard had also seen the group come out of the chapel, but he had been able to use the T80's enhanced vision equipment to zero in for a maximum illumination close-up. Instantly suspicious that the Poro god's costume included the headpiece once again, he calculated that whoever had originally been wearing it might well have had the time – and the cunning – to change. But Richard had no idea what the man who had shot Bonnie actually looked like. His face could well be one of those crowded around the familiar face of Moses Nlong.

He eased the T80 forward slowly now, leaving Squad One to mop up the blazing ruins of the army's hopefully defunct motor pool, keeping a close eye on the group as they shuffled away from the blazing chapel, searching first of all for Celine. She was the lynchpin. The others would have a good idea of what was going on immediately around them. The medical team from Malebo, the nuns whose names he did not know. But only Celine was likely to have the wider view that was vital; only Celine would recognize friends as well as enemies.

But even when he managed to identify her, it would need some kind of a small-scale surgical strike to get her away from Nlong and his men unscathed. A T80 main battle tank was capable of many things, but a small-scale surgical strike was not one of them.

Then he thought of Bonnie. Bonnie had seen the other Ngoboi without his headdress – at point-blank range. And that thought became important, suddenly, as he realized Celine was not amongst the little group he had under enhanced observation. Which meant she was either still in the chapel – or she was in the costume of Ngoboi or one of his masked attendants. It was impossible to calculate which was more likely because he could make neither head nor tail of what General Nlong and his men were up to. Always assuming that any one of them had thought further than the immediate imperative of simply getting as safely as possible out of the burning building – even though under the circumstances that was like getting out of the frying pan and into the fire. Could this stand-off be part of some wider, cleverer plan? Did he have time to work it out if it was?

'We need to get over to them,' Anastasia insisted. 'They're not going to stand there for ever.' She opened the door, preparing to step out.

'Wait!' ordered Richard. Luckily. For a machine gun opened up instantly, sending a line of bullets out of the shadows to splinter the wood of the door and the walls beside it. The sniper was cut off mid-attack as Mako's men came pouring in through the hole Richard had cleared for them. But his short-lived assault served as a potent warning.

'Anastasia. It's Richard. I'm coming to get you,' Richard said brusquely. 'Use the tank for shelter. And Sanda and his men can guard your rear.' He rolled the T80 up to the door and split the screen so that he could see straight ahead and to the left of the massive vehicle at the same time. On one half of the screen, the group of figures hesitated beside the chapel. On the other, the doorway loomed, a massive shadow sliding over it as the tank came between the hut and the blazing building. Half a dozen figures burst out into the protective shadow. Anastasia's voice called, 'Go!' and Richard obligingly eased the tank forward at walking pace.

'Bonnie. Richard here. Can you see the man who shot you?'

'Not yet. What are they doing?'

'Running out of time, unless there's something going on I haven't worked out yet. What in hell's name could they be waiting for? Mako. Mariner. What are your men encountering?'

'Not much resistance. Only Squad One are facing any stiff opposition. I'm sending support round to them now. There are still some diehards out in the bush there. Did you take out all the technicals and four-wheel drives?'

Richard never answered. For at that instant the brick-built generator house exploded.

# TWENTY-THREE
## Technical

There was a dazzling flash, a detonation that reduced even the thunder to startled silence, and darkness fell once more as all the security lighting died. *Damn!* thought Richard. He had underestimated Nlong or Ngoboi or whoever was in charge. There had been a plan in place after all. His mind raced through seeming infinities of implication in the instant that it took him to hit the T80's searchlight control. A beam of pure white light slammed across the shadowed compound to the point where the group from the chapel were beginning to scatter. Ngoboi and his two helpers were running towards the shattered generator house – one helper apparently more reluctantly than the other. General Nlong lay stretched out on the ground and the harsh light showed how terribly damaged his right leg was – a fact that had been hidden by the press of bodies around him. The supine general gave a spasmodic twitch. His chest seemed to burst open. The white-coated nuns and nurses around him leaped back. The left-looking half of Richard's screen showed Anastasia taking aim for a second shot. Already too late, by the look of things, to be delivering the *coup de grâce*. The taller of the nuns came forward and knelt for an instant at his side as though in prayer, her face half hidden by her coif. Or was it a wimple? Richard was no expert on the headgear of nuns.

If the general was out of the picture – had always been out of the picture – then that put Ngoboi back in the frame as the mind that was marshalling this mayhem, thought Richard. And 'marshalling' was the right word. The resumption of the head-dress was a clever double bluff. For whoever was giving the orders holding the remnants of the Army of Christ together must be using a battlefield communications system like their own. And the headdress hid that fact for those few vital moments. And as he completed these lightning calculations, he knew what was coming next. 'Anastasia! It's Ngoboi after all. Can you see him?'

'No. He's vanished into the—'

Anastasia's sentence was cut off by a pair of Toyota Hilux technicals that roared in past the ruins of the generator house. The only flaw in the well-executed surprise seemed to be that they switched their headlights on. Ngoboi was framed against the brightness. Anastasia squeezed off a shot at once. The tall god staggered, but ran on doggedly. Then the two technicals slewed round in front of him, protecting him with their bodywork as the men in the back of one swung a pair of heavy machine guns towards Richard's tank, while those in the other zeroed in what looked to Richard suspiciously like a French Milan anti-tank missile. That explained what happened to the generator hut. 'Gunner! Get out!' he ordered brusquely. 'ATM zeroing in on us.'

The headlights picked out Ngoboi's helpers for an instant longer – just enough time to see that the reluctant one had torn off her mask to reveal Celine's face. The other one was running along the headlight beam towards her when Anastasia's rifle spoke for the fourth time. The pursuer went down and Celine staggered away into the shadows.

Richard hit the coaxial the instant Celine was clear, flicking the automatic fire toggle, even as he began to scramble out of the tank on the heels of the gunner. 'Clear the tank area,' he ordered as he went. 'If that missile hits she'll go up like Guy Fawkes . . .'

Then he was out into the stinking humidity of the battlefield, drenched in perspiration at once running forward at Anastasia's shoulder, fighting to get to the protection of the hut before the missile hit his tank. The hammering of the coaxials persisted, sending tracers towards the pair of Toyota pickups, disorientating, confusing – with luck even killing – the men with the missile. They all bundled into the shelter together just the very instant that Richard's hope for good fortune failed. The Milan hit the tank full-on and blew the turret off. Anyone inside it would have died. Even those, like Richard, safely in the hut, were half deafened and shaken by the shock wave. But the power of the explosion was mostly directed away from them so that was all they suffered. Except for Richard whose right ear was pierced by Robin's shriek of '*RICHARD!*' the instant that the tank went up.

'It's OK,' he grated. 'The gunner and I got out.'

'Bloody man!' she spat, as Richard pulled himself up off the floor. But she sounded satisfyingly relieved.

The hut was almost empty. Sanda and his men had spirited the girls out of the back door by the look of things. Richard, Anastasia and Bonnie picked themselves up, rubbed the dust from their eyes and ran outside. They swung right at once, heading for the technicals' headlights. It was only after he had taken half a dozen strides that Richard realized he was at the heart of a little phalanx of well-armed women and girls, all in black. A phalanx of girls and one tall, powerful-looking youth. All naturally black-faced. Narrow-eyed. And no one was smiling. No wonder they were all but invisible out here in the stinking darkness. He didn't need to ask where they were going or what their objective was. Anastasia was here to get Celine and she wasn't the sort of person who changed her mind too easily.

'Now I understand what your shrink meant about penis envy,' he growled.

'What?' gasped Anastasia, distracted.

'I'm the only one here who hasn't got a gun.'

'You'll get over it,' she laughed.

'I'll probably be scarred for life . . .'

The technicals snarled away from the ruins of the generator

house, following their headlight beams towards the palisade and the river. Trying to trap the fleeing Celine, thought Richard. Unless they had another trick up their sleeve.

Speculation and conversation died then, because the first of the technicals caught the figure of the fleeing Celine in its headlights. She staggered to one side, seeking the shadows at once.

But the tall nun who had apparently prayed over Moses Nlong's corpse stepped into the light, with one arm round Celine. And the gun that had failed to kill Bonnie Holliday pressed to her head. The technicals braked hard, skidding to a halt just in front of the two women. 'Run!' gasped Richard. 'Faster!' He realized with a sickening lurch that a battlefield communications headset could go under a coif or a wimple as easily as it could go under Ngoboi's headdress. Ngoboi had been a triple bluff after all.

'That's him!' wheezed Bonnie as the face beneath the wimple caught the light. 'That's the guy that shot me!'

'Anastasia. Can you get a clean shot?'

'Not from here.'

'Then we need to get closer. Fast.' He reached down as he ran and scooped up the dark red mud at his feet. It smelt of iron as he smeared it over his face. It was almost hot against his skin. It reminded him, in all sorts of ways, of blood.

'Colonel Mako? How are things going on the broader front?' he wheezed.

'Squad One are still finding it hard going, even with more men coming round as back-up. The other men are moving through the camp in standard pincer, but the GPS shows you, Bonnie and Anastasia in the last army stronghold in the compound itself. I'd say they're setting up a line of retreat into the bush where we'll never find them.'

'Looks like someone else has taken command now that Moses Nlong is no longer with us,' said Robin. 'Someone with some military nous.'

'Correct. And he's got Celine Chaka.'

'That could be a problem,' said the Colonel.

'*Will* be a problem,' added Robin. 'Given her father's change of heart. She's quite a bargaining counter, all of a sudden.'

'Important enough to get whoever's got her safe passage out of the country?' asked Anastasia.

'I'd say so,' answered Robin. 'It's a father–daughter thing.'

'Do tell,' grated Anastasia in a tone that made Richard automatically glance over at the back of her T-shirt. But it was too dark to see 'AND F*** YOUR FAMILY' written there.

This conversation all but covered the time it took the little squad to get to the hindmost of the two technicals – and for the man disguised as a nun to drag Celine to the door of the first one. Because they were moving so fast and so silently through the noisy darkness that was full of revving engines, gunshots and shouting – not to mention the roaring of flames from the guttering tank, the blazing chapel and the still-burning palisade – the squad of women with Richard were able to take the men aboard the second technical by complete surprise. A surprise aided by the madness of what Anastasia and her cohort were trying to do, coupled with the distractingly hypnotic sight of a man dressed as a nun with a gun wrestling with the nearly sainted folk-heroine daughter of the country's president.

The feral women simply erupted up out of the darkness, using their guns as clubs, and silently overpowered the three men in the back of the pick up and the two men in the front. Richard was able to spring up on to the flatbed and grasp the double handle of the massive weapon there. 'This is the Shipunov self-powering four-barrelled Gatling designed mini-gun,' he said, awestruck. 'God knows where they got a piece of cutting-edge Russian hardware like this, ladies. But I think it'll certainly help me get over my penis envy.'

No sooner had he finished speaking than the door of the technical in front of them slammed and the vehicle lurched into motion. Anastasia hauled the unconscious driver of the second technical out on to the mud and gunned the motor as the others clambered aboard, then they were off. Richard hung on grimly, straining his eyes to assess whether the Milan that had decapitated the T80 was the only one the lead Toyota had carried. Although he held the Shipunov – held on to it for all he was worth, in fact, as Anastasia's driving matched her approach to the rest of her life – he did not want to fire it as that would put Celine at risk. The men in front would have no such worries about launching another missile at him, however. And even as the thought occurred to Richard, he saw the three men in the vehicle in front start to prepare another Milan. There was still an outside chance they didn't realize their friends had been replaced, he calculated grimly.

But the instant the nun in charge gave an order on the headset under his wimple and got no reply, then he and the girls in the second technical were toast.

Unless, of course, the men in the lead would also be putting themselves at risk if they launched. 'Anastasia,' he called. 'Keep as close as you can.'

'I'm aiming to get more than fucking *close* . . .' grated the Russian woman, grinding the gears as she spoke.

'Good, good,' he said paternally. 'That's the ticket. If we fall back, he'll nuke us, as likely as not; same as he did to my tank.'

The two Toyotas roared along the inner wall of the stockade, beneath the Roman candle that was all that remained of the watchtower overlooking the jetty, and on towards the bush. Richard was sidetracked for an instant, calculating whether Sanda would have had time to get the girls from the hut across the war-zone they were heading for and down to the safety of the Shaldag and the river. If not, then the two careering vehicles were all too possibly just about to decimate a crocodile of terrified schoolgirls on top of everything else.

But then his worries became less speculative. The men in the back of the Toyota immediately in front started shooting at them. Or two of them did, while the third got the next Milan ready to fire.

The Toyota lurched forward as though Anastasia had found a nitrous oxide canister to gun the motor. The vehicles ground along, side by side, smashing brutally up against each other. It was only when a bullet smashed into the body armour on his chest that Richard was shocked into action. He realized that if they were side by side he could deploy the Shipunov without endangering Celine. If he was careful. Somewhere between a nanosecond and a microsecond after that thought occurred to him, the back of the other Toyota was empty – of men, guns and Milan missiles. All of it chewed into nothingness and hurled riverwards by something that sounded like a mad blacksmith trying to shatter an anvil with the biggest hammer he possessed.

Then he realized that if he could depress the mini-gun's elevation sufficiently, he could do to the Toyota's back axle what he had just done to its on-board weapons system. Even as he pressed the trigger, Anastasia hurled her vehicle right, ramming the other technical, while its driver reciprocated. The far side of the Toyota's flatbed followed the men and the Milans into oblivion. But even as it did so, the palisade wall vanished and there was only river-bank beside them – and jungle dead ahead. Anastasia threw the technical sideways once again and the other vehicle began to slide. The riverbank was slick mud, sloping downwards to the water. The racing tyres had very little purchase here – hardly enough to carry them safely to the dry and level safety of the undergrowth half a kilometre ahead. Anastasia threw the technical sideways a third time and the eight tyres driving the two vehicles forward lost their grip at last. The bullet-riddled Toyota began to slide away from Richard – even as he felt Anastasia beginning to lose control of hers. But his gun was still at the maximum depression, and each foot that separated them brought that back axle more surely into his sights. So that at last he was able to pull the trigger and see the whole flatbed dissolve as the mad blacksmith took up his hammer once again. The back of the speeding vehicle broke. The cab slewed round and round. For a moment it looked as though it might roll. But no. Instead it settled as the square-cut end behind the cab sank down on to the slick mud, holding the front steady as it slid down into the water with all the stately grace of an ocean liner being launched. Anastasia's Toyota followed it, swinging round as though it was still under her control, so that the headlights shone on to the wreck as they slid to a halt. Richard ratcheted the mini-gun back on its mount, keeping the shattered technical in his sights.

The shore-side door opened and Celine wearily pulled herself out to come floundering up on to the bank. Anastasia threw herself out of the Toyota and ran down to her, sweeping her into the most enormous bear hug. *Only a Russian . . .* thought Richard.

'Where are the others?' he called. 'Celine, where's the guy who kidnapped you?'

'Gone,' answered Celine wearily. 'His name is Odem and he's gone. Out through the other door. Upriver. Like a ghost.'

'We have Celine,' said Richard into his headset. 'But it looks like there are still some bad men out there. Heading upriver by the sound of it.'

'We'll get them,' said Mako. 'In time. No matter how far upriver they go.'

'Not,' added Robin, 'that there *is* anything much upriver any more.'

'You never know,' said Richard automatically, watching Bonnie, the girls and that one tall young man gather round the two women still lost in their embrace. 'There could be anything up there . . .'

'Don't tell me,' teased Robin gently. 'Tarzan's Lost City. Prester John. King Solomon's Mines. You'll never grow up, will you, my love?'

'You never know,' said Richard with a weary chuckle. 'You never know . . .'

# TWENTY-FOUR
## Pearl

'Satisfied?' asked Richard, his voice deep and lazy.

'Completely,' answered Robin. She pushed away the plate which had contained a fluffy mound of golden scrambled egg and several slices of wheaten toast, and lifted the breakfast tray on to her bedside table. Then she rolled out of bed, wearing only the napkin she had tied around her neck soon after Richard had brought the food through from room service. Crossing towards her bathroom, she paused in front of the mirror. 'We'd better get home soon, though, before all this satisfaction goes to my hips . . .'

Richard climbed out of bed and reached for his bathrobe. 'We can go when you like,' he said, knotting the belt around his slim waist. 'Your mission is accomplished. Celine is in hospital and safely back within her father's orbit. Their reconciliation appears to have sorted out a lot of local difficulties. The sight of her seems to have melted his heart, as they say – elections are promised for next year. Free, fair and internationally observed. My mission is on hold until Chaka gets things settled in the delta. The IMF and the World Bank seem happy with the idea of bridging loans, and everyone else will be back in the spring – Max and I first in the queue.'

'I thought the Army of Christ the Infant had all broken up.'

'Vanished, more like. Into the jungle along with that chap

Odem. Or Ngoboi. Smoke and mirrors. Gods and ghosts. Now you see them, now you don't.'

'Do we need to be worried about Anastasia, then?'

'What, after investing all that money in her? Freudian psychoanalysis and so forth?'

'No. You know very well what I mean. Because she's gone back up to her orphanage . . .'

'Someone had to clear up . . . She's got help. Bonnie and Caleb – and a squad of Colonel Mako's men. And she's organizing some of the older kids into a defence force. Ado and some of the girls. Esan's helping. She'll be fine.'

As he was talking, Richard walked through into the suite's big sitting room, and he noticed something strange. There was a disc he had never seen before sitting on top of his laptop case. 'Robin, do you know what this disc is?'

Robin came to his side, also tying her robe shut. By the time she arrived, he had opened the Apple and started the media player. He slipped the disc in.

Audio started at once. The voices easily identifiable.

'Yes. I do know where they come from,' said Minister Ngama. 'A Japanese company built a facility upriver in the seventies and proposed to produce black freshwater pearls in commercial quantities. There is apparently a man-made lake on the slopes of Mount Karisoke away in the impenetrable jungle of the interior. May I ask how you came by them?'

'My daughter Anastasia gave them to me. She and Mrs Mariner brought them to me. A kind of peace offering, I think, to get the girl back in my good graces.' There was a sneer in his tone. 'One of the children from her orphanage apparently discovered them on the riverbank after the floods. Just before the Army of Christ the Infant attacked.'

'They must have washed downriver for quite a distance, then.' Ngama mused. 'Why did she give them to you?'

'To sell. Anastasia wishes to raise capital to rebuild her orphanage.'

'I see, but I am hardly in the business of buying pearls. Even such unusual ones as these.'

'That is because, with all due deference, Minister, you do not know just *how* unusual these pearls actually are.'

'Then perhaps you would be good enough to explain.'

'Certainly. When the girl gave the pearls to me I took them to my people, naturally, and in the process of assaying what they might be worth on the market, one of my mining specialists got the idea of checking what it was that had made them so uniquely black in the first place.'

'The black volcanic sediment on the bed of the lake, of course.'

'Of course. And that is where things became interesting enough for me to contact you and request this meeting. Because the black sediment on the bed of the volcanic lake that gave these pearls their unique colour is the purest example of coltan my mining engineers have ever seen.'

'Coltan!' breathed Ngama.

'Coltan,' Max confirmed quietly. 'The most valuable and sought after of all the conflict minerals. And if what you said about the Japanese and their pearl-production company is true, there's a lake full of the stuff out there somewhere. *At least* a lake full of the stuff. And, with my Zubr *Stalingrad* we can get closer to it faster than anyone else in the game.'

'This is information that we should keep very secret indeed,' purred Ngama.

'Absolutely,' agreed Max.

'No one outside this room should hear even a whisper about this,' Ngama emphasized. 'No one.'

'Absolutely,' said Max Asov once again. 'Absolutely secret.'

The media payer hissed with static for a moment – a click made it clear one recording was over and another one was starting – then a third voice, also familiar, explained, 'Mr Asov also carries a Benincom phone, you see, Captain Mariner.'

'That was Colonel Kebila,' said Robin. 'What on earth is he up to? Come to that, what is *Max* up to?'

She turned, expecting Richard still to be at her side. But he was over by the French window overlooking their balcony and the swimming pool. His eyes were fixed on the far blue distance where volcanic mountains rose behind the brash green of the delta. She knew that look and it frightened her.

'Not Tarzan's Lost City or Prester John after all,' he whispered. 'Better than King Solomon's Mines: a lake full of black pearls and coltan . . .'

# Acknowledgements

*Dark Heart* follows on from *Benin Light*, although it is not a sequel. *Benin Light* made use of Tim Butcher's *Blood River* for some of its inspiration, and in the same way *Dark Heart* makes use of his *Chasing the Devil*. As well as researching in Tim's excellent books, I reread Graham Greene's *Journey Without Maps* and *The Heart of the Matter*. Michela Wrong's *In the Footsteps of Mr Kurtz* supplied me with more research material as did Ronan Bennett's *The Catastrophist*. And mention of Mr Kurtz, of course, leads me to acknowledge my debt to Joseph Conrad – *Heart of Darkness* and *An Outpost of Progress* in particular. A chance encounter placed Jon Evans' *The Night of Knives* in my possession and that too became grist to the mill. But most influential in many ways (next after *Heart of Darkness* and *Chasing the Devil*, at least) was Chinua Achebe's *Things Fall Apart*. To all of these fine writers and their outstanding work I freely acknowledge a great debt.

I must also acknowledge a huge debt to my wife Charmaine. She edits my manuscripts – often nightly as I'm writing – and suggests improvements. But on this occasion it was she, as we discussed how the 'dark heart' could be symbolized most effectively, who came up with the idea of the black pearls, and with that one flash of inspiration changed the nature of the book. I must also thank my brother Simon, who became editorial backstop after Charmaine on an almost daily basis. And also George Johnston, my uncle, who is tireless in his efforts to make my books better, as is Kendall Stanley, one of my oldest and dearest friends.

Beyond all this research and advice, everything from the Ghost Orchids to the Shaldag FPBs, the ill-fated corvette (whose ailments are all well-documented 'teething problems' of the breed), the mighty Zubr hovercraft and coltan, came from the Internet; a huge amount from the maligned but absolutely invaluable Wikipedia.

Peter Tonkin, Tunbridge Wells
and Sharm el-Sheikh, Summer 2011

ML     6-12